The Bretton Woods Legacy

To Barry, with thoughts of times long since lost!

Dave.

By
DAVID ROSE

©David Rose 2020

All rights reserved. No part of this publication may be reproduced, stored in a retrieval system or transmitted, in any form or by any means without the prior written permission of the publisher, nor be otherwise circulated in any form of binding or cover other than that in which it is published and without a similar condition being imposed on the subsequent purchaser.

All characters, other than those recorded in history, are fictitious and any resemblance to real persons, living or dead, is purely coincidental.

ISBN 9798655566613

Published by:
Pejoro Ltd, Kemp House, 160 City Road, London, EC1V 2NX, UK.
Reg No 12015657

Cover design: fiverr.com/design9creative

Prologue

BRETTON WOODS, JULY, 1944.

+

All historical events and financial institutions in this book are real.

+

Winning a war that has razed half the world to the ground brings its own challenges. To meet the greatest challenge of all a conference was called by British Prime Minister Winston Churchill and U.S. President Franklin D Roosevelt. Both leaders believed that the lack of any structure in the global economy was the root cause of events leading up to the war. It must never be allowed to happen again. The brief for the conference was to discuss and agree the world's post war economic order.

Thus on July 1st, 1944, just three weeks after D-Day, 730 top experts in economics, commerce and politics from all 44 allied nations assembled at the exclusive Mount Washington Hotel **(now the Omni Mount Washington Resort)** in Bretton Woods, New Hampshire.

Referred to ever since by the global banking, finance and economics community simply as 'The Bretton Woods Conference', it has attained iconic status across all those sectors as well as the wider business and political communities, worldwide.

Churchill deployed his secret weapon, influential and hugely respected economist John Maynard Keynes, then an advisor to His Majesty's Treasury, who had developed a revolutionary process to create new money. It was to become a vast and deep lake of funds which would underpin the massive reconstruction and development needed to repair the devastation of war.

After three weeks, the conference had mapped how the world's economy would be structured for as far ahead as anyone could see. The following May, victory in Europe was declared. Then in August 1945 the first atomic bombs were dropped on Hiroshima and Nagasaki. Presaging the end to the war in the Pacific, and the dawning of the nuclear age.

The conference gained only passing comment in the media. No-one cared about an obscure highbrow talking shop in a posh hotel in New Hampshire. All people wanted to know was how soon the war was going to end so they could start rebuilding their lives. But the legacy of that event has reverberated down the decades to this day. As much as D-Day, victory in Europe and those atomic bombs ever did.

Along with the G7, the Bretton Woods conference spawned the International Monetary Fund, IMF, and the World Bank, both of which we have all heard. These were followed in 1948 by the reinstated, and lesser known, Bank for International Settlements, BIS, previously ostracized by polite fiscal society for inadvertently holding looted Nazi gold on behalf of the German Reichsbank.

Together, these three institutions now form the 'holy trinity' of the global monetary order. But most of the many other structures and treaties which came out of the conference were overtaken by the mid-1970's by events. But far moreso by technology that could not even be conceived of in 1944.

But Keynes' spectacular 'money creation' process survives. The presentation was made exclusively to the most senior financial experts in a closed door plenary session. They sat dumbstruck at the awesome potential of his brainchild. It has remained a secret exclusive to the global financial elite, and those privileged by exceptional wealth, to this day.

His process was, and still is, exquisitely simple.

Debt instruments are created and backed with cash. This cash is then used as collateral by banks to provide loans to the traders. The loans, always off-balance sheet, use money that does not exist (hence not repaid) and is usually ten times the cash backing on the instrument. Then follows a 40-week pre-arranged, risk-free trading cycle, known as 'arbitrage', with the new money manifesting as profit on the trades.

With the loan increasing the deposit to the power of ten at the get-go, the profit coming out the other end is magnified times ten.

Genius. Pure genius.

There has been speculation that Keynes' revolutionary process created the money behind the post-war Marshall Plan. Also

President Eisenhower's re-booting of F.D. Roosevelt's 1930's 'new deal' with the construction of tens of thousands of miles of new highways in 1950's America. As well as many other initiatives since that have appeared to conjure money out of nowhere.

Over the following decades Keynes' process has evolved into what are now known as Private Placement Programs (PPP's). ***Reader caution:*** *if you Google PPP's please be aware that most of what you find there will be the scams perpetrated around this ultra-secretive market. There is no reliable information on PPP market participants anywhere on the internet.*

PPP's finance hundreds, even thousands of billions of dollars in massive infrastructure, energy and humanitarian projects around the world every year.

So far, so good. But if you still think high finance is boring, please read on…

The minimum deposit, or placement, required to enter a PPP is one hundred million dollars, meaning they are the exclusive domain of the super-rich, known in the financial markets as Ultra-High Net Worth Individuals, or UHNWI's. These are the .02 of the world's population who own 90% of its wealth (depending on whose data you believe).

The loans against the UHNWI placements are made by just ten or a dozen of the world's top global banks which 'host' the **PPP** traders. Their off-balance sheet loan exposure across all active PPP's hovers around five trillion dollars at any one time.

Yes. You read it correctly. Five *trillion* dollars.

Which is five times the sub-prime mortgage exposure that triggered the 2008 banking crisis, from which the world has not fully recovered more than a decade later.

Five trillion dollars issued as unsecured, off-balance-sheet debt by no more than a dozen of the world's top global banks. The loans are made to the half dozen or so genuine PPP trade groups that exist, and which will never be found through Google.

The process has moved on since the 1940's, 1950's and even the 1960's when it was all paper, ink and documents delivered by bank messengers travelling all over the world. From the 1970's it all started to become automated once the arbitrage trades were set up.

It is then that the process started to become supported by the global electronic banking network, Swift (Society for Worldwide Interbank Financial Telecommunications) operating from a village in Belgium.

Through its system of Message Types, MT's, Swift provides the deposit 'blocking' mechanism (ensuring the deposit, the placement, cannot be withdrawn or used for any other purpose while the trades are in progress).

A failure of those systems would see five trillion dollars of off-balance sheet debt, with non-existent money, transferring automatically onto those banks' balance sheets making that debt, and the liability it incurs, real in every crushing sense.

Then would follow the implosion of the global banking network from the top down.

Yes, it would be the long anticipated global economic Armageddon, and the tsunami of worldwide anarchy that would ensue. But the technology has backstops, fail-safes, firewalls and all kinds of other safeguards.

There has never been a problem in almost eight decades of the program's operation.

One

Antigua. April.

As dawn broke the children began hurling themselves on bellies, backsides and each other down the twenty foot sloping incline to the beach. Over generations, their screams and shouts had become a regular part of the morning ritual, and could be heard in the village just a hundred yards back from the shoreline. The grown-ups still do it, without the screams and when they think no-one is looking.

The grey rock had been smoothed to a lichen-covered gloss over millennia by the constant, gentle trickle of water finding its way to the sea, helped along by the anatomies of countless generations of children. It was way off the tourist track on the west side of the island, and they visited each morning to beachcomb for things they could polish up and sell to the tourists as souvenirs.

...ning the screams were different. Shrill, sobbing wails ...en gripped by fear, bringing startled villagers running to ...e cove in seconds.

They were grouped in a terrified huddle as far away as they could get from the two bodies, left where they were by the receding tide a few hours earlier. They were lying on their sides facing each other. They could have been a couple relaxing and having a private conversation on the pristine white sands of the isolated cove.

But the zip-tied wrists and neat .22 calibre wounds in the back of their heads, washed clean by the sea and clearly visible, told a far different story.

There was no ID, until the next day when their hotel contacted the police to report two missing guests.

+

Before ending his days on the sands of an unnamed Antiguan cove, Valiece Davey had been a role model for African-American Detroit manhood. What you saw is what you got. Larger than life and all-round good guy. Likeable and born to his relationship manager job at Wells Fargo bank. He liked his customers, and they liked him. He had been married to his doting wife Daphne, now lying next to him with empty, lifeless eyes staring into eternity, for almost thirty years.

A few months before he had been wondering what had possessed him to accept the offer of this new job from one of his customers. Sure, it had doubled his salary and he and Daphne were living a completely different lifestyle. But it was nothing like as enjoyable as the bank.

He missed his customers and the banter he used to enjoy with them. The buzz of being out and about meeting them which he now realized, too late, he had come to take for granted.

The corporate finance law firm he was now grafting for had been contracted by an obscure European wealth management outfit to set up fifty new banks. Fifty banks in itself was no big deal. There are many kinds of banks and Valiece knew what all of them were for and how they worked. These were fifty 'private capital' banks across twenty offshore jurisdictions. Nothing more than a depot to 'store' funds for those who own the banks, and operate them for themselves and their clients, which was usually no more than their close circle.

He ploughed his way through the same mind-numbing process to set up each one of them. Hire a local law firm specialising in company registrations, have them provide proxy directors who, in turn, register as owners of the new bank with the company as the sole stockholder.

Provided the people behind the banks can show they really exist, and can capitalize the bank with anywhere between five hundred thousand and five million dollars, depending on where it is, they are set to go. It was no big deal, but fifty of them in one hit was a challenge. More to his sanity than anything else.

Valiece knew how private banking and the secretive 'wealth sector' worked. Confidentiality and discretion reign supreme. So there was nothing strange in setting up fifty different banks across twenty jurisdictions, owned by fifty different companies, in turn owned by fifty different people, sitting behind proxy directors, all hidden behind a wealth management firm somewhere in darkest Europe.

The proof of funds had been sent in one lump sum of $40 million to an escrow account over which Valiece and his firm had sole discretion, concealing the identity of the wealth management firm and, in turn, their clients.

If absolute anonymity for their clients was what they were looking for, this European outfit was going the right way about it. And then some.

This was a new departure for his firm. Previously they had focused on corporate finance law, but now they had an opportunity to diversify into wealth management, a rapidly growing market, and Valiece was told it was his to build on. He had never heard of the European firm itself, Median Private Wealth, but they were obviously of some substance to be setting up fifty private capital banks for their clients.

After almost a year of solid grind he was on the home stretch with the last couple of banks, and in desperate need of a vacation. As with a few other jurisdictions, Antigua had already asked for a 'wet' signature, in ink and signed by a human being in front of a regulator in his office. So he had left this particular job till last.

He checked with his boss if it was okay to take a couple of weeks' vacation after he had signed off the last bank in Antigua. He would go on from there to do a bit of island hopping with Daphne.

No problem, and his boss even offered to cover all the air and hotel bills and told him to get his secretary to set it up for him. "You can go business class, if they've got it in that neck of the woods. And make sure she fixes up decent hotels for you."

He told him 'well done', and that a sizeable bonus would be waiting for him in his account, paid out of the several discretionary millions that were left in the escrow account when he returned. So, just maybe, all this monotonous graft had been worthwhile after all.

The secretary had booked them on Delta Airlines for the four and half hour flight from Detroit Metro to Antigua. From there, over the next couple of weeks, they were taking in Curacao, Grenada and Bermuda. A leisurely amble through the Caribbean which he thought he had well earned. Daphne too. He had lost count of the times he had told her he was going to be kept late at the office.

+

Come the day, they were a skittish middle-aged couple laughing and giggling as they waited for the cab to arrive. They had not had a proper vacation in a long time. Their only son was now an avionics engineer with USAF in Germany, so they had no real obligations to anyone.

Six hours later, early evening in Antigua, their cab dropped them at the Blue Waters resort where they were going to spend the first three nights of their vacation before flying onto Curacao. The suite was unaccustomed luxury and the view, mostly filled with the flat calm Caribbean under a stunning sunset, was four stars up from what they had from their bedroom window in Detroit. This was the moment it registered that they were actually, really, at long last on vacation.

Valiece's appointment with the regulator the next day was at 1pm, so they took their time over breakfast before enjoying a leisurely bus ride to his office in the capital, St John's. Signing took just 30 minutes. With his final piece of business settled, they carried on with their exploration of the town.

They were gazing into a shop window, a jeweller, holding hands and soaking up the sun when a cab pulled up at the kerb behind them. The driver sauntered over. Nothing happens in a hurry on Antigua.

For a very reasonable fee he offered a personal guided tour of the island, after which he would drop them off for dinner at a friendly restaurant he knew in English Harbour on the other side of the island. He would then come back, pick them up and return them to the Blue Waters.

He looked a decent enough guy. Clean and well-spoken with a British accent, just trying to make a living, and they only had a couple of days to take in the whole island. Perfect. What could go wrong?

They got into the cab, a spotless silver Mercedes and drove off. Already in relaxed and friendly conversation with the driver.

+

The police recorded their murders as a mugging gone wrong, or possibly drugs-related. When Valiece's employer was tracked down through their hotel booking they were called with the news. After an almost audible stunned silence, his boss offered any assistance he and his firm could provide.

A copy of the file was sent to Detroit PD, with a request for them to arrange collection of the remains. ASAP.

Two

Singapore. April.

There are times I feel like a stranger in my own life. And this was one of them. It was sunset, and I was gazing through the wall-length window of the presidential suite at the Four Seasons in Singapore. Luxury that once upon a time I hardly knew existed.

The heat haze rising from the mostly concrete covered island was making the mesmerising red orb dance in the sky. I'd showered and now Kelly, my partner, was in there having hers. Although with three bathrooms dotted about the enormous suite she hadn't really needed to wait for me!

I watched her come back into the bedroom lost inside a fluffy white bathrobe several sizes too big for her. With just her blond bob showing out the top, she attempted what was meant to be a sexy little sashay across the huge bedroom, before falling flat on her face. Giggling to herself under a pile of white towelling…

What the world saw of her was not the Kelly I'd come to know and hopelessly fall for over these past couple of years.

Heathrow to Singapore is a bit of a haul and for some reason I get more of a jet-lag hit than most. So I'd timed it to arrive that Saturday afternoon so I could get my head straight before the event the following evening. Where I'd be meeting my new boss and colleagues, at the start-up wealth management firm where I was going to head up the PR.

She'd come along for the ride because she was curious about this new job of mine, and wanted to meet my new boss as well. She was due in Sydney on Tuesday anyway, so it was no great shakes for her. She was one of those who could travel across ten time zones, get off the plane whip-smart and walk straight into a meeting fresh as a daisy.

She shucked off the bathrobe and, for a moment stood there in all her five foot six, 110 pound glory with a hillock of white towelling around her ankles and giving me that cock-eyed grin of hers. I loved her in many ways and for many reasons. But mostly for what she lacked in stature, she made up for in sheer devastating intellect. Besides that, there wasn't an investment bank on the planet that wouldn't pay this amazing woman top dollar for her know-how.

And did.

+

The four years since I was stretchered off the transport, in an induced coma after taking three rounds from an AK wielded by a lad of about 13, seemed to have gone by on fast forward. On seeing the young guy appear out of nowhere in front of me I'd hesitated. He hadn't.

The poor little blighter was shot to shreds in a split second as my four-man squad reacted by emptying half their magazines into him. But the damage had been done, and I saw the strangely bewildering sight of my own blood pumping from my chest before I blacked out.

I'd left my body armour behind as the whole mission was about setting up my sniper's hide. Ever tried lying on your belly for days on end in body armour?

This had all happened barely ten hours before near an abandoned factory in Helmund. But in that ethereal place the drugs had taken me, dark but somehow light at the same time, I'm sure I still picked up the stench of cordite and sweet coppery smell of too much blood clinging to me.

When they revived me a week later they told me that one round had shaved my aorta, almost opening it, and two others had shattered my right femur and tibia. The wound in my chest had been stabilized at Camp Bastion and a transport back to the UK held up so that I could be medevac'd without delay.

The leg, which I could see but not feel, hoisted up in front of me encased in a spider's web of matt black scaffolding was a different matter. They told me that when the scaffolding was removed, in a couple of months, there would be more of it left screwed to what was left of the bones inside the leg binding everything together, which would heal and re-set over time.

Probably a long time. And with a strong possibility that it would all need to be adjusted at some point. It was only when they told me it had come close to amputation that I finally took on board that my army career was over.

I'd certainly be no use to the Regiment any more, which came as a bit of a blow. I was a SAS sniper, and very good at my job. I'm no psycho, but there's something deeply satisfying about seeing that distant blood-red misty plume through the 'scope telling me my aim had been true.

Every one of those targets I'd dealt with was, in some way or another a real and present threat to my country, friends and family. I knew I'd never achieve the same level of job satisfaction again. And it was hardly a skill-set I could put in a CV.

When I was shunted back to our Hereford HQ my CO had my medical discharge waiting for me, but with 12 months delay to give me plenty of time for recuperation. I was found a post at the Ministry of Defence, MoD, in London.

I'm convinced the CO did that only to get me out of the way. My moaning, after sitting around the base doing nothing for weeks on end, was driving everyone barking mad.

But at least I was now doing something worthwhile, researching the next generation of sniping weapons, something that could be common across NATO. I went along with it knowing full well that every sniper in every army in the world, NATO or not, has their own weapons preferences, and nothing I did would change that.

But this was progress, I was in London with a proper day job, of sorts. By now I was getting around on one crutch, rather than two, and the physio was becoming less painful and nowhere near as exhausting as when I'd first started on it.

I was coerced into going to a dinner party organized by one of the civil service drones, who I happened to like, at the MoD. He told me I was spending too much time in the pub, and didn't accept my argument that it was the default destination for the army when there's nothing better to do. He has a sister, and I don't think he was expecting what happened next. I know I wasn't, and it takes a lot to take me by surprise!

There were about a dozen people there, but the two of us clicked on sight and ended up being very impolite by ignoring everyone else for pretty much the whole evening. The chemistry hit us both like a train.

We were still sat talking on a sofa in her brother's study at 2am when he came in and told me that it was time for me to bugger off home. Everyone else had.

And that's how it was when Corporal Derek Fox met the dazzling Kelly Murchison. It's the first truly grown up relationship I've ever had. Nothing on this earth is going to screw it up.

+

Since then, I'd hardly been able to keep up with events and I'd found myself living and working in a completely different world, far removed from what I'd been used to. But, after another look around the suite I was standing in I thought it had all been worth the ride.

Somehow through circumstance, fate… call it what you will, and with hardly realizing it, I'd been carving out a career and reputation for myself that was far beyond any expectations I'd ever had. I'd always lived for the moment but now, with Kelly in my life, I was becoming more circumspect in how I went about things. I wanted this new life of mine to become the norm.

While I'd been gazing at the sunset, day-dreaming, she'd turned in and was already sound asleep. I took off my bathrobe and tossed it onto the sofa behind me. The sun had gone down and I gazed at my reflection in the huge window, with the lights of a night time Singapore behind.

The six-pack hadn't yet morphed into one big-pack. I was still in good shape. The ugly white scar that ran diagonally across my chest from where the medics had dug out the AK round was not going to go away. Nor was the web of scars running down my right leg from the top of the thigh to the ankle.

That didn't mean I had to get used to it, I never will. But it doesn't bother Kelly, so that's alright then. She thinks I've got a bit of the Prince Harry about me, especially when I grow my stubble. Fine by me.

As always, I gave thanks that my crown jewels had escaped damage from that poor lad's AK by just a few inches.

And wouldn't be needing scaffolding any time soon.

Three

La Hulpe, Belgium. April.

Spring arrived in northern Europe with a procession of soft showers drifting in from the Atlantic. In La Hulpe, a village nestled amongst fields 20km south east of Brussels, the last shower had left the air fresh and village sparkling in the sunshine that followed. Mature trees, now starting to bud, overshadowed the well-tended square bordered with coffee shops, bistros, bars and other outlets. Boutique hotels and up-market cars on the village streets overtly signal that La Hulpe is somewhat more affluent than your average rural Belgian village.

The font of all this wealth and wellbeing is an oversized Palladian structure on the village outskirts. This colossal glass, marble and sandstone clad edifice is the global headquarters of Swift, the Society for Worldwide Interbank Financial Telecommunications.

The chateau, in its grey stone and ivy-covered splendour crowning the hill behind, gazes down disdainfully upon this intruder. As if willing it to move onto a neighbourhood where it might feel more at home. Wall Street maybe.

Established in 1973 by a few hundred founding banks, Swift's membership now extends to more than 11,000 institutions worldwide. They exchange over 15 million messages every day carrying and transacting untold billions and trillions in every currency in the world with them.

Over the decades a system of MT's, Message Types, has been developed to streamline an endless array of transactions between the banks, their clients and the multitude of different players in the global financial services industry. If they want to send ten dollars, or ten billion dollars from one point on the planet to another, as cash or as part of a wider transaction, it will go through Swift one way or another.

Supported by the entire global financial firmament its 2,000 staff, working 24/7, sustain La Hulpe and the rest of the countryside for miles around. Google images show the sheer size and gravitas of the building, but no pictures of what goes on deep inside have ever made it into the public domain. And never will.

Mobiles and cameras have to be left with security before any staff go into the operations area. Instant dismissal, with security instantly escorting you out of the building, no matter who or what you are, if you are found to have one on you after that point.

With its original construction in the early 1970's, a cavernous void was gouged out beneath the building to construct three massive underground levels in reinforced concrete.

The vast computing and telecommunications power contained in this subterranean structure rivals GCHQ and NSA combined.

Mohammed Ibrahim, Head of Network Security, had watched the shower pass over the village as he shared a coffee in the second floor glass walled staff restaurant with a few colleagues, halfway through his last day at the office.

They noticed he was more pensive than usual, and put it down to this being his last day at Swift. He had always come across as preoccupied, maybe distant, some would even say taciturn. Other times he would look downright haggard, leading some to believe he was suffering from a progressive illness. Others thought he carried a secret burden he was unable to share.

But most ascribed it to the enormous responsibilities that came with his job. People noticed that he often got into his UK-registered Renault, headed for the Eurostar terminal and drove back to Dartford in Kent to visit his parents. His devotion to his parents was considered to be a little excessive by some.

In his very first job at a bank in London's City, network security had clearly come across as being his future specialism. He put forward just a few but significant changes to the bank's network which transformed its integrity. After that, he was allowed freedom to work directly with Euroclear, a trading settlements operation, to make the back-office system for the bank's traders far more secure.

It was a natural progression for Mohammed to move to Euroclear's Brussels headquarters from where, within less than two years, he was head-hunted into Swift.

For three years he had been working below ground, in a huge space nicknamed 'the hole' by its occupants, building a future-proof network security system.

Rather than keep on talking about 'the project' or 'the system', and as a bit of a team building exercise, Mohammed, or Mo as he was soon to become known, had organized a ballot to give the new security system they were building a name. Everyone was confident that what was now known as 'Dreadnought' provided ultimate security across Swift and all its 11,000 member institutions.

Over the past few months Dreadnought had been rolled out across the entire network. Everything was working smoothly. On this his last day, a series of final system tests and trials had been scheduled which he knew would go without any hitch at all. Starting at 6am, his day ended at 8pm, when he was fully satisfied that everything was as he wanted it. He was leaving a legacy that anyone would be proud of.

That evening he walked back to his car, the ground still wet beneath his feet and the air fresh from another shower, carrying the few belongings from his workstation which all fit comfortably into his backpack. It was well outside office hours when he had handed his pass into HR, and both the two people on duty recognised him and wished him well in his new job, whatever it might be.

In exchange for his pass he was handed a temporary card that would let him out of the building and the car park, for the last time.

A couple of his colleagues watched from the restaurant window as he walked slowly to his car. His weary posture gave the impression that he was rather lonely and miserable. One of them remarked that whatever this new job of his was, it must be something very special if he was so sad to be leaving Swift.

Mo *was* lonely. And miserable. And sad. And just plain *scared*.

+

He was thinking back to the two texts he had received just the week before. One giving the serial number of a PC, the other of a laptop. The security system he himself had built demanded that every new device used to access Swift needed specific authorization for it to be automatically recognised and approved before it could be accepted by Dreadnought.

He needed to add these two serial numbers to the long, forever fluctuating list of hundreds of thousands of authorised devices. Easy for him to do from his control desk.

As he did it, he felt a black cloud of despair come over him. The texts were from an old acquaintance, Ashar, who he had come to know while they were both working at his first bank. One evening while playing a computer game at Ashar's flat, he had been surprised but intrigued to learn of his hard line Islamic, verging on jihadist attitude. But, as far as he was concerned, there was nothing to it. Hot air that would never amount to anything.

He had let his friendship with Ashar cool when he moved to Brussels to work with Euroclear.

+

On joining Swift three years ago, and within days of moving into his small one bedroom apartment in La Hulpe, there was a soft tap on the door. Followed by an encounter that had haunted him constantly through every hour, day and night, ever since.

Casually but expensively dressed, the man stood at the door gazing at him for a few seconds before he spoke. He told Mohammed that he was a friend of Ashar's and asked if he could come in for a quick chat. Taken completely by surprise he just shrugged and asked the stranger in. His offer of a drink was politely declined.

His visitor stood over six foot tall, maybe early-50's, looking vaguely middle-Eastern but with blue-grey eyes. His dark wavy hair was showing the first signs of greying on the sideburns. He gave a friendly smile and opened with "Ashar speaks very highly of you. You are... if I may say... held in very high regard by our movement."

Mohammed blinked. *Movement?*

His guest spoke amiably, as if Mohammed was an old friend. "We'd like to congratulate you on your new appointment. You and your parents must be very proud…"

Parents? An unfamiliar cold bolt. Deep inside.

"We know that your brief at Swift is to completely overhaul security across the network. Quite a task, and long overdue from what I understand. Of course, you'll apply your own special talents. A member of our movement is one of your new colleagues. He's actually working in the same office as you." This last sentence uttered with a smile, as if it was a pleasant surprise to his visitor.

There was a short pause. "When you've completed your task, you'll leave Swift able to access the entire network without being detected by the security system you're going to build. When that's done you'll meet with Ashar at a place we'll advise you of come the time."

Another pause. "You'll need to set up your, er… do we call it 'back door'…? so that you can access every area of the Swift system itself and every account in every bank on its network. Around eleven thousand banks all over the world I hear…" said as if he was genuinely impressed.

Then, still smiling, in the same tone as he would offer an invitation to a dinner party, "Now, I have to ask, is that understood?"

Mohammed sat frozen. Stunned. Expressionless. After an eternity of silence he managed to blurt out through a forced grin, "Ahaaaa..! You're having a laugh! Did Ashar put you up to this? If he did, you can tell him from me it's *not* funny!"

He finished with a half-hearted laugh. But he could feel the dread stirring deep inside.

The visitor sighed as he looked down at the floor. Then looked up, straight into Mohammed's eyes. For the first time in his entire life he felt that cold steel grip of pure, unalloyed fear as he looked back into those soulless, blue-grey eyes.

His guest spoke softly. Cajoling. "Please, Mohammed. Please don't think this is any kind of a joke… or game. There *will* be consequences if this conversation is mentioned to anyone. We'll know instantly. We know you're more than capable of doing as we ask. Don't betray us."

Mohammed shook his head hard, as if doing this would somehow delete the past few minutes. "*No.* I'm not one of you and I'm nothing to do with your… your *bloody* movement! I'm not going to do what you ask! In fact, I'll be reporting this conversation to security first thing in the morning!"

He had wanted to sound bold and fearless but his insides were churning. He could not stop his voice shaking as the panic rose within him, no matter how tough and resolute he tried to sound. On legs that felt like jelly he rose and made towards the door, ushering his visitor out.

The man, still sitting comfortably on the sofa, continued to stare at Mohammed with tight lips and unblinking eyes.

His voice was quiet, assured, as he looked up at him. "Mohammed, please don't think for one second that you arrived in your exulted position in Swift through your own attributes. We have ensured that your career path has led you to where you have now arrived by saying the right things to the right people at the right times…"

The bombshell revelation that he had been manipulated through his entire career came as a tectonic shock. He reached out to the wall to steady himself and he felt his mouth hanging stupidly open. But somehow could not make himself shut it.

The stranger was still talking, "You are the third generation of your family living in the UK. I would think your parents would probably not be interested in martyrdom for the cause, but they will become martyrs if you fail in your mission… or talk about it with anyone.

Do as I say and you'll save them. And yourself." The man seemed to be taking pleasure from inflicting this pain on him.

An adrenaline powered rush of terror coursed through his entire being. He felt suddenly cold and clammy. The man stood and moved to the door to let himself out, while Mohammed stumbled to the bathroom. This was no idle threat. He was overcome with remorse, and nausea.

He felt his eyes welling up and heard himself groan as he cursed the day he had ever met Ashar. In his wretched state he hardly realized he had soiled himself as he sobbed and vomited into the toilet.

The following evening, there was a visit from another man. Speaking with an Eastern European accent and with no preamble he was told to keep himself to himself and avoid friendships.

Do not attempt to contact Ashar. Just do the job he was contracted to do by Swift, with the added task given to him by his previous visitor. He was being observed at all times. He pushed a flat, black presentation box into Mohammed's shaking hand and then left without another word, leaving him trembling at the door.

On weakening knees he sank down the doorframe to the floor. Then opened the box, to find a framed picture of himself and his parents in their garden, having a barbecue. He recalled the day, last summer. The picture would have been taken from one of the flats behind their house.

As if from a distance he heard his own helpless, despairing sobs.

+

Now, three years later, on that early spring evening he walked in the shadow of the chateau silhouetted by the setting sun on the hill before him.

He sat in his car for a moment looking back at the huge Swift HQ building through his rear view mirror, where he could have made so many friends and had a settled and happy career. Tomorrow, he would do a final clean up before vacating his small apartment and driving home to Dartford.

Everything neat and tidy. Finally released from three years of living a lie. And a cold, fearful dread deep in the pit of his stomach.

Four

Detroit. April.

The new Detroit PD headquarters was a world away from what the time-served cops had grown used to. The eerie silence throughout the building gave the impression that it was preparing itself for whatever challenges might come in the week ahead. Arlene Smith had moved to Detroit with her father's job a few years before and found herself feeling right at home. She had always wanted to be a cop, much to her parent's natural concern, and DPD had made her very welcome.

Now a rookie, almost at the end of her year of probation, she actually enjoyed the peace and quiet of working the Sunday evening shift. It was a bit spooky without all the usual noise and chaos that permeated the place during the week, and with only her corner of the huge basement with any lights on, but no problem. She enjoyed company, but it was good to get some me-time.

The Department had moved to these new headquarters, which had once been an MGM casino, by the time she had finished her training at the academy. The previous DPD building, which had been in use for over a century, finally gave in to the battle against plaster falling on desks and disintegrating plumbing and electrics being eaten away by rats. She had heard some hair-raising tales about a large window falling out and other structural horror-stories that eventually forced City Hall into making the move.

She got on well with the older hands which, for her, was just about everyone. She was no longer asked to make the coffee after she had let everybody know what she thought about *that* by the end of her first week out of the academy.

You can take the girl out of the Bronx, but, "How old are you? And you *still* don't know how to make freakin' cwawffee?" had earned her a level of genuine, albeit bemused respect that no rookie had ever commanded before.

She had got in ten minutes before her shift started at 4pm so she could get changed into her freshly pressed uniform hanging in her locker even though, for this shift, it was not compulsory. With no real effort, it was just the way she was, she had made herself popular among her colleagues. The men knew their limits, and the women welcomed her into their fraternity. She could call on any one of a hundred new mothers whenever she needed to.

All rookies on the Sunday evening shift have the task of going through 'the bins'. In effect a mailroom in the basement with four cavernous blue fibreglass bins which, in another life, would have lived at the bottom of a chute collecting hotel laundry. They are stencilled in big red letters 'Det' (Detroit), 'Mich' (Michigan), 'OOS' (Out of State) and 'Foreign'. Into these bins are thrown incoming letters, dockets and packages depending on where they come from, ready for distribution. Sundays was the day to clear the backlog.

She was starting to get used to some of the grotesque images that came with the crime reports. The worst she had seen after just a couple of weeks on the job, and took her weeks to get over, came with a package in the 'Mich' bin from Ann Arbor. At the top of the file was a picture of a naked, gagged girl about 14 or 15 dangling from chains by her wrists in an abandoned, freezing factory.

It looked like an old car plant with overhead, tracked cranes once used to carry heavy loads across the vast steel and concrete structure. She had been strung up by the chains from one of these cranes. Snow had fallen through the gaps in the roof stretching far away behind her onto the grey, cracked concrete floor.

Blood and other matter from her beaten, broken and blowtorched body had drained into a large pool beneath her feet. The discarded baseball bat and blowtorch were left lying in the middle of the pool.

It was as if her tormentors had simply got bored and walked away, leaving her to freeze or bleed to death in her own good time. Worse, if that were possible, the autopsy showed she had been raped by two men. Two stupid men. It was their DNA on her and all over the crime scene that led DPD straight to them.

They had not touched her face. The expression of utter abandonment, bewildered terror and excruciating torment was forever seared on the memory of all those who saw it. If it had not been for the gag, she would have been screaming for her daddy.

Daddy was a C.I., a criminal informant. A snitch. And he shot himself on the DPD lawn a week later.

Ann Arbor was inside DPD's field of operations and the perpetrators were found and 'dealt with' as only DPD cops know how, resulting in their court appearances being put back several weeks. The delay presented to the court as giving plenty of time for their hapless lawyers to prepare their defences.

By the time she got into work this Sunday evening, the Det, Mich and all but a few items in the OOS bins had been sorted. She cast her eye over what was left and decided she would probably be done by the time she clocked off at 10pm. By 9pm she was down to the last couple of items in the 'Foreign' bin.

Still with some trepidation, even after being pre-conditioned by the stream of gut-wrenching images she had pulled out of these packages, she sliced open the docket from Antigua. But what came out was just plain sad. A harmless middle-aged Detroit couple, dressed in colourful tourist garb, on a faraway beach. Both with zip-tied wrists and shot clean through the back of the head.

There was some seaweed, and what looked like dozens of small pink crabs crawling over them. They were lying on their sides facing each other as if, even in death, still wanting to be together on the pristine white sand. There was no blood anywhere. Meaning they had been killed and thrown overboard from a boat of some sort out at sea.

The couple's passports along with the contents from their room safe, some cash and airline tickets, sent to Antigua police by the Blue Waters resort, were also in the docket. The passports showed the home address of Valiece and Daphne Davey in Livonia, a quiet and respectable Detroit suburb. The file had been sent onto DPD for them to try and find next of kin, and deal with the estate. There was a request for assistance with the investigation if it could be arranged.

But it looked to Arlene as if the Antiguan police were trying to wash their hands of the whole thing, as if it were the Davey's own fault. They were asking DPD to arrange for the remains to be collected and taken home for autopsy as soon as possible.

She read through the report that came with the photographs. Well-written, factual but with a conclusion that could only be described as bizarre. Are you freakin' crazy? Mugging gone wrong? Drug-related? *Oh, perleeeze! Gimme a break!*

Realizing she had blurted the last few words out loud she quickly looked around the shadowy basement, relieved to see that there was no-one else there.

She dismissed the 'drug-related' speculation out of hand. Even with her limited experience, she had never heard of a drug dealer staying at a classy vacation resort, with airline tickets onto other Caribbean islands and reservations in even more classy resorts, over the following fortnight. And taking the wife with them.

The report also showed that their hotel booking had been made through a Detroit company, with an address just two blocks away.

Something was telling her that this case had 'different' stamped all over it. It was neither a mugging nor drug related and it was like no other homicide she had encountered in her short career. It needed special treatment.

She decided to put it in her sergeant's post-box and then, when she had had the chance to give it some more thought, go along and see her as soon as she got on shift tomorrow. Antigua was asking for a recent photograph of the couple which they could use to help with tracking their movements before the case went cold, so she did not want to waste any time.

By the time she had done all this she had not touched her last cwawffee and it was 10.30pm. She got changed back into her civvies, hung her uniform up carefully in her locker and headed home. To a sleepless night.

+

When she got into work the following afternoon she went to see her sergeant, Beth Haydon, and ran through the highlights. Both victims were bound and shot through the back of the head with a single .22 round. Even after just a year on the job, Arlene knew that .22 from behind the ear was the caliber and method of choice for close range assassinations. Do it right and the small slug enters and ricochets around inside the skull, mashing the brain. Heart stops. No blood pumping from a gaping wound to make a mess. All in a split second.

She also gave her forceful views about the drug-related and mugging-gone-wrong conclusions that the Antigua police had come up with. She clammed up suddenly, after realising she could well be voicing opinions that were still well above her pay grade.

Beth was in her mid-50's, been round the block many times and knew how everything worked. And she liked Arlene, as they all did, seeing a bit of herself in her. Maybe it was time to cut her loose. "Well, what do *you* think are next steps?"

This took Arlene a bit by surprise, but it was exactly what she had secretly been hoping for. She had worked through what she thought how it should be dealt with during her sleepless night. This could be a big break if she got it right. She was only a week away from finishing her probation.

A long drawn out "Weeeeell…" and then she put into words all those thoughts that had been rattling around her head the night before. "We go to Valiece's firm and get his HR file… see if there's any next of kin other than, um, Daphne, showing there. See if we can get a handle on what his job entailed… Fix up a warrant to enter their house and see if we can find any clue to anyone who might want them dead... It's motive we need to focus on if we're going to get anywhere on this one."

Now that she had been able to offload what had been filling her thoughts since she had opened the docket, it all seemed a bit of an anti-climax. There was a pause before she finished with a resigned sigh and her body seeming to deflate.

"I dunno… It's another homicide. Write it all up and send it to whoever at City Hall deals with murdered Detroit couples washed up on foreign beaches."

Beth was quiet, looking at Arlene with a pensive expression for a few moments, lightly tapping her pen against her chin. She was thinking how quickly Arlene had started growing the protective cynical skin that all cops grow over time.

At the same time Arlene was wondering if she had screwed up until Beth responded with "Good start. But you missed out a financial background check, which may help with motive... You can organize that. We're really hammered right now. I agree that there's something weird about this one. Go plain clothes so you don't draw attention to yourself and just show your badge. Be discreet. Use my authority to set up warrants where you need them, pull in all the information you can and have a report on my desk by close of play on Thursday."

Yesss! This was all she needed, but she knew she was being tested. The warrants could be arranged by filling out a few forms on her screen. She would have those back and printed off by the end of the day.

She called Valiece's employer, Collins, Day Corporate Finance LLC, to fix a meeting with their senior partner, Eric Day, for 9am tomorrow, Tuesday morning.

They had been expecting the call.

Five

We had the day to ourselves before meeting my new boss and colleagues in the evening. Dress was formal, which I read as a signal that he expected discipline and standards from his small team, which I couldn't argue with. I'd hired a tux from the tailor in the hotel lobby. Kelly had bought her (and my) favourite LBD with her. When she wore that dress… well, even a eunuch would sit up and take notice!

Sunday in Singapore is like any other day and the streets were heaving. We found our way to the botanic gardens and a few other hotspots but for both of us, and especially this mangled leg of mine, the heat and humidity were just a bit overpowering.

+

As we mooched about the place I was recalling the chain of events, driven by some other-worldly momentum that had brought me here.

While I was at the MoD I'd touched base with an old mate, Colin Wood, a sergeant I'd shared a few ops with. When he left the Regiment he started a security firm, innocuously named Corporate Security Associates, CSA.

He provided discreet bodyguard and security services to the ultra-wealthy and their families and, when called upon, looked after a few other matters for them as well. He took a long-shot on me and told me he was looking for someone to head up his PR and marketing operations.

I knew absolutely nothing about it but told him I was a quick learner. He knew that anyway. And then, as if under its own momentum, I was suddenly a civilian with a proper job. Even better, he would rent us a flat at the top of his office building, a Georgian town house in Belgravia. Kelly was more than happy to move out of her brother's house.

While I was still in the army I'd bought a run-down old timber-framed cottage, the sort you see on chocolate boxes, close to the base in Hereford and done it up over the past few years. It was in a small village in a part of the country I like to call 'forgotten England'. I could let it out through the base. The rent would cover the mortgage. I was earning good money, and living in a subsidized flat in the middle of London. It doesn't get much better than that.

CSA's clients were the seriously rich, known in the financial world as Ultra-High Net Worth Individuals, or UHNWI's. I felt as comfortable in my new job as I ever had soldiering. I made an effort and did an online PR and marketing course, but it all just came naturally to me.

The job involved going to lots of events and gatherings and meeting some seriously wealthy people, some of whom actually became friends. A couple, good friends. Over time the media started coming to me for comment whenever they were producing anything to do with the wealthy, generally viewed by the public and the media itself with suspicion. Or maybe it was just raw envy.

I always tried to provide some balance and, in return, got the occasional priceless mention in the column inches or tv program segments for CSA.

From there, with seemingly no effort on my part, I'd been propelled from your average, semi-invalid ex-army sniper to financial PR guru. On the way I'd accrued connections among the wealthy and the media across the world that others, who had been in the game a lot longer than me, would die for. Who wouldn't enjoy a ride like that?

The leg was healing, but slowly. The doctors had shown me a scan of the reconstruction work they'd done. It looked like more scaffolding than bone, but plenty of walking was the only way it was all going to heal properly, eventually. I carry a copy of that scan to hold up in front of me when I set off the security alarms in airports.

I was feeling really full of myself after a great lunch with a journalist from *Forbes* and limping the mile and a bit home from the Shangri-La restaurant in the Shard. I was making my way across Hyde Park, with the flat in sight, and leaning a bit heavily on the stick when the mobile sounded off. I didn't recognise the number. "Hello, Dez Fox speaking."

"Hello, Mr Fox and please forgive the intrusion. My name's Roger Watson. I hope you don't mind, but I've been asked to contact you by one of my clients."

When the conversation, in which I was gobsmacked to realise I was being headhunted, had finished I was sitting on a bench under a huge London plane tree, gazing across the park. I'd tried to fob this guy off. I was really happy at CSA, but who am I to stand in the way of anyone trying to earn their bucks?

I didn't remember sitting down, and my thoughts were going in a direction they'd never gone before. I was 35. Was I really intending to stay in the same job forever?

We'd fixed lunch for 1pm at a pub, The Star Tavern, just a ten minute limp from the flat for two days later. I got there a bit early, intentionally, and bought myself a half-pint of beer. I set myself up on a stool at the end of the bar, behind a small group of girls giggling over what sounded like a shocker of a hen party the night before.

I could tell when it was Roger coming through the door. Smart, dark grey pinstripe suit, six foot, blondish hair, early-thirties and a little out of place with the casually dressed crowd, including me, in the pub. I wouldn't have immediately marked him down as a head-hunter. But what do I know? Even then, civilians were still a species I'd yet to fathom. And anyway, when I'd hunted heads, it was through crosshairs.

I left the beer, worked my way through the crowd and tapped him on the shoulder.

We ordered the wine and picked over the menus after a few pleasantries. I thought it was best if someone took charge. "So, Roger. Please call me Dez. What's this all about?"

He was coming across as a bit hesitant and obsequious. I wasn't sure if it was an act. "I can't disclose the name of my client at this stage of course. He's asked me to explain his reasons for opening this negotia…. er… discussion."

I felt my eyebrows lift a tad, which prompted him to continue. "My client believes you're underestimating your own influence."

I couldn't stop the eyebrows elevating even higher, in surprise. Roger nodded and continued. "Oh yes, Mr…er, Dez… Indeed… There are hundreds of so-called 'top' people in the PR business, especially financial PR, that my client could have targ… approached, but there's only one in the world that business and financial journalists actually *want* to talk to, *especially* when it comes to the wealth sector."

I hadn't realized any of this. Maybe coming into the business from the army, rather than from university or some other career route had given me an edge I didn't know I had. More likely it was my connections among what are commonly called the 'mega-rich'. Or maybe he was just trying to massage my ego.

Pointless. If I'd ever had one of those, I'd never have made it past first base with the Regiment.

I couldn't help myself. "So... Where's this business based?"

"It's global of course. Currently being set up. Offices here in London, New York and Singapore... probably Dubai. They're introducing a new wealth enhancement program, in which only UHNWI's have the wherewithall to participate. Minimum deposit, or placement is a hundred million. More if they want to, and some do. Less can sometimes be arranged, as little as fifty million, but the hundred million is what the traders prefer. And they call the shots."

The guy was coming across now as self-assured. More confident. No hesitation.

"They already have a few clients just to set the ball rolling. Your task will... would... be to build that to at least a hundred and maintain it there as people churn through the program. There's over two and a half thousand billionaires around the planet, plus thousands more verging on that status, and you're better placed than anyone on earth to get my client's message across to all of them. Simple as that."

I groaned inwardly and couldn't stop an impulsive snort. "Oh bloody hell, Roger! You're talking to the wrong man... really! I know how many billionaires there are, and I know a fair few of them. But, I'm sorry... I'm just not interested in being the front man for yet another investment scheme. I see them come and go all the time. I think it would also damage the relationships I've built in the market. I can put you or your client onto a good marketing agency if that helps."

He looked hard at me for a few long seconds, then came over all serious. He put down his knife and fork and made direct eye contact with me for the first time. He leaned forward across the table, looking around the room before speaking softly. "Believe me, Dez." A knowing shake of his head. "This is *not* just another investment offering. Have you heard of PPP's? Private Placement Programs?"

I had. And I probably knew more about them than he did, and told him so. One of CSA's clients, Pat Wheeler, a charming Canadian guy who had made his billions in mining had run me through how PPP's work. And how they had developed out of some weird 'money creation' process developed by Maynard Keynes way back in 1944.

The profits from these programs are simply awesome. I don't know why Pat had told me about them, I was doing very nicely, thank you, but I wasn't ever going to be able to afford to invest in a PPP. He also gave me a fabulous little vignette which is known only to those in the high finance stratum.

It was the tale of how, between 1948 and 1951 the Americans had made a 'gift' of thirteen billion, that's two hundred billion dollars in today's money, towards the post-war rebuilding of Europe. But, in fact, that thirteen billion was new money from a series of Keynes' 'money creation' 40-week trading cycles.

So that 'gift' had not cost the USA one single, solitary dime. But that had not stopped them dining out on it ever since. It was also widely considered to have funded Eisenhower's massive infrastructure development program across the USA in the 1950's.

Keynes' process had evolved into PPP's over the following decades, and those with the necessary minimum one hundred million dollar deposit liked the look of them, but they had one big reservation. It meant moving huge sums of money across borders to the bank hosting the program's traders, carrying the risk of drawing attention from regulators and tax authorities.

And who needs a polite knock on the door from their friendly neighbourhood tax collector?

But, even so, this put a completely different complexion on the conversation. "Ok," I countered. "so… if I was interested, where would I be based?"

"Wherever you want. Accommodation, good accommodation, will be provided."

It dawned on me at that moment that I actually knew people who really mattered and they'd accepted me into their very discerning community. Over the past few years I'd become deeply embedded in the global elite of the ultra-wealthy. I'd never looked at it that way before. It would have been even nicer if I'd actually been one of them rather than some sort of hanger-on. *Dream on, Fox…*

For the first time in a long time I was feeling stirrings of excitement. "So, what's the deal?"

Roger didn't hesitate. "All the usual benefits. Car if you want it…"

He took a large, buff docket from his briefcase at the side of his chair. It had obviously been placed so that he could lift it out of the briefcase and pass it across the table without having to rummage around for it. This man paid attention to detail, which earned my respect.

"That's the draft contract. Golden handshake, retainer and commission override, use of private jet account… all in there. Don't open it now. Take it. Read it later. Talk it over with Kelly. Then give me a call. Detailed explanation of the PPP in there too, which is why I need an NDA (non-disclosure agreement) from you. If you already have a grip on PPP's, you'll see how this one's separate to the crowd and what's so special about it."

He passed me the NDA to sign as he finished with a confident grin, no longer the obsequious head-hunter, placing his business card next to my empty wine glass. I wasn't surprised or concerned to hear Kelly mentioned. If I was doing his job, I'd have done my homework too. I signed the NDA.

As we were shaking hands he gave me a long, hard look and said something that has stuck in my mind ever since, "Just remember, Dez… 'luck' is being prepared for opportunity."

This may have been some sort of head hunter's refrain, or just a piece of friendly advice from one professional to another. But, somehow, it's managed to keep popping up front of mind ever since.

I did some due diligence on the company and its boss, which threw up nothing to worry about. After a week of thinking about it, and with Kelly making encouraging noises, I couriered the signed contract to Roger and he sent it on to my new employer, Global Discretionary Wealth Management (GDWM) in Singapore, to be signed off by the CEO, Robert Jaeger.

This wasn't exactly a life-changing opportunity for me, I'd already built a meaningful little pot out of a few deals I'd been invited into by some of the UHNWI friends I'd made at CSA. But it could be another significant step up my personal wealth ladder, and there's nothing wrong with good, positive change. Roger had earned his bucks.

Six weeks later, after I'd worked out my time at CSA with Colin's full blessing and a memorable leaving do, the invitation to Singapore where I'd meet the full GDWM team, arrived. A mews house in Kensington had been found which would be ready for us to move into when we returned. We were looking forward to this new chapter in our lives.

Was I mutating into a big softy civilian at last?

+

The Singapore humidity was making my leg play up something rotten, so we were back in the suite by early afternoon. We had a snack, fell back on the huge sofa and started watching a movie.

But then she started doing that funny thing she does with my nipples, before doing all those other things she does as only she knows how. I think we finished devouring each other on that huge sofa at about the same time as the movie finished. It sure took my mind off that bloody leg.

Strange, but I've never been able to remember what that movie was.

We roused ourselves about six to get ready for the evening's gathering. I'd been told there would be around 20 people at the event where I'd be meeting Jaeger for the first time. I'd found out what I could about him during my due diligence. As with many in the ultra-discreet 'wealth sector', real detail had been hard to come by.

There was nothing of any concern and the best part was that I couldn't find Jaeger on any social network. He was never mentioned in media and I couldn't find him through any search engine no matter how deep I dug. This was all welcome confirmation that he was deeply embedded in the inscrutable ultra-wealth stratum where *money talks, wealth whispers*.

A good place to start from for his GDWM launch.

Six

Mohammed's one-way ticket to Malta arrived a couple of weeks after he got back to his parent's home from La Hulpe. Two days later he was on this plane, in a window seat and lost in terrified thought for the entire two and a half hour flight.

As the Malta Airlines A310 began the last stage of its descent over Gozo he could see the fish farms huddled around the small island of Comino, squatting between Gozo and Malta. Then, the Gozo ferry pulling away from its terminal on Malta's north shore.

A few minutes later he saw the scrubby landscape below as they approached Malta International. Then the old, sandstone buildings still standing from when the airport was a cold war RAF base, reflecting the afternoon sun alongside the runway rushing by as the plane touched down. He had heard somewhere that it had once been the longest runway in Europe, for V-bombers back in the cold war.

He could see that a few of the old structures had been converted into private jet hangars and workshops. As the plane slowed for its taxi to the ramp he could feel the now familiar cold dread return to the pit of his stomach.

He was to wait at the pick-up point at the front of the terminal. Ashar, once a friend of sorts but now his nemesis, would spot him from the car park and swing round to pick him up. When he pulled up Mohammed opened the back door, threw his backpack into the old blue Ford and got in after it. There was no exchange of pleasantries. Mohammed saw Ashar looking at him curiously in the rear view mirror as he pulled away from the pick-up point.

The drive from the airport took about half an hour, and passed in total silence. They arrived outside a ground floor apartment in Marsaxlokk, a fishing village on the south end of the island on a quiet, narrow street leading away from the quayside.

As he got out of the car Mohammed caught a glimpse of brightly coloured fishing boats on their trailers at the end of the street, with the deep blue waters of the harbour behind. After Ashar had let them in he did a quick tour of the apartment. A lounge with two desks facing each other and two bedrooms. When he was back in the lounge he noticed that one desk had a PC with three screen, and the other had a laptop sitting on it.

Bathroom, utility room and a large kitchen/diner. This was going to be home and office for the foreseeable future as far as he could make out. After his peremptory tour he grunted his approval and stared at Ashar as the two stood facing-off across the lounge. They had been friends or, more like, close acquaintances. Now he was here only because of the threat hanging over his parents and himself. He was carrying the entire burden himself. If he had told his parents what was happening it would have destroyed them.

Ashar was acting as if nothing had happened to disturb what he had always thought was a proper friendship, which Mohammed was finding difficult to handle. "I'm sorry, Mohammed, if there was any misunderstanding. I just assumed you knew what our movement is all about. After all we spoke about it often enough."

Mohammed did not think this was worth responding to. "Please give me your passport, wallet and mobile and let me look through your backpack."

He gasped and stepped back. Furious. Astonished. Who the hell did this jumped up little shit think he was? If it was not for his parents, he thought he could have throttled Ashar on the spot, and laughed while he did it.

"Enough of this!! Who the *fuck* do you think you are?!" He rarely swore, never lost his temper but he could no longer hold back the bottled-up tension and impotence of the past three years from erupting.

Ashar sighed and held out his hand to receive what he had asked for. Mohammed threw it all at him.

Throughout his three years at Swift he had tried to spot who it was monitoring him. But, even if he did find out, who could he tell? There was every likelihood that if he went to any of the authorities either in the UK or Europe, word would immediately get back to Swift and it would be the end of the line for him and his parents. Rock and hard place did not come close to describing where he was at. His only hope was that whatever he was going to be asked to do now would be the end of it, and he could get on with his life free and clear of the nightmare he was now living.

After a minute rummaging through his backpack and confiscating Mohammed's laptop, phone and passport, Ashar put it all on the lounge table. He had found the memory stick containing the links to his 'backdoor' and held it up with a questioning look. Mohammed reluctantly nodded confirmation.

Ashar spoke as if he had rehearsed every word. "We're going to be here for as much as six to nine months. You're to call your parents once a week, as you usually do, in my presence. Otherwise your phone will be switched off and I'll give it to you when it's time to make your call. You're free to move around Malta, but not to use the Gozo ferry. Just remember you're under constant surveillance."

He pulled all of Mohammed's bank cards from his wallet and handed him a debit card. "Use this card for everything you need, we'll be checking the statements. Do not attempt to buy any tickets home or to anywhere else. Do as you're told, complete your tasks and you and your parents will be safe. Do you understand me?"

Shaking with impotent rage and too furious to speak, Mohammed just nodded and snatched the card and PIN-slip out of Ashar's hand. It was issued on an obscure bank in the Czech Republic.

Ashar went out to the utility room and came back with two rolled up prayer mats. He offered one to Mohammed and nodded towards a pencilled vertical line drawn on the wall facing the street. "That line points South East towards Mecca. Now, Mohammed, let's pray for the mission ahead."

Mohammed stared in disbelief for a second and then, venting three years of pent-up rage and frustration, backhanded the mat out of his grasp. As it flew across the room he swore once more, picked up the spare keys on the table and stormed out of the apartment. Ashar let him go thinking it was best for him to get it out of his system, after which they could get down to the job in hand. He would go and stay at a hotel tonight, so Mohammed could have some time to himself and cool off.

The apartment was empty when Mohammed got back around midnight. He had calmed down a bit, but the rage returned when he saw no sign of his laptop or mobile. The next morning, after a sleepless night and wondering where Ashar was, he bought some groceries from a small shop on the corner of the narrow street, then got a bus into Valetta to stock up on clothes.

Before going back to Marsaxlokk he took a walk around Valetta, his mind churning and confused. At the end of his tour, he found himself in the Barrakka Gardens by the government buildings at the entrance to Valetta, leaning against the wall looking high over the expanse of Grand Harbour. Lost in thought.

He felt Ashar's presence beside him before he spoke. "Did you know about the Ottoman siege of Malta in 1565?"

A resigned, exasperated sigh. *Is there no escape*? "Vaguely."

Ashar became animated. "Oh yes… the Ottomans tried to invade Malta. But it was held by the Knights Hospitaller with just 2,000 soldiers and 400 Maltese men, women and children. *Women* and *children*! Can you *imagine* that? Awesome courage on both sides of the battle."

He pointed at the soaring fortifications across the harbour. "See those scars on the walls of the Three Cities over there? They're from the cannon and other weapons the Ottomans used all those years ago. It was the last battle between the infidel and Islam. The infidel won… on that occasion."

He took a thoughtful pause, nodding with some secret satisfaction to himself. "That's why I asked to put this part of the operation on Malta. I want to play a part in creating a completely different outcome for this final battle. When we bring down their entire degenerate so-called civilization."

Mohammed was still in such turmoil that most of what Ashar said went over his head. But he had already come to the conclusion that the man had become demented since he had known him before, driven by something that even he was not too sure about. He had resolved to play along for one purpose only, to keep himself and his parents alive.

Then Ashar announced that enough time had been wasted, there was work to be done. He hailed a cab.

Seven

By seven o'clock we were dressed and ready to go down to the Windows East room two floors below our suite. I'd been told that it was going to be more business than pleasure and that Kelly, because of her reputation, was welcome but could leave whenever she wanted. But I knew Kelly, she'd be there to the bitter end.

Half an hour later we stepped out of the elevator and into the room where there were just half a dozen people standing in a group by the window, holding their drinks as they stared out over the Singapore evening skyline. The same view I'd been looking at from two floors above about the same time yesterday.

With subtle lighting and decor, it was just the kind of setting in which professionals providing discreet financial services to the world's ultra-wealthy would feel comfortable. There was a time I would have felt completely out of place in these surroundings. I'm truly working class, but I'd found myself growing more and more comfortable with all these trappings after all the events I'd been to while I was at CSA.

It all seemed quite natural to me now, even wearing a tux, though I sometimes chided myself for 'turning civilian' and taking it all for granted. I'd promised myself that I'd keep hold of all those survival instincts instilled in me during my time with the Regiment after I left. But I knew I was getting lazy. Going native.

A receptionist, a local girl, pointed to name badges on a table by the door and indicated for us to pick ours out to hang round our necks. I did. But no torture on earth would induce Kelly to ruin her appearance with one of those things. And who could disagree?

Jaeger stood slightly aside from the small gathering, a trait I'd noted was common among those with significant wealth, although not so much with your bog-standard millionaires. Even when a group of these ultra-wealthy are together, their instinct is to give themselves more space than the norm.

He gazed a little longer than was really necessary at Kelly. Not surprising as in her LBD, set off with discreet diamond and emerald necklace and earrings sparkling just beneath her blond bob, she looked a long way north of merely stunning. The slight tan she'd picked up from walking around Singapore yesterday was the icing on the cake. It was hard even for me, who knew her better than anybody, to tear my eyes away from her.

He pasted a welcoming smile onto his far too bloody handsome features, put down his glass and came across the room towards us. He looked first again at Kelly not even trying to hide his admiration, if that's what it was, then at me.

Shaking hands, he said in a soft, beguiling tenor, "Welcome to the team, Derek… It's a genuine pleasure to meet you and we're all looking forward very much to working with you. We really do appreciate you joining us." I couldn't tell if this was all bullshit or not.

Dark wavy hair, slightly greying at the sides and blue-grey eyes that were at odds with, but somehow complemented his dark features. And charisma oozing from every pore. I decided right there and then that I wouldn't trust him even to walk my dog, if I had one. But I somehow managed to muster a nice smile for him.

He turned to Kelly, leaned down and kissed the back of her hand. I could sense her recoiling inside, as she would from a snake. If Jaeger had picked up on it, it didn't show.

He made eye contact. "And welcome to you, Ms Murchison… Kelly. We're delighted to have you with us this evening… We'd hate to see you go, but if you find yourself getting bored, please feel free to leave. We'll be disappointed… but not offended." He was now holding her hand with both of his and smiling at her in the way any man smiles at a woman he fancies. A lot.

Unbelievable. The guy was hitting on her right in front of me! If this had been a few years ago, the paramedics would already have been called out to him. But it was a long time since I'd lost my cool. I leave that to others. I just smiled.

If this idiot had known how solid we were, he wouldn't be embarrassing himself like that.

There he stood. Oily charm itself. The obligatory dark brown voice. I couldn't see a time when we'd be swapping yarns over a beer or two.

I was wishing I'd insisted on meeting him before signing off the contract. I could still be having a ball working with a team which I had come to know, like and respect at CSA. I felt my sixth sense, which had lain dormant since the shoot-out in Helmund, splutter into life and then begin firing on all cylinders. But, right then, I couldn't figure out what it was trying to tell me.

He said he looked forward to seeing me at the office tomorrow morning. "Come casual, Derek. It's going to be all work."

He invited us over to be introduced to his little group and took complete charge of Kelly with his hand on the small of her back as he guided her across the room. I walked behind and saw the expression on her face reflected in the window. I could tell she was not comfortable. Anyone else would think she was completely relaxed.

My digging had thrown up that Jaeger was born to an Egyptian mother and German father fifty-five years ago. Dark hair with distinguished grey flecks just showing on the sideburns going well with his evenly tanned complexion and those pale, blue-grey eyes. Nauseatingly perfect.

At a slim six foot two he cut an impressive figure, which he obviously used to great effect over lesser mortals. From where he sits, that'll be about seven and a half billion of us.

While I had a moment alone with him, I thanked him for providing such a luxurious suite at the Four Seasons, it really wasn't necessary. "Oh that. Think nothing of it, Derek. I'd booked it for myself, but my apartment was ready sooner than expected. I wasn't going to let it go to waste as it was already booked and paid for. It was quite lucky for you actually, finding a decent hotel room in Singapore at short notice is more difficult than you might think. You could well have wound up sharing with the cockroaches in some two-star hovel if it hadn't worked out that way."

He was trying to connect with me through a bit of banter. It wasn't working. "Well, thank you anyway…" I said, into our chemistry-free zone.

Sometimes buried for days or even weeks on end in my invisible sniper hide, I'd grown closely acquainted with a few quite personable cockroaches, some other critters too. I was thinking that I would have preferred to be spending my time in their company right now rather than his.

More people began to drift into the room and it soon became clear that Kelly would be the only woman at the gathering. The men, all in their late-30's or early-40's, at the peak of their careers were giving her the once-over, sometimes the two-or three-times over, as they arrived.

Two large, round and highly polished sandalwood tables reflected the subdued lighting and filled much of the room, with places set for the 20 guests. There were no place names and people just found seats for themselves and settled in after filling their plates at the buffet.

I watched as people introduced themselves to their neighbours, and we joined in. A comfortable buzz of conversation grew as waiters started filling glasses. I could see that this was obviously the first time anyone had met, but that they all came from the same background. Relaxed, confident and settled in their safe little worlds.

We chose seats directly facing the lectern so we wouldn't have to crane our necks to see Jaeger speaking. Just after 8pm there was the traditional ring of knife on wine glass as he gained the room's attention.

I'd found myself feeling really quite laid back and was mildly surprised to realise that I was becoming totally acclimatized to this good life. But my sixth sense just would not let go. I then thought that maybe I was being a little harsh on the clones who had now filled out the room.

For all I knew, they could well have been regarding me as a bit of an outsider. I was surrounded by people who were top of their game in the wealth management and private banking sector, in an environment that exuded wealth and privilege.

Was I wrong to feel at home in all this? I didn't think so, I'd done more than my bit for Queen and country, so now it was time for a bit of payback. And, just maybe, that overactive sixth sense of mine was crying wolf. I didn't have to like Jaeger to work with him.

As everyone settled down, he looked across the room towards the door and gave an imperceptible nod, a signal for someone to close the doors. Out of curiosity I glanced over and saw the muscle, also wearing a tux, close the doors as the last waiter left. He turned around to face the room standing, feet apart, with hands clasped in front.

There was eye contact and, for a heart-stopping split second, recognition.

Neither of us betrayed it. But the message that passed between us as telepathic lightning was crystal clear. 'What the *fuck* are *you* doing here?!'

In that instant I was a soldier again, with every one of those instincts fired up. I was brought back down to earth with a crash and I had to make a conscious effort to show no reaction. To cover it, I turned to Kelly and gave her a 'glad you're here with me' smile. Did Jaeger notice?

Was that a glance towards the door and then back at me?

After just a moment's pause he welcomed everybody and explained that rather than go around introducing people now, we would all get to know each other over the coming few days at the office.

But he made an exception, and introduced me. "I'd like to make a proper welcome, however, to Derek Fox who's going to head up our marketing and media relations. Our PR man. A job more critical and demanding, from our company standpoint, than it might sound."

Everyone gave me curious nods of acknowledgement, none of them really understanding why I was there or what my role in this set up would be. But next came the bit that this bunch had really been waiting for "…and his partner, Kelly Murchison, who some here will already know by reputation."

At last, an excuse for the whole testosterone-laden crowd to have a really good ogle. She responded with a coquettish smile and a shy little wave that raised the temperature across the whole room. What is it about a woman in an LBD that makes men want to howl at the moon? Coco Chanel has a lot to answer for. I could see too that Jaeger was taking the opportunity to have a really good ogle for himself.

My sixth sense was now up and running again at full throttle. Something about this guy… about this whole bloody set-up.

"And now I think it's time to set out what we're here to do."

He went onto explain the program that GDWM was introducing, the Private Placement Program, the PPP. That it was originally conceived by Maynard Keynes in 1944 and how, over the subsequent decades as it had evolved, it had funded many trillions of dollars in countless major infrastructure and humanitarian projects across the world. All that new money absorbed into the global economy through labour, materials and ever-expanding population leaving no effect on inflation.

The only problem is that to raise the billions of dollars needed for these projects, the program's traders need a minimum deposit of one hundred million dollars, which the host bank can lend against, to start a PPP trade cycle. "You've all been provided with my 'wealth enhancement' briefing, which I hope managed to convey how the PPP, and particularly *our* PPP process works."

No matter what else I might now be thinking about Jaeger, he was a compelling speaker. We couldn't help but listen intently as he explained that it's not the banks themselves which carry out the PPP trades, they just host the trade group of which there are only five or six in the whole world. The investor's deposit, their placement, is held in a blocked, non-depletion account under their own signature at the bank hosting the traders, which loans them ten times the placement.

I looked at Kelly and could see that this was stuff she already knew. But I could see as well that she was looking around the whole room, trying to read the people in it. But not so's you'd notice.

Someone on the other table raised their hand. An Australian accent. "So, Robert… but what if you don't actually have a project that needs all this money?"

"That's the question I've been waiting for." A quiet smile. "It's not something I could actually put in writing in my briefing. But you can enter a program, and take your profits, even if you don't actually have a project to fund. However, this has been happening for a few years now, so I don't know how long the powers that be will continue to tolerate it."

Another pause accompanied by a confident, thoughtful expression as he looked around the room. No more questions. "Now, here's what's so special about *our* PPP… Where all the others fall down is that the investor has to move their funds to the bank hosting the traders, so the host bank has the deposit safe and secure in an account of their own, where they can see it's there as collateral against their loan to the traders.

"But no matter how big or secure that host bank may be, it's still unsettling for the investor."

Then, as if looking into everyone's eyes at the same time "However…with *our* PPP, their money can stay blocked in their *own account, at their own bank*. And *that*'s the whole point of *our* offering and what separates us from the crowd…

There was a few seconds pause before he continued. Conspiratorially,"Everyone in this room knows about Swift and their Message Types… their MT's. One of those MT's is the MT799. When used with our PPP it tells our traders where the deposit is and confirming that the bank will not allow it to be moved or used for anything else, other than as collateral for their loan, for the duration of the trades.

"The MT799 can't be released until it's timed out or an agreed code exchanged between the client's and our host bank to liberate those funds. For the period they're blocked, our bank can then leverage those funds, from a distance so to speak, in order to provide the loan to our traders. The deposit stays in the investors own account. It doesn't go anywhere."

I had completely absorbed Jaeger's wealth enhancement briefing. The addition of the MT799 feature was a stroke of genius. Nothing could have been further from my mind when I was squinting through crosshairs, and buddying-up with cockroaches.

This was what I'd read in the docket Roger Watson had given me back in London, and was the deciding factor in accepting the job offer.

This really did make the GDWM PPP unique. Jaeger had opened the door to a whole new raft of potential investors, the nervous ones who like to keep their money with banks and in jurisdictions they know and trust. That's all of them. Opening the door to a colossal market for us.

+

There was a bit more Q&A, but by nine-thirty people had gathered into small groups and were introducing themselves to each other. The biggest group was surrounding Kelly, of course, and I watched her as she went into her 'intelligence gathering' mode.

She had a way of standing, head cocked slightly to one side and a quizzical look in her eye which implied: *'Just say the right words, chum, and this chat could go in a whole new direction…'*. It was nothing less than flirting, on stilts. But when she did it she could extract anything she wanted to know about anything from anyone… Correction, any *man*.

Jaeger came across the room, led me over to the door and introduced me to the muscle, John Burgess. He told him to come round to the hotel and pick me up for my first day at the office in the morning.

John looked me hard in the eye, with a polite smile as we shook hands. "Pleased to meet you, Mr Fox. See you tomorrow. Seven-thirty."

+

I was psyching myself up for an early start when we got into the elevator back up to our suite.

We were both silent until Kelly said "Did you notice?"

"Notice what?"

"Aside from Jaeger at the start, I didn't see anybody actually smile this evening…" a quiet snort "…except when they were undressing me with their eyes."

"Yeah. That'll be right." Silence again.

We let ourselves into the suite and started getting ready to turn in. I said, "I saw Ted Larkin this evening. He was the muscle on the door. He's a mate."

"Who?"

"Ted Larkin. I'd no idea he'd left the Regiment. I thought he was still on active. Jaeger called him John Burgess. We recognised each other but neither of us gave it away. Training."

Kelly was still on her own tack. "You know what? They were all so intense. It's like it's not a job. It's more like a mission to them. They were all recruited by that guy Roger… you know, the one you met in London… um, Watson. He must have retired on the fees he got if all their retainers are anything like yours. He must have been given a brief that told him to find people in a fixed age bracket, degrees, languages and stuff like that…" and with a little chuckle, "not that *you'd* fit any of it!"

She stopped and thought for a few seconds. "It's weird. These guys are clones of each other. Maybe it's just Jaeger's way, 'tis his first start-up after all."

We were on the same page with that. I was about to answer, as best I could anyway. But once she started, you just didn't interrupt.

"…and as far as that Jaeger goes, you should know I *do not* like that man! He's repugnant, but then again that's only me…" and then, firing that cock-eyed grin at me, "…some people like reptiles."

I didn't know what to say so I said nothing. And I really wanted to know why Ted Larkin, with whom I'd shared just one very hairy op back in the day, was there under a fake ID. Sooner or later I'd find out.

But at least we were obviously of one mind about our Mr Jaeger.

We turned in. Early start tomorrow.

Eight

Once a friend of sorts, Mohammed was now seeing Ashar as nothing more than a scrawny, obnoxious little runt who was obviously getting a kick out of lording it over him. He stood behind him and watched as he plugged in the memory stick, then cut and paste the link to his back door from the stick into his browser. Swift responded by asking for a confirmation code which, again, he was able to cut and paste from the stick.

Immediately, he could see that he had full and open access to the entire system, as if he were back at his control desk in 'the hole'. In fact, he now had even more control because access to individual accounts by anyone at Swift was prohibited, blocked and constantly monitored.

To override that block had been a few minutes work for Mohammed. After all, it was he who had written the code for it in the first place.

Without a word, Ashar passed him a sheet of paper showing the three bank accounts for those who had already signed up to the GDWM PPP offering, Jaeger's 'pilot' deals. Still with Ashar standing behind him he went to the first account, a private bank in Canada. It showed $100 million blocked with a Swift MT799 and a remaining accessible $1.2 billion that, if he wanted to, he could move immediately to any other bank account anywhere in the world.

Ashar grinned and said. "Perfect, exactly what we wanted. You've done well, brother."

Mohammed could not help himself, hissing "I'm not your brother. And never will be."

Ashar sighed, as if there was still hope for Mohammed. "I assume the holder of this account will not know it's been accessed?"

Mohammed shook his head. "No, there'll be no sign we've been near it unless we actually do something with it."

Ashar took the stick out of the PC, walked round the desk and plugged it into his laptop. He then repeated the same process that he had just watched Mohammed go through on the other two accounts but, this time, with the authorization code for his laptop. He gave a smile of satisfaction, with eyes wide open in amazement, as he saw Swift and the entire global banking network open up before him. Almost disbelieving what he was seeing with his own eyes.

Both the PC and his laptop now had full and unfettered access to every account in 11,000 banks across the world. Over 20 billion of them, personal and business, churches to multi-national corporations, pensioners to pension funds. He looked across at Mohammed and then at the wall behind him.

Mohammed turned round to see the 50-inch screen showing everything that was on his three screens. His every keystroke was being monitored. Ashar leaned back in his chair with hands clasped behind his head, looking directly at Mohammed.

He explained that over the coming few months, he would be given the co-ordinates for as many as 100 or more bank accounts. These were the new GDWM client accounts as they bought into their PPP's. Each one would have a minimum $100 million blocked with an MT799, and he was to advise Ashar of what funds remained available in each account that they could move.

He then tossed another memory stick across the desks to him. "You'll find fifty banks on that stick, each with their Swift registration applications that now require verification… by you. Set it up so that all fifty are allocated Swift and IBAN codes. Those are the banks you're to move the funds to. It doesn't matter what goes where, we just need to ensure that the amounts are as even as possible so that we don't get flagged. You'll need to space them all out over 24 hours, so that we don't throw a spike up on the Swift system."

With his head spinning Mohammed reviewed the fifty banks on the stick and could see immediately that they were all private capital banks in offshore jurisdictions. He could also see that they had all been registered over about a year, so someone had been on a mission to get them all set up.

Then, "In the meantime, you'll provide a list of all MT799's and other Swift MT's used to block funds currently in operation and what accounts they apply to."

Mohammed was having trouble keeping up. "Are you kidding? There's thousands, probably tens of thousands of them at any one time! What do you want that for?"

Ashar explained that he was only interested in those blocking amounts of $100 million or more, as these would mostly be deposits on PPP's.

Mohammed was getting ever more flustered and confused. He snapped "What the hell are you banging on about..?! What's a PPP?!"

Mohammed, along with almost 7.5 billion other people had no idea what a PPP was. After all, the first 'P' stands for 'Private'.

"You don't need to know. Our focus for now is on MT799's blocking $100 million or more. Just produce the list for me and keep it updated."

Simmering with impotent fury, and with no other choice, Mohammed set about doing as he was told.

Nine

Arlene's visit to Collins, Day Corporate Finance LLP had gone well. It had been her first experience of showing her badge with no supervision and had been surprised at how everyone in the office fell straight into line. Maybe because they all knew and liked the Davey's. It was all very new for her and she knew she still had a lot to learn. But she could get used to this.

Eric Day, the senior partner, was co-operative and wanted to help in any way he could. He handed over Valiece's HR file where she found that there was nothing suspicious in his career history. She had to have what a 'private capital' bank was explained to her a couple of times before she figured that they were nothing more than somewhere to store money for the seriously rich.

The owners deposit the minimum amount required by the local jurisdiction as capitalization and, provided they do not go below that requirement, they can move their money around other banks and accounts, as much as they like. No-one would bother them.

She challenged Day on why anyone would want to set up fifty of these banks, in twenty different jurisdictions and why the European wealth management firm they were contracted to did not do it themselves.

Day's explanation that for security and anonymity they chose to do everything at arm's length and, besides that, it was really a clerical grunt job which they probably did not want to be bothered with, all sounded plausible enough. It was a world she had no experience of, so she just had to believe what she was being told.

But fifty of them? …fifty? And all initiated from one company in Europe? If she didn't check that out she'd never hear the last of it from her sergeant.

At first, Day drew a line at disclosing the name and address of the European firm, but after telling him that she could quickly arrange for a subpoena, he gave in and handed over the details. The firm, Median Private Wealth, was based in Gibraltar which was somewhere she had only vaguely heard of, and had to look up on Google when she got home that night.

These fifty banks were ringing a whole carillon of alarm bells for her. This just *had* to have something to do with the homicides. She asked to look through the files for all of them and found that they all contained much the same paperwork. Copy passports, utility bills for proof of residency, company and bank registration forms and much more. It was mind-boggling and she could see what Day had meant by it being a 'clerical grunt job'. The paperwork was for people from all over the world, but she kept on digging until she found a file with the application coming from a U.S. citizen.

This was a bank registered in Puerto Rico through a company set up by a Joseph Garcia of Richmond, Ohio. The name of the bank and all the supporting documentation was well organized in the file.

She put it in her briefcase, which had been given to her by her grandpa who had once been a lawyer. An old worn-out, shabby brown leather bag with a flap over the top which was secured with a brass rod. But it was her grandpa's, so she treasured it.

She gave a receipt to Day, and decided to focus on this particular bank as there was a U.S. citizen involved. If there was anything suspicious she would be able to unearth it a lot quicker and easier than working through some foreign bureaucracy.

+

Valiece's HR file gave his wife as next of kin and confirmed his home address was the same as on his passport and there was also the name of his lawyer, Richard Wood. After she realized she had been in Day's office until gone 2pm, she thanked him for his help and headed straight for the lawyer's office. Armed only with her badge and not calling ahead to make an appointment she was there in just ten minutes and announced herself at the front desk, telling the receptionist that she needed to speak to Richard Wood. Now.

After waiting for ten minutes she reminded the receptionist in her very best '*don't mess with me, I'm a cop*' voice that she was still waiting. She had already made up her mind that this lawyer was going to be as obdurate as any she had encountered so far in her short career.

After another ten minutes during which she could feel her blood starting to simmer a suave Richard Wood, buttoning his well-tailored suit jacket came into reception. He announced to her that he was the senior partner.

Good for you, she thought. Then badged him and started to explain "We're gathering background for a homicide investigation..." Before she could get any further he interrupted with a raised hand.

A sharp intake of breath. "Warrant..? Subpoena..?"

"No. But it wouldn't take more than a couple of hours."

He gave a heavy sigh, turned around and started walking away. *Arrogant jerk!* The hostility between cops and lawyers is mutual, just like she had been told at the Academy. In a voice she was finding increasingly difficult to control, she spoke quietly and deliberately.

"This is a homicide investigation. Urgent. One of your clients. You can just help us out or I can get that subpoena and think of a gazillion ways to make your life freakin' hell for years to come. I've got a looooong career with DPD in front of me."

She didn't quite know where this had come from and wondered if she had overstepped the mark. But he stopped short and turned around on his heel with surprise all over him. Who the hell was this green little rookie to talk to him like that? Problem was, she could actually do exactly as she said. "So who's been murdered?"

"One of your clients, Valiece Davey... and his wife, Daphne."

His haughty demeanour collapsed in an instant. He deflated in front of her. It would have been the same if he had gone home to find his house burned to the ground.

He was trying to speak. Eventually he gasped "Val? You mean… You mean Val? And… and Daphne? Are you sure..?" He had gone very pale and she could tell he was finding it hard to absorb this news.

Okay, time to lighten up. Obviously this guy was more than just a lawyer to the Davey's. Walking unsteadily, hands holding his head and giving out the occasional shocked gasp he led Arlene into his office.

When he had recovered himself, he explained that he had worked with Valiece at Wells Fargo and their wives had become close friends. He had left the bank at about the same time as Valiece to set up his own firm, corporate law, but for people he knew he would do occasional family law and had drawn up the Davey's wills.

She learned that there was a son, Paul, in USAF based in Germany who was probably not bothered about not hearing from his mum and dad. As far as he would be concerned they were still gallivanting around the Caribbean in middle-aged abandon. Good luck to them, they had earned it. He was the sole beneficiary of the will, but was yet to be notified of the homicides. She made a note to get in touch with the nearest USAF base to get that organized.

Valiece's file also contained a house key, which Wood was happy to hand over once she showed him the warrant to enter and search the house. At least, this would avoid having to break down the door if they failed at picking the lock. There had been no keys or wallets on either Valiece or Daphne, which was why the Antiguan police had marked the killings down as possibly a mugging gone wrong as one of the motives.

She had found out all she needed to know about the Davey's family arrangements, and left the lawyer sitting, still in shock, behind his desk.

+

To enter the property she needed to be accompanied by another officer and she had arranged for a detective to meet her there. She felt distinctly uncomfortable as she walked through the door with the detective behind her, as if she were an uninvited intruder into the Davey's privacy. She told herself that while this was her first time, it was sure not going to be the last and to just get on with it.

The place was spotless, like a show house. At some 2500 square feet it was around the middle market for Livonia and it was obvious that Daphne had been extremely house proud. Everything about the place was normal. Photographs, kitchen and pantry with what you would expect to find and a small well-kept back yard. Wood had told her that the mortgage, which Valiece had got while working with Wells Fargo, only had a couple of years to run.

There was a huge collection of vinyl records and CD's, and what looked like a very expensive Yamaha keyboard with a carefully arranged pile of sheet music on top. One or both of them must have been musically inclined and, looking at the sheet music showing

Brahms, Rachmaninov as well as some blues and jazz, probably very talented. She felt an overwhelming sadness building deep inside.

Upstairs there were four bedrooms, with the fourth converted into a study where Valiece and Daphne had their own desks. There was a laptop in one of the drawers on what was clearly Valiece's desk which she switched on but found needed a password. She put it in an evidence bag and would give it to the forensic IT guys when she got back to HQ. On the desk was a picture of Valiece and Daphne in a restaurant with a few other people, one of which was Eric Day. It was probably a night out they had when he joined the firm, so the picture was only about a year old. She put it in another evidence bag.

There was a filing cabinet, unlocked but with nothing of real interest. Bills, correspondence, car and house insurance documents. Nothing that would help the investigation. The sadness was slowly turning into rage at such a violent and inexplicable end for this ordinary, inoffensive couple. And then, an overpowering craving to see justice done for them.

She had been taught never to get emotionally involved. Fine for the classroom, but very different when you are out in the field.

Before leaving, she left a note on the kitchen worktop for their son:

Dear Mr Davey,

We're so sorry for your loss and for intruding into your parent's home in your absence. We'll do all we can to find justice for them.

I've taken the laptop from the study as evidence, and the picture of your parents with Eric Day and will return them both as soon as possible.

Please call if I can be of any assistance.

Arlene Smith, Detroit PD.

She only just managed to resist adding: *Don't you worry, Pal. We'll nail these vermin!* She left her card by the note.

She went to her car to get a role of 'crime scene' tape, but then thought better of it. There was nothing to indicate any crime had been committed in the house, and she just felt it would be a desecration of the Davey's memory. It would also advertise that the house was unoccupied. She decided it would be worth taking the hit if Beth Haydon kicked up about it.

+

The first task the next day was to scan the picture of Valiece and Daphne on their night out with Day and send it to Antigua police for them to use in their information gathering. Then she did some digging on Joseph Garcia of Richmond, Ohio. She called his local PD and asked them to check out the address given on the utility bills. She told them it was part of a homicide investigation and to treat her enquiry as a priority.

The message came back a couple of hours later that the people who had been living at the address for over 30 years had never heard of any Joseph Garcia. Further checking through local municipal records showed that the only Joseph Garcia of Richmond, Ohio had been three years old when he had died of meningitis, 37 years ago.

If false ID was behind this particular bank registration, then the chances were that the same would apply to all the other 49. But there was no way she could take on an investigation of that magnitude on her own. It would even be a challenge for the entire DPD to handle.

For good measure she got on the web and found the Gibraltar company registry where she saw that Median Private Wealth had been de-registered just a week before. There was no way she could go any further by way of checking out the directors or get anything on the company bank account. That would take a whole other system of warrants that she did not even want to contemplate.

After a really good day of information gathering, she had now hit a dead-end. But she thought she had all the material she needed to produce a meaningful report, including the dead-end, for her sergeant.

Just to be safe, she called Eric Day to tell him that a DPD van would be calling by the next day with a warrant to collect all records related to the setting up of the fifty banks.

On Thursday morning Beth received Arlene's report, along with a package containing the Garcia file used to open the private capital bank in Puerto Rico. The young probationer had done an impressive job and produced a detailed summary revealing a case that appeared to have far more to it than an ordinary homicide. She had also taken the initiative of finding a picture of the Davey's and getting it away to Antigua. Hopefully that would throw something up.

She took an hour to read through the report and all the documentation Arlene had sent up to her. Then she made a few calls and reserved a meeting room on for the following Tuesday.

On Monday she called Arlene to give her the time of the meeting, and told her to 'come smart'.

Ten

We were both awake early on the Monday morning. Kelly was leaving the hotel at midday to catch her 2pm flight onto Sydney, and I was keen to find out what Ted Larkin and his fake 'John Burgess' ID was doing in all this. Had he got himself involved in some kind of industrial espionage? It'd be good to know.

When I left the suite Kelly was absorbed in her laptop and we were both looking forward to seeing each other again when she got back to London in a couple of weeks. I would have completed the move to our new home by then.

My sixth sense had throttled back while I'd slept and pushed my dislike of Jaeger and worries about him and the firm I was now working for, GDWM, to the back of my mind. I was hyped up about getting stuck into my new job and had a bit of a spring in my limp as I headed down to the lobby.

Ted Larkin, AKA John Burgess, was standing by an immaculate midnight blue Bentley Bentayga, which I thought was a bit of overkill, given that all it had to do was run around an island hardly half the size of Greater London. I was ready with a quip about him playing at James Bond, but the hard stare behind his formal smile prompted me not to start any skylarking.

He opened the rear door for me at the same time glancing up at the CCTV camera surveying the hotel concourse. Signal enough for me to make like I didn't know him beyond our introduction by Jaeger last night.

As I got into the car he smiled and said "Good morning, Mr Fox." and then, putting any ventriloquist to shame, whispered "You don't know me. You'll be contacted in London."

He shut the door behind me and, as he got behind the wheel, held up his mobile shaking his head for a moment, telling me it was as much a bug as a phone. For the benefit of the bug we talked about Singapore's land reclamation program, football and other meaningless stuff through the twenty-minute drive to the GDWM offices on East Coast Road.

He pulled the car up outside a building that looked like a squashed blancmange, except it was blue. No doubt it had earned the offending architect a few awards from those who inhabited the same world. I really don't like using my stick, but the humidity was already overpowering and my leg was really playing up. It was starting to cross my mind that I might have to look for a proper crutch somewhere, which would give me more support.

The lobby was a strange mix of steel and glass disappearing into the distance at odd angles, and I stopped halfway across the gleaming grey and white marble-floored concourse to the elevators to draw some breath. I saw a security guy get up from behind the reception desk which looked like it was half a mile away and walk over to me.

Very polite. "May I ask who you're here to see, sir?"

Equally polite. "I'm here to visit GDWM." I could see from the board behind the reception desk that they were on the top floor.

"Of course, sir. You can see the elevators over there." He said, pointing. And then "Could we assist sir with a wheelchair?"

I've no idea what expression appeared on my face but the little guy took two very quick paces back, turned and almost ran back to his desk.

The elevator opened directly onto the reception area in GDWM's ten thousand sparsely populated square feet on the top floor. Jaeger came out of a door next to the reception desk dressed smart casual, and came towards me across yet more marble flooring with his hand outstretched. I got the impression that he'd followed my progress to this reception area from the moment I'd got into the Bentley. "Derek, good morning. Good to get down to work at last. I understand Kelly's going onto Sydney later today?"

Miss Murchison to you, pal. I looked through the blue-tinted windows soaring up from the floor and curving above us in one sweep across to the wall behind me, where I'd just stepped out of the elevator. I could see Changi airport a couple of miles away across the bay. I checked my watch, surprised to realise how much I was missing her already. "Hmmm… yes, she'll be flying out at two on Qantas."

From here, I'd be able to spot her plane as it took off. He nodded. "Sure… So, let me show you around."

I dropped my briefcase onto a pale green leather sofa that looked like it cost as much as my dear old departed dad would have spent on a car. The receptionist, the same girl who welcomed us to last night's soiree, came over immediately and picked it up. She disappeared with it through the door Jaeger had just come out of.

I followed him through a dark green leather padded door to the right of reception into a vast open plan area occupied by most of the people I'd seen last night. The desks were well spaced on a plush neutral carpeted floor, with opaque glass screens placed strategically between them. Giving everyone privacy when speaking to clients, but at the same time allowing conversation to flow so that information could be easily shared.

There was an uneasy sense of transient impermanence about the place. Maybe the office décor hadn't been finished off yet, or just that this was the first proper working day for the company. But a picture or two on the walls, or even a pot plant here and there would have helped things along. I pulled myself up sharp. When in the name of all sanity did I become interested in office décor?

I could see more activity on the far side of the room behind a partition, yet more opaque glass, through which shadowy figures and computer screens could just be made out.

Jaeger had e-mailed summary profiles of everyone working at GDWM to all of us so that we'd all have an idea of our colleagues' backgrounds. Kelly and me had both been right, all these guys had come out of the same box, with me as the only exception. All of them showed a background in private banking, wealth management and the like, backed up with degrees in some permutation of economics, business and finance.

A galaxy away from my own history and making my few middling GCSE's from my East London comprehensive look a tad inadequate. My army service showed only my start and end date and that I was invalided out. I had told Jaeger to make no mention of my being in the Regiment, but I had bigged-up my time at CSA just to let people know that I knew what I was doing, and understood the world they worked in. But they still probably regarded me as a bit of an intruder into their slick, exclusive club.

All these guys had their own UHNWI contacts, as did I, but it was my job to generate sufficient enquiries, filtering out the dreamers and time-wasters, to be sure they could build a critical mass of clients to reach a steady churn of a hundred or so investors.

Until last night, when Ted made his appearance, I was going to put the program to my own contacts to earn myself some more commission. But something was telling me to hold fire on that until I could work out what it was my sixth sense was nagging me about.

PPP's are not something that can be advertised. There are 'non-solicitation' rules meaning that, technically, you have to be 'invited' into a program. There's no actual punishment if you breach the rules other than total exclusion, forever, from a club you really do not want to be excluded from.

My particular skills in highly targeted, discrete media exposure is what the GDWM program needed, if only to comply with the rules.

I was going to be working hard and pulling every media relationship string I had, as well as calling on a number of juicy favours, to earn the obscene amounts Mr Jaeger was paying me.

After a couple of hours of introductions, education and what I put down as Jaegers attempt at 'forced bonding', I was led into the room behind the opaque glass partition where he made a general introduction. "Guys, this is Derek Fox, the PR man I've been telling you about. Derek meet Gloria, Ken and Asif. These are our traders. We leave them to get on with whatever it is they do."

They were sat around large, grey, circular computer desking. They could all see what each other was doing. There was room for two more similar tables, each set up for three occupants, in the room. None of them, all in their thirties, had been at last night's gathering but they all gave me a friendly wave and smile, obviously preoccupied with whatever conversations they were having in their headsets, and then went straight back to their screens.

On the way back out he explained that these were the guys who set up the arbitrage trades, and that arbitrage means that all the trades are pre-contracted and agreed, eliminating all risk in the 40-week trading cycle. It all happens outside of the regulated markets, which is why no-one ever gets to hear about any of this.

I let him keep up with his spiel, wanting to absorb as much knowledge about the 'product' my PR campaign would rest on as possible. Jaeger said that Private Placement Programs could best be defined as investors *placing* their own *private* funds into the *programs*, which helped give me a different take on it.

What the traders were doing was setting up the pre-contracted trades, which they show alongside the deposit, or placement, to our host bank.

I had just one more gap to fill and asked him who our host bank was. He told me. I knew them. Who didn't? This was one of the top ten global banks with its head office in Canary Wharf in London, and there was no chance they would be involved in anything illicit. In fact, having them involved just reinforced my take on the whole thing that it was real and legitimate, and my sixth sense was getting all fired up about nothing.

Ted Larkin must be using a false ID for his own reasons but, if that was the case, what was all that about being contacted in London?

Jaeger asked everybody to wrap up what they were doing and come across the reception area to join him in the boardroom. Everyone, that is, except the three traders who appeared to inhabit their own mysterious little world.

Everyone made their way across to the boardroom and settled themselves in around the outsize boardroom table. I saw that the receptionist had put my briefcase on the chair next to where Jaeger would be sitting.

At the far end of the boardroom was another office with vertical blinds through which I could pick out a few people busy at their desks. Jaeger's PA and admin back-up I guessed.

+

He took his place at the head of the table as everyone filed in, helped themselves to coffee and find places around the table. He could see that there was already some bonding going on and suppressed a smile. Pity. All that would count for nothing as their pathetic little worlds disintegrated into panic and chaos when his real game plan was triggered.

In all his life he had not formed any friendships. He had countless acquaintances from his banking and finance career but these were always kept on a strictly professional level.

As for women, it was just not sensible to make any kind of commitment, and he kept these relationships purely transient.

He knew he was a lonely man and freely acknowledged it, even though there were times he had found it painful. But this was simply a price that had to be paid. He knew who to blame. Not long now, and sweet vengeance would be his.

He was going to let the meeting find its own way without any agenda. He set things off by asking everyone to introduce themselves, with a little bit about their background, taking no more than a couple of minutes. He told the guy sitting immediately to his left to start off, and then work their way around the table.

With the help of the head-hunter, Roger Watson, he'd covered just about every major language on the planet and all these guys, not one woman among them, had deep experience of working in the rarefied world of the ultra-wealthy and high finance, and the unique culture that goes with it.

+

I was last, and he asked me to introduce myself and explain for everyone what my role was. Take as long as I like. I'd almost nodded off to sleep while listening to almost identical career histories 20 times over. I didn't know there were so many people in the world who could follow almost identical career paths. I took a moment to gather my thoughts.

"Thanks, Robert. Yes… essentially my brief is to keep the new customers coming through the door. You've all got your own UHNWI contacts and no doubt you've already been in touch with them. But our market isn't just the billionaires, it's the multi-millionaires bordering on that status. If you've got a few hundred million bucks, there's nothing to stop you from blocking one hundred of it for forty weeks and earning a few bill off a PPP. That expands our market from around two or three thousand full-on billionaires and multi-billionaires to 15 to 20 thousand when we include those qualifying multi-millionaires with, say, upwards of 500 mill liquid."

I explained my role of maintaining a critical mass of new enquiries through a highly targeted PR campaign. We were dealing with a very tight little community. Two or three thousand billionaires plus about another 20 thousand multi-millionaires bordering on that status to varying degrees.

Add those to the traders and bankers who operate the PPP market and we're dealing with no more than the population of a small town, maybe 30,000 people in the whole world. An exclusive, enigmatic stratum of people who live by the rule that *money talks, wealth whispers.*

I'd already arranged one-on-one meetings with a few key journalists and editors while I was in Singapore. This was definitely not press conference territory, everything had to be targeted. I'd invited the Asia editors from *Barron's*, *Forbes* and *Bloomberg* to private briefings over the coming few days.

"I've produced some background notes for the media, I'll send copies to all of you so we're all singing from the same hymn-sheet. It points them to using the terms 'wealthy individuals', 'private investment program' and 'blocked and protected deposit'. No mention of UHNWI, PPP, MT799's or anything vaguely technical or that shouldn't leak into the public domain."

I told them that I'd be heading back to London at the end of the week. I was setting up meetings with *The Economist, WSJ...* that's *Wall Street Journal* and a few others, including a couple of wealth bloggers who've become very influential these past couple of years. I'd be taking a different approach with each one, depending on their positioning in the market. I was then going onto the U.S. to talk to media over there as well.

With no break to my flow, something prompted me to ask Jaeger "As we're all getting to know each other here, Robert, would it be too much to ask a little about your background? How GDWM is resourced… funded? What other plans you've got for GDWM maybe?"

There was that charming smile again. Or maybe reptilian, as I thought back to Kelly's remark last night.

+

Sooner or later someone was bound to ask, and he was not surprised it was Fox. After all, he knew he had actually had the bald cheek, the *temerity* to run due diligence on him and his company. He didn't seem to show any understanding of the protocols that go with this stratum of business, and the people who populate it. You simply trusted people that their word was their bond and that they were capable of doing what they said they were going to do.

"Of course, Derek. I've been waiting for someone to ask."

No reason not to tell them. It'll make no difference to anything at the end of the day.

"I was fortunate enough to be head of UHNWI business at a private bank in Lichtenstein everyone here will have heard of, but which I'm obviously not going to name, and got to know a few of the clients very well indeed. One of them 'spotted' me with a hundred mill deposit, because he didn't want to use his own identity for whatever reason. I didn't ask. We shared the profit after 40 weeks. None of it went to projects, we split four and a half bill fifty-fifty. Some of my half is financing GDWM."

Purse-lipped, silent nods of knowing approval from around the table.

"As far as other plans for GDWM, those are still being worked on but obviously the PPP is the overriding priority right now. Your contracts are open-ended and you should all be earning upwards, hopefully *well* upwards of ten mill in commissions and fee-shares over the 40 weeks of each PPP trade you generate. Stay on and earn as much as you like."

He hoped he was coming across as a reasonable and generous employer seeking a rapport with his staff. He felt no compunction in playing up their financial prospects and status in the full knowledge that they would be waking up in a few months to a world where rampant, global anarchy will have replaced their delusions of wealth and privilege.

Those that did not have their money in private rather than mainstream retail banks would be overwhelmed and consumed by that anarchy whether they liked it or not.

The self-satisfied grin was hard to suppress as he thought of what was to come. All those years of quiet preparation and planning were soon going to produce the result he had been aching for almost since childhood.

He asked if there were any other questions and one of the guys, an Indian, asked for a bit of clarity on the Swift instrument that blocked the funds in the clients' banks.

He explained patiently. "Sure. Go Google 'Swift Message Types'. You'll see hundreds of them there, all with different functions. You'll see that the MT799 can be used to block the funds in our clients' own banks and can't be lifted unless by a pre-agreed code between the two banks involved, or a time-out. Where we've scored is that our bank has agreed to use the MT799 to keep the client's money in their own bank. So far, ours is the only bank that's agreed to do it, so we need to strike first and hard. Others will follow in time."

+

This covered any outstanding issues. It had been a long meeting and, to a man, everyone round the table was leaning back in their plush boardroom chairs, still oozing the luxurious fragrance of new nappa leather, with arms folded and smiles of quiet satisfaction on their faces.

I had listened to Jaeger thinking that everything was making sense. But there were things I couldn't put my finger on that simply weren't right, or maybe missing. Jaeger himself was definitely withholding something, which I could sense was a lot more than commercial information that any CEO would withhold.

Not so much 'withholding' as 'suppressing' something. Maybe that febrile six-sense of mine again.

If it wasn't for all that, and Ted Larkin appearing out of nowhere, I'd be sitting back with that same self-satisfied smile as the rest of them sitting around the table. As soon as I realized I was the only one not joining in I did the same, as nonchalantly as I could.

I looked at my watch. Just gone 2pm. I swivelled my chair around and looked across the bay. A Dreamliner with the Qantas logo on its tailfin was taking off from Changi. Kelly was on her way to Sydney, and I had only two weeks to wait before I saw her again.

Despite all my reservations, and with my over-developed sixth sense doing backflips all over the place this was not at all bad for a working class lad who, after all kinds of juvenile problems with police, gangs and whatnot, had found his vocation in shooting people who needed to be shot. From a distance. Legally.

But I'd moved on.

Unlike most of the guys sitting around the table here, I was not kidding myself that because I was putting up a good investment offering, I was actually a member of that exclusive billionaire club. As Clint Eastwood once said in one of his Dirty Harry movies: '*A man's gotta know his limitations.*' I decided I would just to do my job, keep my head down, take the shedload of money I could earn out of all this, and run if I had to.

I thought about contacting Ted and meeting up for a drink just to find out why and how he was involved with GDWM, just to see if it would lay my sixth sense to rest. But that would have been a stupid thing to do.

And I don't do stupid.

Eleven

When I got back to London there was a package waiting for me at the flat with the keys to our new house, along with a set of BMW car keys. I wasn't that fussed about a car and had told Jaeger as much. It's easier to jump on a bus or tube to get around London and, if they're not handy, the place is crawling with cabs. But, if Mr Jaeger chose to give me a car, then that was fine by me.

I spent the first day finishing off the packing and managed to rouse myself, still full of jet lag, in time for the moving guys arriving at 8am the following morning. It was a stonking hot day and, by 4pm I was a sweaty, knackered mess gratefully handing over a sizeable tip to the guys who had done all the donkey work.

With my leg the way it was, there wasn't a lot I could contribute by way of heavy lifting. Furniture was mostly where it was meant to be and boxes were in the rooms in which they were going to be unpacked. Eventually.

When the truck had driven into the road, Trinity Mews in Kensington, where GDWM had leased me a nicely refurbished house I'd noticed a pub, the Red Lion. It was at the end the mews facing onto a large lawn sparsely dotted with a few ancient headstones surrounding a small church. By the time all the lifting and shifting was done, and with my leg knocking ten bells out of me, visions of a cold lager were floating before my eyes. I shut the front door and headed for the pub, walking stick making heavy weather of the cobbles, to cool down a bit.

Having a pub on the corner was great. Pubs are a lot different to what they used to be. I could get a meal most any time of the day coffee, beer or anything else. It would also be the place where I get to meet my new neighbours and, maybe, make a few new friends.

So I introduced myself to the landlord before ordering that nice, cold lager and taking it to one of the outside table.

I was sitting in the shade of a large oak tree that had spread itself over the pub from the churchyard, looking down the mews to our house. I laughed to myself when I noticed the garage facing out onto the mews with what I'd been told was a spanking new BMW 5 inside, which I still hadn't looked into.

But then a grubby old red Peugeot saloon pull up outside. I watched a tall lanky chap wearing an ill-fitting dark grey or blue suit, hard to tell and totally out of place on a sweltering day like this, get out and ring our doorbell. But I was enjoying my second cold pint and was still in need of a proper night's sleep, so didn't stir myself to go limping up the mews and ask what he wanted. If it was that important he'd be back.

It was only after he'd done a very tight four-point turn and was driving away when Ted's whispered words came back to me: 'You'll be contacted in London.' Sod it, far better whoever it is talks to me when I'm properly awake anyway.

It was about the same time the next day, when I'd managed to get the house into some kind of order and was pushing the vacuum around when the doorbell rang.

It was the same guy. "Mr Fox." Not a question, just a statement of fact. Whatever this was about, it was 'official'.

I responded in kind. "Correct. Come in."

He made himself right at home on our leather sofa which I had only just managed to shoehorn into the lounge. It was a nice house, but with nothing like the space we had in that sprawling top-floor apartment we had when I was at CSA. I fixed us coffees and sat opposite him across the coffee table.

He leaned forward in his chair and got stuck straight in. "You're still subject to the Official Secrets Act."

I nodded my acknowledgement. There was no introduction or preamble. "Ted Larkin is still with your old Regiment, but he's been seconded to us. We managed to get him inserted into GDWM as their security man, through a contractor, but it's very difficult for him to find out what's really going on. He's not privy to any of the real action. It would really…"

I'd had enough, and held up my hand to interrupt him. "Whoa..! Let's rewind here. Who's 'us' and what 'action' are you talking about? And, come to that, who *are* you? Ted and me didn't have any contact after we recognised each other... Ted made it clear we shouldn't. I haven't a clue what any of this is all about."

This brought him up short and he seemed genuinely surprised as he flopped back into his chair.

He looked at his briefcase and then at me again. "I'm sorry... apologies. Lines of communication obviously screwed up... again." A wry grin and shake of his head. "I'm Tony Jackson and I'm head of project on the Robert Jaeger case at MI6."

He pulled out his MI6 ID and held it up for me. *What the hell have I got myself into here?* We shook hands across the table. It seemed the right thing to do. I held up my hand again asking for a pause while I took all this in.

I didn't want to be any part of this. "Uh huh... Just so's you know, I'm not interested. Right now, I like my life. What do you mean by Robert Jaeger *'case'*? But I'm asking only because I work for the man, nothing else. I did my own full due diligence on him and his company and nothing was flagged up."

Without a word he took some papers out of his briefcase and pushed them across the table towards me. I felt the breath rush out of my body. I'd seen some gruesome stuff in my time, but this was well north of anything I'd seen before.

If this Jackson guy was trying to shock me into taking notice of what he was saying, it worked. "These images are of MI5, CIA and other agents who've been tortured and killed. The one that was skinned alive, and that's the worst of all, was Mossad. One of them is French Special Forces. There are others from over the past five years not included here. Jaeger is not directly involved in any of them, we don't even know if he's aware of this… this…"

His voice trailed off as he slowly shook his head "…no words. But, when we do an association check on all those we actually *know* were involved, Jaeger's always there no more than one or two parts removed. His name keeps coming up as being the common denominator in all of these… these… slayings. The poor bastards in those pictures had obviously uncovered something about Jaeger, or people he's working with, they weren't supposed to know."

He paused for a few seconds. "We think they were being tortured to find out how much they knew and where they got it from. Not to extract any state secrets. None of them were spooks as such. But it's just as likely, knowing these people… these filth… they were tortured and killed for the fun of it."

He carried on staring at me, and then "The entire file on this case is comprised of known jihadists, crime syndicates… and there's also a couple of North Korean agents, and we're still trying to work out why or how they're involved."

I was shaken. Still taking on board and trying to comprehend the depravity of those images. "What about Ted? Is he secure?" I asked.

Jackson seemed to be on top of his game. "He's with Jaeger right now at his compound south of Perth, near a place called Margaret River in Western Australia. That alone is cause for concern. The security he's building at the place is like he's expecting an invasion, or siege... We're calling it Fortress Jaeger. Part of Ted's job is to advise on how all the security around it should be put together. As far as we can make out everything short of anti-personnel mines are being installed and, for all we know, they are but Ted doesn't know about it. Big question here is 'why'? What's it all for?"

I couldn't help myself. Despite my reluctance, I was starting to ask myself the same questions. Jackson sat back in his chair again and looked out the window behind me onto the mews. "We know there's something being planned... formulated... constructed... whatever. But we can't work out what. We've got eyes on Ted all the time."

Then I remembered. "KELLY..." I blurted out. "Kelly. My partner! She's in Sydney right now... I want eyes on her... NOW!"

He nodded and spoke calmly, irritatingly in control. "Already in place. We know how dangerous this man is. Ted also saw the way he was looking at her at your little get-together in Singapore last week."

"Who's doing the eyes?"

"Aussie SAS, their Special Air Service Regiment... SASR. She'll be quite safe and she'll have an escort all the way when she flies home. She's not aware of any of the stuff I've told or shown you."

I'd worked with SASR on a couple of ops and felt a bit more relaxed. They were on a par with our own outfit. He watched me as I thought through the whole bloody mess, and stared at those revolting pictures on the coffee table.

So this is what my sixth sense had been trying to tell me. I should have listened harder. Eventually, I had to ask. Reluctantly. "So, where do I fit into all this?"

He took a notebook out of his case, wrote down an address and tore the page out. It looked like it was a house on a Croydon street in South London. "If you can come to that address tomorrow morning at around ten we can walk you through the file."

I was starting to get confused, and a bit annoyed. "Why do I need to be 'walked through the file'?"

"As I said, Ted can't get close enough to find out what's really going on. We know all about GDWM, the PPP thing – although I don't pretend to understand any of that – but we don't know where all this is heading. We need someone on the inside."

I flopped back in my chair. *Oh crap.*

Twelve

Margaret River, Western Australia. May.

Ted had been shown the images of the torture and killings before accepting the assignment. He had been 'tortured' during his SAS training, but that did no justice to the helpless agony showing on the faces of the wretched men in those pictures.

What if they were ever seen by their wives… parents? That had been his first thought when he had seen them. Beyond imagining.

He knew the unthinkable consequences that would follow if his cover was ever blown. But in some strange way it had only strengthened his resolve to see the mission through. The most hairy moment had been when he had spotted Dez at the Singapore meeting but, for both of them, their training had kicked right in and he was sure they had covered it well.

Despite all that, he really did like it here at the bottom left hand corner of Australia. Under any other circumstances he would have seriously thought about moving here. The climate, the people, everything about the place. He had never been anywhere that was more laid back. But he just wished he could work out what this whole Jaeger show was all about.

He was being kept at arm's length from all the real goings on, making him worse than useless to the investigation. He just had to go with the flow and soak up what he could, without raising any suspicion about himself.

Maybe now, if Tony Jackson could convince Dez to play a part, they might be able to get a better handle on Jaeger's scheming.

He took some comfort from the fact that he was under constant surveillance by an SASR sniper, with clear views across the whole compound. They had the entire site under constant surveillance from a fire watch they had built as a cover, thirty feet up a massive karri tree back on the main road.

He was standing at the top of the cliff overlooking the Indian Ocean talking to the fencing contractors who were now drilling the long line of footings around the perimeter of the three acre compound. Beyond that there were sensors covering some thirty acres in all directions around the site.

Each fence post had a three metre deep anchor with an outward leaning post of six metres. There was no way this razor-wire tipped fence was going to be breached. A second, duplicate fence, this one standing upright, would sit three metres behind the first.

Right now, the first row of posts was being installed from the back of a truck using a hydraulic system to insert a thick polypropylene 'sleeve' into the footings. A second truck followed to drop in and fix each post, followed by a further truck which was standing by ready to roll out the steel mesh fencing which would be attached to the posts. The posts and the fencing itself had a light green powder coating so that it would not stand out too much against the surrounding landscape.

But the coating would not inhibit the flow of direct current into anyone who tried to scale it, or even just leaned against it, human or otherwise. The fencing was not pulled taut between each post, but left hanging slightly loose making it absolutely impossible to scale.

This was the last stage of his security brief for the compound. Then he would be spending the next couple of days checking and re-checking the day and night cameras, laser alarms and other systems for which he had designed and overseen the installation. After that he was going to take a week off and head over east to do a proper de-brief with his SASR oppo's in Sydney.

He had told Jaeger he was simply going to take a week's break before heading back to Singapore to oversee the security being installed at his apartment.

He was quickly coming to understand the lifestyle that bottomless wealth can bring, and how it can separate you from the rest of humdrum humanity.

+

Jaeger was at his desk monitoring GDWM progress on the three screens in front of him. His team appeared to be doing well, especially Mr Fox whose PR efforts were producing precisely the results he had hoped for.

His meetings with those Asian editors the week before had already produced some discreet column inches, which all the editors believed would add to the 'insider knowledge' credentials of their publications. Intentionally, no contact details had appeared in the articles and GDWM did not have a website.

But Robert Jaeger was mentioned and, with that, those inhabiting the secretive and close-knit UHNWI stratum knew just how to track him down. *Money talks, wealth whispers…*

Within a week, ten new clients had been signed up with each of them now at the stage where MT799's were going to be applied to their accounts, blocking their deposits and starting the trading process for them. Most were 100 million deposits, but another had gone for 250 million and yet another 300 million.

A further 25 deals were already in the pipeline and the PR campaign was hardly out of first gear. All because the clients could leave their money safe and sound in their own banks. As with everyone else he had recruited there was no real personal connection with Fox, but his track record showed that he could do the job he was being paid very well to do. He could respect people's abilities, and was happy to pay for them, but he did not want deep and meaningful relationships with any of them.

Fox had told him that he had further meetings with journalists in London lined up for next week, and that he was heading to the USA a couple of weeks later. He estimated he will have generated enough interest through targeted media exposure to deliver the first 100 clients signed up and ready to go within the coming two months.

Profits were paid out monthly to the investors and, at least for a couple of months before Jaeger's real plans kicked in, Fox would be seeing a sizeable commission. This would be paid in line with profits to the investors on top of his retainer, landing in his own private bank account in Geneva.

Mr Fox had obviously taken sound advice from some of his old firm's clients. Most likely, it was one of those who had opened the door for him at the private bank, which were always very fussy about who they took on as customers. He had done his own due diligence and seen that Fox had taken a minor stake in a small consortium led by one of CSA's clients which rescued an ailing hotel chain in Europe.

Within two years it had been sold to a global hotel operator for forty times the purchase price and Fox had earned enough to qualify him to open a private bank account. The minimum requirement for which is always into seven, or sometimes eight figures.

He had carried on working at CSA, even though there was no real need to. Jaeger deduced that this was simply so that he could maintain his connections within his UHNWI network and stay involved with similar schemes. Which, from the size of his bank balance, he had managed to do.

He got up, stretched, looked at his watch and walked over to the drinks cabinet and dropped a few ice cubes into a cut-glass whiskey tumbler, followed by a couple of fingers of his favourite Aberlour single malt Scotch, which had to be the ten year old.

He liked his office. It had only been finished off a few weeks before and still had the 'new-build' scent about it. His large antique solid rosewood desk and plush executive chair, on patterned grey and black marble flooring, were positioned facing the door, so that he would not be distracted by the view behind him which looked out over the Indian Ocean.

A large oriental rug, with a grey and red pattern, for which he'd paid several tens of thousands of dollars, rested under a rosewood meeting table, yet another antique, and six soft leather boardroom chairs at the far end of the room. The walls were hung with his favourite art, individually lit.

Among his collection was a series of sketches on a large sheet of paper divided into quadrants framed under glass. It was obviously Turner trying out different concepts for his Fighting Temeraire. He tried it with two tugboats, the ship itself with and without her masts and then, the bottom right sketch with one tugboat towing the ship with all masts and sails furled. Which he obviously went with for the final masterpiece.   These sketches did not appear in any catalogues, but was traded and passed around those inside the

UHNWI stratum. If you were offered 'the Turner sketch' as payment for a special service, you did it willingly, as Jaeger had done.

He looked around the expansive office approvingly. It could have been in any major financial centre around the world. London, Hong Kong, New York or wherever. But this compound, in this corner of Western Australia was now going to be his home for the foreseeable future. He had no problem with that.

The sun was now just touching the horizon, getting ready for the best part of the day when thousands of people all along Australia's west coast line the cliffs and beaches to gawk at the magnificent sunset over the Indian Ocean. He appreciated the finer things in life, and stood looking out of his window to enjoy the view.

He considered this particular part of the country, Margaret River, to be the one of the finest wine producing regions in the world. Superior even to France and the other supposedly loftier and more mature European regions. And remote enough from the rest of the world to escape the immediate effects of the chaos and anarchy he was about to unleash.

He chuckled quietly to himself as he congratulated himself on stringing all those idiots along, convincing them he was either a full-on jihadist, anti-capitalist revolutionary or just a criminal mastermind, depending on who he was talking to. He could deliver what they wanted, but he shook his head in disbelief at their pathetic naiveté.

He had been stunned at some of the things he had seen as their vicious, murderous instincts overrode any inkling of common sense. None of them except, maybe, the North Koreans, had picked up that he was in this for his own, deeply personal motives. Driven by some force they were not interested in, so long as they got what they wanted.

But he was starting to enjoy the incredible buzz that came with exercising the power that had taken him decades to accumulate.

Everyone was going to get what they had bought into. More money than those idiot so-called jihadists, assorted terror groups and crime syndicates had ever dreamed of or could possibly need.

The Pyongyang crowd would even be getting what they wanted, which was totally in line with his own core, life-long mission.

He had enjoyed every moment of the project intensely. The planning leading up to this imminent point of execution had given him an almost sexual buzz and, now, here he was just waiting for everything to climax. The insect screen around the veranda took some of the glare off the sunset and he could see John Burgess talking to a couple of the contractors out towards the top of the cliff. Jaeger had decided to have the fence installed even there as well, so that he could relax about anyone attempting some kind of fantasy adventurous intrusion from that direction.

Ten clients had brought the security and comfort he was offering through the compound he had been building here for the past three years. In fact, it was well known that a great many UHNWI's had been buying properties in secure, gated communities in the more remote and pleasurable parts of the world in anticipation of coming events. Most could see what was really coming, even without Jaeger's help in making it happen.

They were expecting a global financial meltdown that would overshadow the 2008 crash, the 1930's depression and even the Covid-19 aftermath to the point of insignificance. They had started moving their money out of mainstream banks into private banks so that they were removed from the ever more febrile inter-bank capital markets in which the mainstream banks played.

This had been going on since long before the 2008 crash. It was the mainstream banks and their over-leveraged lending and fragile balance sheets that were going to be the trigger for the next crash. Which would be unmitigated global economic Armageddon.

Those in informed wealth circles believed that, this time, it would lead to outright anarchy and the disintegration of civilized society. The ten suites built into the compound had been bought for 25 million dollars each as a last bolt hole for his ten customers, who would evacuate their own villas and gated estates if they could see things going the wrong way.

Violence driven by resentment, envy and primal survival instinct was a given. Anyone showing the slightest sign of wealth or privilege would be number one targets because, naturally, it would all be their fault.

Jaeger had argued that it was going to happen anyway so why not get it over and done with, and move on.

He had been very careful in his selection of customers, or 'guests' in that none were over fifty, all in good shape and with no immediate family to concern themselves with, other than their wives or partners. One was a leading surgeon, whose fortune had come from owning the rights to a unique surgical procedure and whose wife had many years of nursing experience. He had been allowed a slight discount as, between them, they would provide all the medical expertise his small community would need, backed up with a well-stocked pharmacy.

Everyone had been given weapons training and the same weapons they had been trained on, along with many more, were kept in his armoury. That training would continue even after they had moved in. It was a condition of their tenancy.

Soon now. Very soon.

He took his whiskey out to the veranda and leaned back in a comfortable patio chair. He gazed out at the sunset for a moment, took a sip of whiskey and picked up his phone

Thirteen

I took a cab to the address Jackson had given me which turned out to be a small, two storey office converted from a detached Edwardian house in need of a facelift. The same as you'd find on thousands of streets across London. The weathered wooden sign screwed onto the wall next to the front door said 'CR Software', which was for the benefit of the neighbours and would account for the small number of people who went in and out of the building every day.

Inside, it wasn't quite as shabby as the outside said it might be. It was just a workplace and, with the number of screens dotted around, could easily have passed for a software company. But this was an MI6 outstation.

I was introduced to half a dozen people who, between them, were monitoring everything about Jaeger and his known associates. About twenty of them with profiles to set your teeth on edge. Plus a few on which there was no history at all and, for all anybody knew, were in this just for the kicks. But Jaeger seemed to be right at the epicentre of it all. The file was comprehensive and well put together, with input from not just MI6 but also agencies in the USA, Australia, Canada, various European countries and elsewhere. It left no doubt that there was something very big being put in place, but with no clue as to what.

The file had been built over five years. There was even a detailed three-page profile on me which, to my deep consternation and not a little embarrassment, was totally accurate.

There were registration documents for various companies, including GDWM and a few pictures of Jaeger's compound, 'Fortress Jaeger', which had been taken by Ted and the SASR guys, and others that looked like they were taken from a drone. It showed a large red brick, two storey villa with a first floor veranda running around the entire building, shaded by an overhanging roof. Probably about 300,000 square feet across two floors of very solid construction. It could have passed for a golf or country club, or a boutique resort hotel.

It looked out over the Indian Ocean from a 100 foot cliff to one side and a local single lane road leading back to the forest and main road to the other. Falling away to each side there was open, rolling grass and scrubland and I could see tree stumps from where the land had obviously been cleared. Sniper's heaven. Nowhere for anyone to hide from your crosshairs. It really was a fortress and, like everyone else in the room, I was now asking myself *what's this all about?*

One of Jackson's team spoke up. "Ted's given us a pretty good handle on this property," he said "and what you can't see is a huge basement stocked with food, medical and other supplies that'll last for a couple of years if there's thirty people living there, which looks to be about right when you add in the staff quarters. There's also a couple of small prison cells down there.

"There's no images of the inside as Ted hasn't wanted to risk being caught at it. There's been no real evidence of anyone else moving in, but there's ten self-contained apartments with their own kitchens, bathrooms and all that. Really big and quite luxurious, according to Ted. If it was a resort hotel you'd be paying top dollar."

Jackson stepped in and explained that although the property was on all mains services it had its own septic tank sewage system and the underground diesel tanks would keep the two Toyota SUV's, a couple of pick-ups and a Humvee in the large garage cum workshop and generators in fuel for as far ahead as anyone could see.

Ted had told them that there was even a well that was still being sunk away from the compound, which would provide their own water supply if ever it was needed. Solar panels were scheduled to cover the entire, massive roof area on the main and outbuildings.

There were fenced off areas which were thought to be for a chicken run and, maybe, a pig farm. Everything was pointing to the whole compound becoming totally self-sufficient.

Jackson pointed at a large garage block, set off at an angle behind the main building, with a helipad alongside. "If you look at the floor above the garaging there, you'll see that there's accommodation for what looks like half a dozen or so service and maintenance staff."

There was something missing. I asked, "If these people are laying in for a siege, which it sure as hell looks like, where are the perimeter defences? Walls… fencing? Ditches maybe?"

Someone else in the room said "That's what Ted's working on now. And at the end of the garage block there, the last garage… That's an armoury. Ted only managed to get a quick glimpse, but from what he said it would probably compare with what your old Regiment's got in Hereford." Somehow I doubted that.

The briefing went into more depth. The North Korean contingent appeared very rarely but first contact was made between them and Jaeger when he was working at the Berne office of a Swiss private bank. GCHQ had found its way into the bank's systems, which were surprisingly poorly defended, to discover that they had a number of key people high up in the North Korean military, as well as some ruling family members, as clients.

There were no records of any communications, meetings or other contacts between them and Jaeger, but the same names had kept cropping up intermittently across the five years of ongoing surveillance.

There were plenty of pictures and recordings, although many were barely decipherable, of meetings between Jaeger and a whole collection of assorted terrorists and other havoc-makers. Some already known, some new.

But what no-one could get their heads around was that if the PPP investment offering was so secure and successful, what could Jaeger possibly be planning? There was no incentive to rip-off any of the investors, as the returns on the investment and the fee income to GDWM and its team would make anything like that completely pointless.

Everyone stood to make the kind of money that any normal person would count as life-changing. And, from what Jaeger had told me at the briefing in Singapore only last week, he had a couple of bill stashed away already. So what's the motive… and the objective… if it isn't money?

I was asked to give a background on PPP's and I went through the whole thing. I knew it all off by heart now.

At the end, Jackson asked. "What's this Swift thing?"

I explained what it was and how the MT799, one of many Swift Message Types, blocked the investors funds in their account at their own bank for the duration of the PPP arbitrage trading program. Like anybody else who wasn't really into high finance and the technology and systems it was wrapped up in, like the way I had found myself becoming, he just nodded. A grunt that confirmed he had at least heard what I had to say, even if it hadn't stuck.

By mid-afternoon we were all sitting around the room in a state of complete confusion, and with no clue as to where to go from here. I couldn't do any more than say I'd find out what I could, but that I had no reason to go back to Singapore or to have any further meetings with Jaeger for at least a couple of months. Everyone was just getting on with their jobs. Even if I found some excuse to go back to Singapore or ask for another meeting with Jaeger, it would set off alarm bells.

What couldn't be done on phone, Skype, Whatsapp or whatever? All I could do was keep my ear to the ground and let them know of anything I heard that might help.

But something had caught my eye. Among all the reports from various agencies was a note from Mukhabarat, the Egyptian intelligence agency. It had no direct record of Robert Jaeger, but the name had prompted their system to throw up another Jaeger, which turned out to be his father.

He had worked for a British merchant bank in Cairo. It looked like he had been accused by the Nasser government of collaborating with the Israeli's in the six-day war in 1967. But it didn't say anything about what the outcome was. Jackson agreed it was something worth following through on and would get back in touch with Mukhabarat.

+

It was coming up to four o'clock and I still needed to start work on scheduling my meetings with U.S. media, so decided to get back home. This was turning into one humdinger of a summer and I was feeling the heat as I limped slowly to the end of the road, and found a bus that was heading back into central London.

My leg had settled down a bit, although I still had the walking stick and I was wondering if it was ever going to be anything like normal again. But, ever compliant with instructions to use it as much as I could, I went up to the top deck where I was lucky enough to find a seat at the front with a good view of the road ahead. It was coming up to rush hour and would be a good 45 minutes to where I wanted to get off.

Take it from me, there's nothing more soothing for an overworked mind than watching the city streets pass by from the top deck of a London bus. It's impossible not to ponder on those thousands of lives sitting outside pubs and cafes, going in and out of shops and offices, all going about their business just a few feet below. Thousands of anonymous triumphs and tragedies that put your own life into perspective.

Suddenly, I had an overpowering need to hear Kelly's voice. I called her, forgetting that it would only be about 3am in Sydney. She answered on the second ring. "Sorry, I forgot. Did I wake you?"

"Don't worry, it's good to hear your voice. What have you been up to?"

For a moment I almost told her, but common sense prevailed. "Well, the house is all but sorted. Just a couple of rooms to get straight. It'll all be ready for when you get home. Nice pub on the corner."

She could switch to wakefulness in an instant. We talked about work and some domestic stuff and then we both fell silent, just happy knowing that we were both at each end of the line.

Eventually she said "I've been missing you. I'm really looking forward to getting home. The flight gets into LHR at half five on Sunday morning."

I really meant it when I said "Missing you too. Badly. I'll be there to meet you."

There was some shuffling around. Then, from 10,000 miles away "I'm on top of the bed… just my panties… and thinking about the things we do…" silence for a few seconds, then "Anything we can do about that do you think?"

Hmmm… we'd done this a couple of times before when our schedules had kept us apart. And, if I was anywhere else I could have come up with a few good ideas. Instead, using my legendary Noel Coward impression I replied, "Unfortunately, my dear, I can think of nothing that would not cause an unseemly disturbance on the top deck of a London omnibus… in rush hour."

She dissolved into one of her giggling fits, so the best thing to do was hang up.

The next morning my heart sank when I had an e-mail from her telling me that she was going to be stuck in Australia for at least another week or two. With every possibility she was going to have to go and stay in Canberra while she was sorting out whatever problem she had. Some government department wanted her around while they reviewed the deal she had been working on. Funding for a new railroad from what I could remember.

That brought home just how much she had come to mean to me. After a brunch meeting at *The Economist* the next morning I took myself and my stick, in a cab, over to Hatton Garden where I found an engagement ring I knew would make her melt. She really went for diamonds and emeralds, and I couldn't wait to give it to her.

A romantic weekend in Barcelona for the proposal maybe. It struck me then that my transformation into a whimpering civilian was all but complete.

Fourteen

Malta. June.

Ashar was in a trancelike state and deep into writing the code that would trigger Jaeger's ultimate plan, separate to what Mohammed had been tasked with, ready for execution when the time came. His phone sounding off pulled him back to earth. On this phone it could only be Jaeger. He glanced across the desk at Mohammed, picked up the phone and asked Jaeger to hold on a moment while he put his laptop into his backpack before going outside. The laptop was never out of his reach. That and Mohammed's PC were the only two devices they had with serial numbers acceptable to Swift.

He walked down the narrow street towards the quayside café on the corner where he could sit with a coffee while he was talking. Ashar was slightly built, indeterminate features, and one of those people you just do not see or take any notice of. He liked it that way.

"Everything on track?" Jaeger asked.

"Looks like it. Mohammed's behaving himself and writing his code ready to execute. Right now I see eleven clients, and his program is set up to move, so far, fifteen point something bill into our fifty banks, when we're ready."

There was silence at the other end before Jaeger came back. "How are you doing on the MT799's?"

"Well… According to what Mohammed's retrieved out of the Swift system it looks like there's just shy of 800 PPP's in progress aside from ours. Those deposits have been transferred to the traders' banks under the old system. We know who they are and, out of those, mostly in London or Hong Kong."

Another thoughtful silence from Jaeger before he replied. "Okay. Perfect. Have we heard anything from our friends in Pyongyang?"

"No, but didn't we agree that it was radio silence until execution?"

A thoughtful chuckle from Jaeger. "Indeed we did."

Another silence while Jaeger realized that throughout the call he had been staring across the compound at John Burgess doing some work on the CCTV cameras on the garage block. Something prompted him to ask, "Ashar… have you begun monitoring the dwellings yet? I'm monitoring mobiles here and there's nothing to be concerned about. But the bugs in those homes we've managed to get them into are stored on your server. Have you looked in on any of them yet?"

"Sorry, no" Ashar replied. "The MT799 string has taken a lot of coding if I'm going to have it ready on demand for whenever you want it."

"Understood. But please listen in when you can. In particular Mr Fox in London. He's performing very well, but I just want to be sure of his… um… loyalties."

"Sure. No worries. New phones?"

"Yes. Number six."

They ended the call. Ashar stayed seated finishing off his coffee gazing at the market further up the quay and the throng of tourists and locals milling around the quayside. He picked up his backpack and walked across to the edge of the quay.

After quickly glancing around he removed the battery and SIM from the burner then dropped the phone, SIM and battery into the water separately. He followed the meandering descent of the dissembled phone to the bottom where it came to rest among the previous four he could still see about six feet down.

It was hardly distinguishable from the detritus found on any shallow quayside floor. The phones rested in the watery shade of a decaying wooden rowboat that had not been moved from its mooring, with the same frayed rope, ever since Ashar had organized the lease on the apartment six months ago.

He would get his next burner, number six, charged up tonight. Everything seemed to be going well. He had dealt with any risk of exposure to the first stage of the project by eliminating the Davey's on Antigua.

Valiece was the only one who could compromise the operation as he had dealt directly with Median in Gibraltar and handled all the paperwork. Daphne was collateral damage. Shame about that.

He and his two friends had made very short work of them after they left the restaurant in English Harbour. They had found them at the end of the jetty, probably taking in the romantic Caribbean moonlight, while they were waiting for him.

They were standing directly above the boat they wanted to get them into. The idea had been to carry on their friendly chat and just lead them out to the end of the jetty where the deed could be done. But they had made it much easier for him.

Valiece and his wife had both gone down quickly and silently after a touch to the back of their necks with a stun gun. Amazing what you can buy with fifty bucks on the web. They had not been unconscious but both lay still, paralyzed where they had landed on the jetty, unable to move or speak.

Their wrists were quickly zip-tied behind them before they were rolled into the boat. A couple of hundred yards out from the beach they were able to sit up just in time to be relieved of wallet, purse, keys and everything else besides, shot in the back of the head and lifted over the side.

Job done.

Fifteen

Arlene had three uniforms. Two that were cleaned and rotated every week and another that was kept clean and in its cotton cover in her wardrobe for special occasions. It had so far been used only once, at her graduation from the academy. Beth had told her to 'come smart' so she intended to do just that, but was nervous as to why.

She walked into the squad room that morning with creases on her trousers you could shave with and shoes that shone for America. A few of the team put their shades on and stepped back with arms raised as if shielding their eyes from the glare.

Cop banter, which made her feel part of something much bigger than herself, and always played along with.

No-one knew quite what it was she was involved in, and she was not too sure herself, but all of them knew it was something out of the ordinary and not day-to-day policing. There was no territorial protection or jealousy. After all, it was sheer chance that this probationer had found herself in the middle of what everyone knew was going to be a major, international investigation.

All she got was just genuine offers of help should she need it. DPD prided itself on being a team like no other.

She went to her hot-desk and took over her shift. There was half an hour before the meeting so she spent it going through the entire file on the Davey's killings, then got in the elevator up to the meeting room. Why was it so important to 'come smart'? She did not have the usual butterflies in her stomach, more like a flock of crows. As soon as she entered the small meeting room, she could see why.

Standing by the window, in deep conversation with Beth was the police Chief, Hal Bedson. A bear of a man with a reputation for getting things done, and giving the Detroit gangs and crime syndicates a run for their money like they had not seen in decades.

His presence dominated the room and, as always, he was impeccably turned out in his uniform. A columnist on the *Detroit Free Press* had once written that hc had emerged from his mother's womb wearing his uniform. Freshly pressed.

That was two years ago, but the prevailing relationship between the *Detroit Free Press* and DPD was still frigid, at best.

He had turned a blind eye to the treatment meted out by his officers to the men responsible for the rape, torture and killing of the snitch's daughter, and seen to it that both of them had gone down for life. More if it could be arranged.

This was one of those times he was really pleased that Michigan did not have the death penalty. Those vermin were going to suffer for decades. He did not use 'vermin' lightly, it was a word that had become popular across his whole Department and used by cops determined to eliminate the crime syndicates, as they would with rats.

This was an old school cop who *did* take prisoners, and kept them. Arlene just could not help herself. She was nervous as hell.

He looked across the room directly into her eyes and walked over to her holding out his hand. His six foot six topped with determined features set off with an imposing black moustache towered over her and, for a moment, she felt utter confusion as she tried to recall the protocol for saluting indoors.

Did she salute if she wasn't wearing her cap or, if not, did it matter? What was the rule for saluting indoors, rather than outdoors? Or, should she just hold out her hand to be shaken? She went for the latter, hoped for the best and watched in awe as her tiny probationer's hand disappeared into the Chief's huge paw.

A deep baritone. "Probationary Officer Smith, I presume." His eyes crinkled with a warm, heart melting smile. Well, hers anyway.

She managed a weak "Yes, sir."

"Sergeant Haydon has brought me up to speed on this case. Thank you for the work you've done and, if I may add, the initiative you've shown. Have we had anything back from Antigua yet?"

She gave Beth a wide-eyed glance, whose response was the barest hint of a smile.

"Er…" *pull yourself together, girl* "Um…" *STOP IT – just tell him what he wants to know.*

"I got an e-mail listing the newspapers and tv channels they're going to put the pictures into. To make it… er, cleaner… they're cropping out just the faces of Valiece and Daphne from the picture so there's nothing to distract from them and working up a press release to pull in as much info on their movements as possible. There's a couple of newspapers on Antigua but there's also other media, including tv, covering the whole Caribbean. But, so far as we know, they arrived in Antigua from Detroit just the day before, so the best response should come just from the Antigua media. Shouldn't take too long." She was a little breathless when she finished.

She saw Beth give an imperceptible nod as the Chief stepped back and looked across at her. "Thank you, officer. You're on top of your brief."

He could not have paid her a higher compliment and she tried to conceal the rush of pride and satisfaction that surged through her.

She had hardly noticed Valiece's old boss, Eric Day sitting nervously at the meeting table and she gave him a nod of acknowledgement as she took a seat. The chief relaxed the atmosphere a little by helping himself to some coffee from the jug on a sideboard behind Beth Haydon.

Everyone followed suit and, while this was going on, Beth opened the proceedings. "Well, we all know who we are and thank you, Mr Day, for agreeing to join us. We think we're going to need all the help we can to get to the bottom of this case. This meeting is confidential although it is being recorded. So, when we're all coffee'd up I'll kick off with a summary of what we know so far."

As everyone settled down she went on to review everything from receiving the case file from Antigua, through Arlene's meetings and interviews, and her final report. She added that, because of the international nature of the case, it was procedure to send a copy of the report to the Chief of Police.

He had a reputation for reading everything that crossed his desk, but she had not expected a call from his PA asking to be notified when the follow-up meeting was taking place.

At the end of her review she paused and looked around the table. "It's obvious to all of us here… at least the cops among us… that this homicide is neither a mugging nor drugs related. The purpose of this meeting is to dig as deep as we can for any other motive behind these murders. And that, Mr Day, is why you were invited along. Without motive, we're not going to be able to move this case forward. Obviously the false ID behind the one bank…"

There was a pause while she looked through the briefing notes, "…yes… um… private capital bank, that officer Smith identified separates this from a normal homicide case."

Day had been just as taken aback to see the Chief in the room as Arlene, and his defences were up from the get-go. "Do I need to get lawyered up?"

Beth leaned back in her chair, shrugged and, with a deep sigh "Entirely up to you, Mr Day. But all we're doing here today is trying to get a grip on some facts, get them into the right order if we can… and we believe you can contribute to that. Unless you've been up to stuff you shouldn'ta you don't need a lawyer. But, again, your choice. But what we've got here are two law-abiding, respectable Detroit citizens who died for no good reason on foreign soil. And we're going to find whoever did it. First things first, can you just clear up for us what a 'private capital' bank is?"

Day forgot about getting lawyered up and went through the whole structure explaining that they were different to what they would expect a normal bank to be. Provided it kept above the minimum capital requirement for the jurisdiction concerned, money could be moved in and out at will by whoever owned the bank.

The Chief raised a hand and interrupted. "Ok, so let's pause right there. This is what Officer Smith picked up on when she asked why would anyone want to register fifty of these, erm… private capital banks?"

Day explained that there was a type of firm that had made an appearance over the past ten years or so calling themselves family offices. Some were multi-family offices providing tax, investment and other services, which might be called concierge as well as financial to their wealthy family clients. Many of these firms set up private capital banks for their clients, so that funds placed in them are out of reach of the mainstream banks.

Beth was confused. "Why would they want to do that? Surely those big established banks are for more secure than some rinky-dink piggy-bank of your own in some place no-one's ever heard of."

Day paused for a moment, so that he could get everything boiled down to basics in his head so that it was all easily understood. "If there's another banking crisis, funds in these private capital banks as with most private banks, will be insulated against the worst imaginable financial meltdown. This would happen with some kind of collapse in the inter-bank markets and the instruments traded in them, such as the sub-prime mortgage instruments which triggered the 2008 crash."

He finished by saying that most of those with serious wealth now believed there was a much bigger financial meltdown on the way, which would probably be triggered by some sort of derivative trading or technical failure.

He could see from the deadpan expression on the faces of his small audience, he still had work to do to get the message across. "Okay… World indebtedness is now at a place where, if it was a household, it was borrowing twice as much as it was going to earn over the coming 30 years. Completely unsustainable. It'll take only a minor tremor for the whole global economic edifice to come crashing down."

Everyone was staring at him, their expressions showing disbelief and scepticism. Bedson leaned back in his chair. "Phew!"

Day was warming up. "'Phew' would be right, Chief. Have you ever researched what we call the 'wealth sector'?"

Everyone around the table just shook their heads and gave him looks which said '*Why would I*'?

"Well, currently there's about 25 million millionaires around the world, that's people defined as having at least one million dollars free and clear liquid cash in their banks, with an aggregate worth of about seventy trillion bucks. That's like .02 per cent of the world's population holding some 90 per cent of its wealth. Most of this is dry powder… money that's waiting to be used for something.

"At the top of that pile are about 2,500 billionaires with some eight trillion between them. I know all this because, as corporate finance lawyers, we're often involved in structuring investment deals that are funded by these millionaires and billionaires – or UHNWI's… Ultra-High Net Worth Individuals. They invest directly in growing companies, support M&A… that's merger and acquisition deals and also major projects like roads, bridges, energy and things like that."

He continued getting the blank stares as his captive audience showed they were only vaguely taking on board what he was trying to explain to them. The numbers were incomprehensible. He waited for someone to say something.

It was Arlene, hoping she wasn't going to make herself look stupid. "Well, if money's a motive for this Gibraltar outfit and their banks, from what you're saying there's plenty… billions or trillions of motive there. But something I don't get is, if these private capital banks don't actually have any accounts, how do people move money in and out of them?"

Bedson gave her an approving nod and then looked expectantly at Day, who was now really enjoying his fifteen minutes. Well, like I said, some of them do operate accounts if they need to and, if they do, they're mostly for friends, family, trusted contacts… their close circle. It's no big deal, there's off-the-shelf banking systems you can buy to provide basic banking services. But whether to move funds between accounts or as capitalization for the banks it's all done through Swift."

No response. More blank stares. "Swift… that's the Society for Worldwide Interbank Financial Telecommunications. They're based in a village in Belgium. If you make any movement of money from one bank to another, whether it's within the USA or anywhere else in the world, the chances are it'll be carried on the Swift network at some point or another. It's a massive operation which serves every branch of every bank on the planet. It's Swift that sits behind the IBAN number… the International Bank Account Number… on your bank account. You'll see it somewhere on your statement or other bank paperwork."

Beth said "If it's so big why haven't we heard of it?"

"Because you've no need to. It's just there." He paused and looked around the room again. No response. "Er… you can call it the engine that powers the movement of money around the world… between banks, people, companies… It's owned by all its bank members and it's there just to serve the banking industry and others who need to move money or set up specific transactions involving money."

He was going to go on and start explaining the Swift Message Type system but, after another look at the expressions on the faces around the table, thought better of it. He stopped to think for a moment and wound up his impromptu lecture with "Now I'm not the cop in this room, but I can't see how any of this helps us find a motive for homicide."

The room went quiet until Bedson asked "I saw something about forty million dollars being paid into an escrow account at your firm by this Median outfit in Europe. Is that right..?"

Day did not hesitate "Yes, that's right. Forty mill… million. That was to cover the initial capitalization on all fifty banks as it's different in each jurisdiction. They didn't ask for full reports on each bank, although we sent them anyway, and there was a residual of just shy of six million bucks, which the terms of the agreement said we were allowed to keep as operating costs. I paid five hundred thousand to Valiece as a bonus…"

He stopped short in mid-sentence, as if he had had a sudden revelation. For a moment Arlene's eyes narrowed as she was sure he was going to ask if he could have his five hundred thousand dollars back, before coming to his senses and seeing how crass that would be. That would go to the Davey's son, Paul, who had just returned to Detroit from Germany, after USAF had advised him of his bereavement.

They all watched the Chief stand up and walk the two paces over to the window, his muscular six-foot six-inch frame almost blocking out the light, with hands clasped behind his back. Beth was thinking how she should have booked a bigger room. It was starting to get stuffy in here.

He let out a great sigh, slowly shaking his head and looking down at the street below. This was going nowhere. His gaze lingered on the spot on the lawn where that poor guy, the snitch whose daughter had been tortured to death, had blown his own brains out.

After a while he turned and faced the room. "We haven't made a cents worth of progress here. Aside from the background that Mr Day… Eric here has given us," he nodded his appreciation at Day "we still haven't found anything like a motive. All we know is that the Davey's were bound, probably after being knocked out somehow, put in a boat, shot and dropped into the Caribbean. We don't even know if they were shot before or after being put in the boat…" he went quiet for a moment.

Then, frowning "Like they just needed to be disposed of… one or other of them, probably Valiece… knew something they shouldn't…

Somehow or other this case revolves around those fifty banks and the fake ID's, assuming that's what we'll find, behind them."

He stopped, no-one interrupting while they watched him deep in thought for a short while. He turned and looked out of the window again.

An intake of breath. "There's something else bugging me," he said "with all these numbers you've been throwing around, Mr Day… Eric… All that debt. Dry powder..? That's a new one. Seventy trillion bucks and all that other stuff…" A further pause. "I'm no economist but I do know something about conspiracies. And fifty banks, at least one registered under a false ID, two homicides with no apparent motive and trillions of dollars… adds up to a conspiracy. A big conspiracy. Although what the hell it is, God only knows."

He sat back own at the table. "This Swift outfit is in the mix somehow… even if it doesn't know it, and we definitely need help on this. There's no shame in admitting it. This is your case, Sergeant Haydon but my input would be that we get all the details we have up on the Interpol search database and see if that can pull in any further information. It's monitored by the police and security services of most countries so we must be able to flick someone's switch with the information we've got."

"Agree" Beth said. Then, "Officer Smith, see to it that we get all relevant information onto Interpol ASAP. Put yourself up as main contact. We're going to need to provide access to the case file for the FBI as this involves a foreign police force. See to it that that's done and set up liaison with someone in the FBI Detroit field office. I think we're all done here. Thank you for coming in, Mr Day… Eric, we really do appreciate it. You've been a great help to us."

If it wasn't for the non-disclosure form he had signed before the meeting started, he would have been dining out on this for years to come.

Arlene said "Thank you" to the room generally and left clutching her file tight to her chest.

What the freakin' hell is Interpol when it's at home?

Sixteen

Every two or three days as new GDWM client accounts were added to Mohammed's task list Ashar sent a text to Jaeger with an update in a fixed format. Today it was '18/20.2' which told Jaeger that Mohammed had accessed 18 GDWM client accounts through his Swift 'back door' which had 20.2 billion dollars ready to be taken after allowing for the MT799's blocking the PPP deposit funds in each account.

He had been putting off monitoring the GDWM staff dwellings, those that were bugged anyway, for as long as he could as it was time-consuming and boring. But, today, he thought he should make an effort. He liked and admired Jaeger for his precision and focus, but he could be a bit OCD sometimes.

Jaeger had not introduced him to, in fact appeared to make an effort to keep him separate from the other people involved in the project which, at first, had annoyed him. But as time went on he had come to appreciate the privileged, confidante position Jaeger had put him in. He especially valued Jaeger's agreement to put this part of the project on Malta, which he considered to hold a very special place in his religion's history.

He looked across the desk at Mohammed, whose strained features were reflecting the grinding pressure he was under.

He put on his headset and logged into the monitoring site. Out of all the people recruited by Jaeger, five of their homes had been bugged. It was not a crucial part of the operation, just something Jaeger had said he would like to have done as security back up by his own people. It was something he did not want entrusted to the outside security contractor, John Burgess. So Ashar had arranged it.

Fox's residence had been the easiest of them all as GDWM had taken the lease on the property and had full access to it before he got back from Singapore. But they only had time to put a camera in the lounge and two mic's downstairs before he returned. That should not cause a problem as they were not interested in whatever went on upstairs.

The system was sound activated, so only recorded sound and video when there was something going on, and the video opened with Fox limping through the lounge carrying a box. He had not realized that Fox was disabled in any way. The box looked like it contained a kettle, coffee and what anybody would want to have handy on moving day. He carried on watching for another ten minutes as the removal men carried Fox's belongings into or through the lounge. The view was just of the lounge, but the microphones were picking up the sound of the men's grunts, conversations and other noises perfectly from all over the house.

He fast forwarded through the following few hours and slowed back to real time when he saw Fox handing over some money to one of the men. He noted he was learning heavily on his walking stick. There was a shaking of hands and then the sound of the front door shutting after the moving men had gone. There were some sounds from the kitchen and then Fox left the house.

The video then seemed to make a false start, as if there was a burst of noise coming from somewhere, before starting up again an hour later when Fox returned, which he fast forwarded through till about 10pm when he went to bed. It started up again at just gone 7am the next morning and he could hear Fox going about his morning business upstairs before he came down and went into the kitchen. Music started playing on a radio somewhere.

After that it was just what anyone would do in a house they had just moved into. Unpacking with boxes being flattened and put outside, followed by the sound of a vacuum cleaner from upstairs. He had fast forwarded to about four o'clock with no let-up to the boredom, and book-marked the video so that he could come back to it in the next day or two.

In the meantime, he still had a lot of coding to do and that was his priority right now. What he was doing would achieve the ultimate aim of the project.

Not long now. Not long.

Seventeen

Detroit. July.

It had not taken Arlene long to find her way into the Interpol system once Beth had given her the DPD station identifier. She eagerly explored the system which opened up a whole new world to her and was genuinely surprised when she got a response from the UK through the system. A phone call was quickly set up.

There was no preamble. "Hello, is that officer Smith?"

The accent was unmistakably British which she had expected but, when she actually heard it, the full-on realization that this Davey homicide case was spreading its tentacles all over the planet and growing a life of its own came home to her. Big time.

"Er… yes… Hi… Is this Tony Jackson?"

"Yes it is. May I call you Arlene?" Very polite and formal. The smooth deep baritone giving the impression of a tall, lean, enigmatic secret agent. She pictured a Pierce Brosnan lookalike at the other end of the line.

"Sure, if it helps."

"Well, yes… I'm sure it will. Thank you. Please call me Tony."

They confirmed identities through the Interpol protocol and then Jackson opened with "Thank you for putting this case up on Interpol, we think it could be relevant to a case we've been working on for a few years now."

She interrupted before he got too carried away "No problem, we need all the help we can get on this. But can you tell me what MI6 is? Are you a police department? Part of the CIA… FBI..? What?"

She heard Jackson's sharp intake of breath. He cleared his throat… "Ahem. MI6 is Division Six of Military Intelligence here in the UK. We're responsible for deploying and managing British intelligence agents. We work closely with agencies from many other countries, particularly the USA. But no, we are *not* a part of the CIA, FBI or anyone else for that matter. We're responsible *only* to the British government."

The last sentence was spoken with some emphasise. She sensed that somehow she had offended him and immediately apologized. "I'm sorry, but I'm still trying to find my way around all this. This is way outside our envelope. Yours is the only response we've had to our posting."

With the initial misunderstanding out of the way, and Jackson quickly realizing he was dealing with a rookie, he replied "Okay. Not to worry, Arlene. Let's move on... If I may ask just one, short question. Does the name Robert Jaeger appear anywhere in your investigations?"

To which he got one, short answer. "No."

He went on to explain how MI6 had seen her posting on Interpol and how Jaeger had shown up as associated with one of the directors of Median in Gibraltar, which Arlene had used as one of her long list of key words.

It was a long shot for them to make the call to DPD. "So far, it appears that the only keyword we have in common in all this is Median. Is there anything you can add to that?"

"Well, aside from Median, there's this Swift thing. Does that appear anywhere in your case?"

There was a short silence in which she heard the tapping of a keyboard. "No, nothing like that in our files. Is that an acronym of some sort?"

Arlene explained what Swift is and what it does. "It just seems to keep popping up but we're not quite sure how they fit into anything." She then went on to explain how Swift had become somehow relevant during the conversation with Valiece's old boss, a corporate finance lawyer, who had revealed that he had been tasked with setting up fifty new banks by Median. And how the one bank they had investigated had false ID behind it.

There was silence, then a gasp, then "WHAAAAT? *FIFTY FU…*" a cough, *"BANKS?!"* Jackson shouted so loud she winced and had to hold the phone away from her ear. "Do you have the files there for all those banks?"

She confirmed they were all now in the DPD evidence locker, which in fact was a whole floor full of evidence from thousands of cases. But they simply did not have the resource to check them all.

"Arlene, thank you. *Thank you*!" She heard a sigh, which she thought was one of huge relief. "I think what you have there could shed an awful lot of light on this whole case. Can you please arrange for us to visit and have access to those files? We can work from your offices and link to our own resources here. We'll make all the necessary protocol arrangements. We'll have an FBI agent there with us as liaison. We'll be setting up our travel arrangements immediately."

Arlene was on top of her game. "I'll talk to my sergeant and come right back to you. We're already liaising with FBI Detroit field office and we'll advise them directly."

"Thank you again, Arlene. Please understand this is *very* urgent."

"Gotcha…" As she hung up she heard him exclaim again, "*Fifty* bloody banks?! *Bloody* hell!"

+

Jackson's call came just as I was switching my phone off when we were queueing up for take-off from Heathrow. As Kelly was going to be much later coming back from Australia I had brought forward my meetings in New York so I could be home in time to meet her. The flight passed quickly and once I was through immigration at JFK and in a cab on my way to the hotel I flashed up the phone again.

The voicemail from Jackson told me that there were major developments which he didn't want to discuss on the phone. He was going to be in Detroit PD headquarters from the following day with an FBI agent and one of his own team from Croydon, and could I join them? I replied that I had meetings the following day with some U.S. media, but I would fix a flight onto Detroit tomorrow evening and asked him to arrange a hotel for me.

Half an hour later I had a call from an officer Smith saying she had booked me into the Westin Detroit hotel, and that she would be at Detroit Metro to meet me when I arrived the following evening to take me there.

I was pre-occupied throughout the whole day of meetings with bloggers and media, and had to concentrate hard to produce follow up e-mails to the people I had met with during the two hour hop to Detroit. It seemed no time at all before I was at Detroit arrivals where Officer Smith was waiting for me. There was hardly anything of her, a slip of a girl, wearing her uniform and holding up a sign proclaiming 'MI6'. I grabbed it out of her hand, screwed it up and threw it in a bin.

My reaction as I grabbed the card must have scared her witless because she backed off and a couple of people nearby looked like they were going to come to her aid. There was no way they were going to allow some guy with a limp to assault one of Detroit's finest. I was getting some hard looks and, for a moment I was wishing they would try something. I wasn't so damaged that I couldn't still do a lot of damage myself. But, just as quickly, I came to my senses.

I forced a smile and told her in as much of a whisper as I could over the airport noise 'MI6 is a *secret intelligence* agency. You should have just put my name up. Fox."

To be fair her answer was an immediate and downcast "Oh my God… I'm sorry."

"No worries." I said, trying hard to calm down. I took her arm and said "Let's get outa here."

She opened the trunk and dropped my cabin bag in there among enough weaponry to fight a small war. While she was doing that and still a bit jet-lagged, I stupidly opened the driver's door and only just managed to stop myself getting in. She looked at me as if I was mentally challenged before I told her that it was just habit, in the UK this would have been the passenger door. We were not getting off to a very good start.

Along with anybody else who didn't live in a cave, on the moon, I'd seen countless Crown Victoria's, the American cop's vehicle of choice, in movies and TV programs. But this was the first time I was going to get a ride in one, complete with DPD livery. Fair to say, it was as good a ride as I'd had in any armoured personnel carrier.

Detroit was a busy town that evening and it was a slow drive as we made our way to the hotel, the first five minutes of which was spent in a strained, embarrassed silence.

I filled the vacuum with "Sorry. I think we both screwed up. Shall we start again? Can you bring me up to speed on what's going on?"

To her credit she let out a great guffaw. A lot of noise from a little lady. "Sure. Great to meet you! I'm Arlene." I was completely floored by her broad Bronx accent.

She held out her hand for me to shake. This was a young twenty-something with a lot to learn, but came across with a lot of common sense and maturity. She apologized for still being in uniform, but she had come straight from work to pick me up, and then had to return the car to the pool before she went home.

She spent the stop-start late evening rush hour drive under what seemed to be an ever-darkening sky, going through the whole case. She started at when she opened the package from Antigua to Jackson and one of his colleagues and the FBI liaison, Drew Farron, turning up that morning and diving straight into all the files. She was working as part of the small team and was in the middle of compiling a list of all the ID's and document references behind each bank registration to send off to Interpol, who would then check them all out through their own network.

She could e-mail the list of banks and ID's, but all the other paperwork showing the supporting passports, utility bills and other documentation were being copied ready to be go to Interpol HQ in Lyon, France tomorrow by FBI jet.

But everyone was assuming that all of them would come back as fake. Meaning that there was *"...one freakin' monster outfit..."* behind whatever was going on.

I asked her if anyone had worked out how Swift figured in all this but, so far it seemed, if they had a role they had not worked out what it was. They were waiting for me to arrive to try and get some more clarity on the whole PPP ("...*whatever the freakin' hell that is*...") structure and to see if Swift had a role in it that might have a bearing on the case.

By the time we got to the Westin, we had forgotten the initial screw-ups and were getting on well. She said I'd be expected at the office at 9am in the morning. Just ask the cab to take me to DPD HQ. I was on the point of telling her that I wasn't on the MI6 payroll so I'd get there when I damn well felt like it, but then thought better of it. After all, we had managed to get onto first name terms. You could even say we'd developed a rapport.

Eighteen

Although it was mid-July there was an unseasonal bitterly cold, brawny Michigan squall coming off the lake and driving freezing rain through the city the next morning. There was a bit of a queue waiting for a cab at the hotel, only just kept under control by the doorman and, after waiting a while I finally got to DPD HQ at nine-fifteen. Arlene was waiting to take me upstairs to the large meeting room on the second floor that had been commandeered for the investigation. I saw her glance at my stick before asking if I wanted to use the elevator. I told her I preferred to use the stairs.

"Oh, that's quite a limp you've got. I just thought…"

I hadn't realized that it was all that apparent. Probably all the travelling, and the weather wasn't helping.

"What happened?" she asked.

Stock answer. "Motorbike. The truck won. It's best I walk as much as possible on it as that'll help it heal." Saves a lot of explanation. It wasn't mentioned again.

In the meeting room there was a lot of paper all over the place but I could see that someone had put a stamp of order on all the chaos. This turned out to be Arlene's sergeant, Beth Haydon. She came across as experienced and in control.

Jackson walked me through progress so far, which was not a lot, repeating pretty much what Arlene had told me on the drive to the hotel last night. The list of banks and the ID's behind them had just been e-mailed to Interpol, and copying of the paper files was nearly complete. These would be in the air and on their way to Lyon by FBI jet by close of play that day.

Strange how a voice on the phone can so misrepresent the person behind it. Jackson's lanky, awkward frame completely different to the muscular, confident one Arlene had visualized, was all over the room as he moved between different documents and people.

Amid all the bustle he told me "We've come to the conclusion that Swift has to figure somewhere in all this but I'm afraid a lot of what you told me has gone in one ear and out the other. What was all that you said about empty 799's …or something like that?"

I had to do a double-take to figure out what he was talking about. "Oh, you mean MT799's. That's MT for 'Message Type', not 'empty'..." I laughed. He didn't.

"So, what is it then?"

No emotion, just demanding answers. I had been far too flippant as I recalled those sickening pictures of torture and death he'd shown me and, of course, the Davey's murders. We were dealing with dregs of humanity. Nothing to laugh about.

"Yes, sorry... Swift MT's, message types, are different formats and functions for messages... um... they structure a whole gamut of different transactions between banks and their customers and even inter-bank transactions. MT799's, in particular, block an agreed amount of money in an account so they can't be moved 'til it's timed out, or a code agreed between the two banks using the MT799 says so. There are many other MT's that perform the same or similar functions, but the 799 is specifically to keep funds blocked and unused for anything else at a bank other than your own. With the client's agreement of course."

I could almost hear him thinking.

"And that's it?"

"That's it..." There was nothing more I could really add, but I tried anyway. "People can block funds for any reason... like cash on delivery, or awaiting completion of some transaction or other. In the case of PPP's, it's to block any movement of funds placed as collateral for the loans provided to the PPP traders by their host banks. The MT799 guarantees that the funds are going to always be there as collateral against the bank loan to the traders, usually ten times the deposit..."

I could see Arlene looking at us, trying to make some sense of the conversation, as she stacked a pile of papers.

Jackson continued, his face a study in concentration as he tried to work out what might be happening. "You mentioned a hundred million dollars…?"

Arlene's expression changed from merely interested to incredulous.

"Yes," I confirmed "that's the minimum placement to enter a PPP, that's why it's the exclusive domain of UHNWI's…" I saw everyone looking at me with questioning looks on their faces. "That's Ultra High Net Worth Individuals in capital markets-speak. Their hundred mill is then leveraged up as a loan for the traders to set up the debt instrument which they trade with. It'll be leveraged times ten, so they're actually trading with a billion dollars. We've got one client who's deposited three hundred mill, so he's kicked-off his trades with three bill."

I thought Arlene's jaw was actually going to hit the deck.

"That's PPP for 'private placement program'?" Jackson asked.

I nodded. All the bustle had stopped and everyone in the room, including the FBI guy who I hadn't even been introduced to yet, was watching Jackson and me. But I noticed his eyes couldn't help straying to Arlene, and struggling to stray away again.

Jackson was staring hard at some distant point only he could see. "So, just to be clear, what's your role at GDWM?"

I explained that my job was to secure highly targeted editorial exposure in media that UHNWI's followed. They didn't take anything they saw on the web seriously so I was working mostly with UHNWI-specific print media who had their own online operations which had to be subscribed to, not cheap, separately. Those whose interest was fired up by what they read would know how to contact GDWM and take their own PPP's forward.

I also explained that our host bank had agreed to accept the MT799 from accounts in banks other than themselves, in other parts of the world. It was this that separated the GDWM PPP from all the others, making it uniquely attractive to investors. Everyone knew our host bank, a tier-1 global institution and just accepted that they would not be part of any scam or conspiracy. But this still was not getting us anywhere. Until Jackson asked "So what happens when one of these UHNWI people contacts GDWM?"

I explained that they fix a meeting with one of the relationship managers, and said that I'd met them all in Singapore. If they want to move forward, they agree how much the deposit, or placement, is going to be. The MT799 is all set up so their funds are blocked on their account, the traders schedule the arbitrage trades, show these to ITCD who then provide the leveraged loan, ten times whatever the deposit is… The traders set up the debt instrument and the trades, all contracted and agreed in advance, commence.

"…It may sound complex but it is, in fact, sublimely simple and from start to finish only takes a few man-hours to set up. Scheduling the actual trades takes a few days, but that's more due to the different time zones that have to be covered than anything else. Everyone makes a shedload of money. It all sounds kinda flaky but it works, and has worked for coming on eighty years. GDWM takes a five per cent fee from each monthly pay-out of profits."

"So where," Jackson almost cried "WHAT is the point of all this? There's no NEED for a conspiracy if everyone's making more money than most people don't dare even *dream* about!"

The room was silent until Arlene said quietly "Cwawffee. That'll help. Cwawffee." A couple of the other ten people in the room stepped up to help her out.

This lightened the mood just enough for people to start talking amongst themselves. I took the chance to introduce myself to the FBI guy, Drew. I knew he was the FBI guy because of the neat haircut, impeccably-cut dark navy suit, crisp white shirt, deep maroon silk tie and shiny shoes. I was tempted to get behind him to see if he had 'FBI' sewn into the back of his suit jacket in big yellow letters. But I resisted.

I wondered if he was all decked out like this because he was representing the FBI at an important meeting, or to impress the young officer Arlene Smith, who he clearly had the hots for.

He explained that the FBI was involved because the homicide had happened outside of DPD's jurisdiction on foreign territory. In those cases the FBI had to be in the frame and were the primary liaison between the foreign jurisdiction and DPD although, in practice, Arlene was working directly with Antigua and just keeping him in the loop.

Arlene announced that cwawffee was ready and we all filled our mugs, took chairs and just started chatting generally amongst ourselves, doing a bit of brainstorming in hopes of *something* coming out of it.

+

There was a large situation board against one of the walls with GDWM, Swift, PPP, MT799, ITCD, '50 banks' and a few other things scrawled on it along with pictures of Jaeger, the Swift HQ and copies of the supporting documents on the fake Garcia ID from Arlene's 'sample' bank that had ignited the whole investigation. Jackson had taken the decision not to show the pictures of the tortured and murdered agents to DPD. It would not help this end of the investigation.

Lines were drawn between the various items, all searching for the right connections. It looked like a bag of Christmas tree lights waiting to be unravelled.

Drew's voice interrupted the hubbub "Something's missing here." He carried on staring at the board for a moment and then, quietly, "The customers. Where are the customers?"

And then it dawned on me too "Of course! The investors. The clients." Arlene was standing by the board. "Arlene, can you just write 'clients' alongside 'GDWM'?"

She did and then, in that moment, everything started to fall into place. "Now, draw lines between 'clients' and 'GDWM' and then between 'GDWM' and '50 banks'."

The picture was taking shapee. "Now… lines between customers, fifty banks and Swift."

There was a collective murmur of realization around the room as the pattern started to emerge, and everyone was looking at me for answers.

I gathered my thoughts. "Okay… okay… er, let's not forget we're dealing with billionaires here. There's about 2,500 billionaires in the world. Aside from the funds blocked with the MT799's in those GDWM client accounts, there'll be additional billions just sitting there as well… *that's* where we should be focusing our attention. GDWM has all their account details, the question is, how are they going to get into them..? All in different banks and jurisdictions all over the world don't forget… and manage to move the unblocked funds away and into those other fifty 'private capital' banks? It *has* to be the unblocked funds, because trying to move those blocked by the 799's, or even other MT's doing the same job, would set off every alarm across the entire Swift network and shut it down in a heartbeat."

Jackson asked "So how many customers, clients, investors, whatever… have signed up to this PPP thing then?"

I thought it through for a few seconds. "Good question. I'll ask." I'd not been in touch with Jaeger since I was in Singapore, so I thought it wouldn't be out of order to drop him an e-mail to check out progress.

I got out my mobile and fired it off.

> Hi Robert,
>
> In USA, continuing media meetings. Just checking in to see if I'm holding up my end of the deal. How's progress so far?
>
> Regards
>
> Derek

I didn't know when to expect his reply as, at 2.30pm in Detroit it would have been 5.30am in Western Australia, and no-one was sure he was even still there. But half an hour later the reply came back

> Derek,
>
> You're doing a great job. Thank you. Top quality enquiries coming through with, so far, 30 MT799s in place with trading under way, a further 15 in the pipeline. Funds blocked between $100m and $300m for each investor. Looking forward to paying out your first override.
>
> Thank you and well done.
>
> Robert

I read it out to the room, leaving out the bit about override, and followed through with some more explanation. "So that means that, right now with 30 MT799's in play, there's some thirty billion dollars at risk – at least. Like I said, many of these people will have more than just *one* billion. And we still have no idea how Jaeger's planning on getting into those accounts to move that money. Swift's firewalls should be among the best in the world, if not *the* best. He could hack directly into the individual banks but that would mean you'd need to breach a whole load of different firewalls. Setting up the 799's is an inter-bank function, GDWM is excluded from the nitty gritty of the process."

General nods of understanding from around the room. Then Arlene said "Well, maybe this is where we figure out what this Swift outfit's involvement in all this might be. Maybe we should just ask them."

Who could argue with that? This girl was going to go far. Jackson was straight onto Croydon to get them to set up a meeting with the head honcho's at Swift for the day after tomorrow. And to fix connecting flights on our arrival at Heathrow straight onto Brussels. As an afterthought he gave instructions to find a senior Interpol agent and have them present at the meeting with whatever warrants or other documents were needed to leave Swift with no option but to disclose any and all information we might need.

We were all packing up to leave when it all suddenly became clear to me what my overworked sixth sense had been trying to tell me. The empty walls with no pictures at the office in Singapore, the transient feel of the place and, above all else, the focus on just one product, the PPP. If this was a proper wealth management firm where were the tax specialists or the alternative investment managers, or the private equity and debt teams?

Everyone stopped what they were doing while I voiced this revelation. No, this was not a wealth management firm but something set up for no other purpose than to relieve a great many billionaires of their fortunes. Nothing else. How and when were now the big questions that had to be answered and, if we had this little bit of wind in our sails, maybe this Swift outfit would be able to fill them out even more for us.

+

We could put a stop to Jaeger's whole scheme if I could find out the identities and account details of the clients we had so far. But we could be sure that Jaeger would have any attempt by me or anyone else at doing that stopped in its tracks. Whether through talking to the traders behind that opaque partition in Singapore or having GCHQ find their way into his systems. It would be immediately flagged up somehow or other. He was no fool and would have covered all his bases. No, if ever there was a time for 'softly, softly, catchey monkey', this was it.

Everyone got back to packing up and preparing to leave. Arlene was overseeing the loading up of all the documentation to go to Interpol. She told me she would be downstairs in ten minutes to take Jackson and me to our hotel, and then onto the airport.

Then, "Y'know... If the Davey's hadn't been murdered like they were, we still wouldn't have a clue about these fifty banks or everything else we've uncovered. By killing Valiece and Daphne these jerks actually alerted us to what's going on. How stupid is that?"

Yep. Irony lives. But maybe, at long last, we were heading towards a breakthrough.

Everyone was packing up and leaving, with Drew's yearning eyes following Arlene out of the room.

Nineteen

After clicking 'send' for his reply to Fox, Jaeger walked out to his veranda and surveyed the view before him. All the fences were now in place and he could see Burgess signing off something on a clipboard with the contractor by the fence at the top of the cliff. They walked around the fence until he got to their trucks and he watched them shake hands before the contractor and his crews drove off.

He locked his office and made his way downstairs to meet with Burgess to review the security installations. He heard his burner sound off in his pocket with a text, but decided to ignore it until he had finished his meeting with Burgess.

The next two hours were spent reviewing the entire security set-up for the compound, those that Burgess knew about anyway. Annoyingly for him he was kept clear of the armoury and what he assumed was some sort of control room next to it. They went to a room adjoining Jaeger's office where he demonstrated the CCTV set-up from its bank of monitoring screens. This would be manned by one of his close staff, three obviously well-trained guys, who always seemed to be on hand.

Ted Larkin, alias John Burgess assumed these were Jaeger's goons who did whatever dirty work needed doing. Even with his SAS training, he knew he would have trouble dealing with them if ever it came to it.

He had always kept the relationship professional, with no attempt to befriend this unfathomable man, taking a totally passive role while soaking up as much information as he could to pass back to Jackson at MI6.

But there was nothing wrong with trying a bit of repartee anyway, just to see if he could get him to give anything away. "Quite a set-up here, Mr Jaeger. Expecting an invasion are we?"

Jaeger seemed surprised, *what the hell's it got to do with you?* But simply gave a short laugh, smiled and said "No. Not really. Merely meeting a market need."

This left Burgess completely baffled and simply replied "Oh well. You know your business."

Indeed I do, Mr Burgess. Indeed I do. Now go away and leave me to get on with it.

✢

He watched and waited as Burgess put his bag in his car, drive off the compound up to the junction and turn north towards Perth on the main road. He looked around the empty compound, then made his way to his private control room next to the armoury. Here he could remotely control the locks on most doors in the property, including the ten apartments, watch and listen into each of the apartments and keep stock control of food, fuel and other supplies.

While supplies were available through normal channels, including the Coles supermarket in Margaret River just two miles down the road, he would continue to use them. But, as these eventually closed down or had everything they had looted to exhaustion they would fall back on their own stocks.

Heating is only an issue for a few months of the year and there were wood burning stoves in each apartment and all the main reception areas, with a bountiful supply of timber in this south western corner of Australia. From where he stood, everything was now set to go. But best wait till he had reached his target of 100 new GDWM clients, which reminded him to take a look at that text on his burner.

He checked Ashar's latest text update, 33/48.3. 33 accounts with $48.3 billion available to, shall we say, liberate. He smiled at the thought. He had brought in three clients at the start to get things rolling but Fox's endeavours were working far better and quicker than he had ever hoped for.

He was a little disappointed to see that Ashar was also reporting that some of the accounts had been set up just to hold the placement money, with no other funds being available for them to remove. A natural enough security precaution, but it made no difference to Jaeger, it was not all about the money. Far from it.

He replied to the text:

 Tks. How's monitoring?

The reply came back ten minutes later:

 Boring so far. Will continue tomorrow.

Everything looked like it was on the right track and after a few calls to others working on the project, during which he was able to exercise his command of a couple of north African dialects, he decided to take a few days off and do a short tour of some of the Margaret River wineries.

He deserved a break. Aside from his goons, there were two maintenance crew on-site with a further half dozen due to arrive over the coming few days. They could sort themselves out and look after the place while he was away.

He went to his private apartment, packed a bag enough for a few days and, taking the Humvee from the garage, headed south.

+

Mohammed, now suffering a severe loss of weight and with dark, hollow eyes had taken himself off for one of his aimless bus rides around Malta. Ashar leaned back in his chair and after a few seconds decided to go down to the quayside and have a coffee. When he had psyched himself up sufficiently, he would then spend an hour or two monitoring the bugging devices in those staff dwellings where they had them.

He could not see the point of it as it looked like most of them were hardly occupied as the relationship managers were travelling most of the time to see clients, and Fox was away doing whatever it was he does.

But he did not want to get on the wrong side of Jaeger. His coffee had failed to get him psyched up sufficiently, so he decided he would get himself up to date on all the monitoring tomorrow.

The pressure was off a bit now as the majority of the coding he needed to write for Jaeger's main plan was done. Oh, how he was looking forward to pressing that 'enter' key when the time came! A passing elderly tourist couple did a double take of this nondescript young man sitting alone drinking coffee, as he gave a deep smirk and loud snicker at the thought of what was to come.

He made a phone call and, after ten minutes, a scooter with a young rider pulled up. The two sat at the table having another coffee, deep in conversation for twenty minutes.

As much as Ashar trusted and respected Jaeger, he was wise enough to know that plans are made to be screwed up, and he was not going to be around if or when that happened.

He decided it was time to restrict Mohammed to the apartment. No more bus tours for him.

Twenty

The flight from Detroit to Heathrow was no joke. We were on the busiest Delta Airlines flight of the day and it had been too late to get us into business class. Instead we were crammed into coach after, I think, Delta had bounced a couple of other passengers on the instructions of DPD.

My leg was hanging in the gangway to try and give it some relief. The flight was packed, mostly with business folk but there was a hoard of screaming kids somewhere behind us so it was hardly worthwhile trying to sleep. As soon as we were in the air Jackson leaned towards me. Speaking as quietly as he could.

"We've had some feedback from Mukhabarat in Egypt. Well spotted."

Great. Anything to take my mind off the discomfort of this flight, of which there was still another five hours to go.

He stopped and asked. "You okay? You look like shit."

"Thank you. Leg." We seemed to be developing some sort of rapport with no need to waste words.

He carried on. "Okay... Seems that after the accusation of collaboration with the Israelis, and just before the police were sent to arrest him, Jaeger's dad and Robert were smuggled out of Egypt by the bank he worked for. Seems they got him onto a British destroyer which was parked up at the time in Port Said, and which they used to evacuate embassy staff and other people."

He pulled some screwed up paper out of his pocket and looked at the notes on it. "But, by the look of it, when he got back to London they fired him…I guess because they needed to separate themselves from him so as not to get in the way of any business they wanted to do in Egypt or the Middle East.

"So… from being the regional director for the Middle East and North Africa of a top merchant bank, a big deal at the time, Jaeger Senior could not find any work in any bank anywhere in the world. Don't forget, this was the 1960's when it really was a matter of who you knew, and if there was something whiffy about you no-one would come near you."

That sure fills a few gaps, I thought. "So why'd they have to fire him? They could at least have allowed him to resign if they wanted to distance themselves."

"Who knows? The stroke of someone's pen and a man's destroyed. Seems he wound up grubbing out a living as a small-time insurance salesman, but…" he looked around to make sure no-one was listening, not that anyone could hear anything over the racket coming from those screaming kids, "…he still managed to earn enough to put Jaeger junior, Robert, through private school and uni, even though it meant a life of near penury for himself."

So, here was a father dedicated to ensuring a future for his son. Nothing wrong in that. And hardly a motive for Jaeger to get involved in torture and murder and, it seemed, a plot to defraud dozens of billionaires.

I told Jackson that while all this was very interesting, it still didn't make any sense. It didn't provide the motive we were looking for. Not enough motive for what we had learned of his plot so far anyway.

He looked around furtively and then leaned closer into me. "Maybe not but the fact that his mother, an Egyptian, a model apparently, was taken by Nasser's government and never seen or heard of again… we can only assume in retaliation for his dad's bank getting him out of the country, might well do. He must have got separated from her somehow in all the confusion. It's hard to verify but it looks like the bank was more interested in getting him out of the country than they were about seeing his wife arrested and probably tortured and executed for treason. Wouldn't surprise me if they told the Egyptians exactly where to find her, just to take the heat of Jaeger senior."

Now, *that* would turn anyone's world to ratshit. Career destroyed, shunned by an industry in which he had gained huge respect and prestige, wife taken into who knows what kind of hell and left to raise a son alone. Yeah. That would sting. But, despite all that

Jaeger senior had seen to it that his son was fully equipped to make his way to the top of the industry that had destroyed his family.

"So what happened to his dad?"

Jackson nodded to himself. "Well, according to what the guys in Croydon have managed to dig up, looks like he died a lonely man, prematurely of a heart attack, aged just 51 in a flat on a council estate in Peckham, south London. He didn't even survive to see Robert's graduation. He was cremated and Robert was the only mourner."

This put a completely different complexion on the man I'd met just a few weeks ago in Singapore. If I didn't know better, I could almost feel sorry for him. I now understood that he was a loner, driven by something that only he and his late father understood. Somehow though, relieving a few dozen billionaires of their wealth did not seem adequate retribution against an industry which had destroyed his entire family.

You might upset a few billionaires, but it would hardly register on the global banking firmament's Richter scale. Which is what, I figured, is what Jaeger was really looking for. Most people would have just taken the hit, no matter how painful, and tried to move on. But I was learning that Robert Jaeger was made of different stuff. And I knew he had the means to do a far more thorough job of it if he wanted to.

The rest of the journey passed with both of us trying to grab what little sleep we could, with nothing further said between us until we arrived at Heathrow.

+

Instead of booking onward flights MI6 had arranged a helicopter to collect us at Heathrow and fly us straight onto Swift. It was a short flight, during which I remembered to flash up my mobile. A text came in from the young police officer, Arlene Smith.

> Drew called just after I dropped you off at Detroit Metro. He said there was an FBI jet waiting to take you to London or Brussels. Wherever you wanted to go. I was unable to contact you in time. Sorry. Hope you had a good flight.

You just gotta laugh. I decided not to show it to Jackson. Poor guy had enough on his plate without getting all upset over something like that.

As we watched the Swift helipad come up to meet us I could see a chateau up on a hill to my right and the glass and sandstone-clad edifice of the Swift HQ building to the left. I was impressed, it was much more than I was expecting, even from what I'd seen of Google images. There were half a dozen people waiting for us on the edge of the helipad. I checked my watch, 3pm, and I felt like I hadn't slept in a week. Like there was sand in my eyes.

Both of us were in a sorry state when we climbed out of the chopper. DPD had fixed a flight for us with just under two hours to spare meaning a rush back to the hotel, stuff everything into our bags and then Crown Vic with Arlene driving on blues and twos to get us to Detroit Metro, in driving rain, with 20 minutes to spare before gate closing. DPD had arranged an escort to take us straight through to the plane without knowing about the FBI jet that was waiting for us on one of the private ramps.

When we had got to the airport Jackson had jumped out and gone to the trunk to get our bags.

On impulse I leaned across to Arlene "You do know that that FBI guy, Drew, fancies the pants off you don't you?"

She sat bolt upright and gave one of her guffaws "Get outa here!"

I was out of the car and taking my bag from Jackson when, over the howling wind I heard "Hey, you!"

I bent down to look back in the car, squinting against the freezing rain. Something had gone seriously wrong with July in Detroit. She was leaning across the front seat looking up at me. For a moment the probationer cop from the Bronx was just a pretty young girl full of hope for the future. "Really?"

Through the noise of the drop-off point, I could hardly hear her. There was even a parking jobsworth loudly trying to move this cop car, still with its blues flashing, which had pulled up less than half a minute ago, out of the way. Street life USA.

"Yeah. Really. Seeya." I shouted back over the din. And couldn't help but give her a big grin and a wink before limping as fast as I could after Jackson.

This happy little vignette evaporated as the welcoming committee looked curiously at the arrival of their two red-eyed, unshaven guests.

The Interpol agent, the regional commissioner, was a German guy, short, moustached and with small gimlet eyes called Klemens Beringer. He stepped forward and introduced Swift's CEO, Dick van Druten along with their operations, technology and security directors. Van Druten was plainly in 'defend Swift' mode and was looking at us with suspicion.

Riding all the way across the pond in coach, and then the cramped chopper meant that I had needed to fish out my collapsible walking stick from the bottom of my cabin bag, which I was now leaning on heavily. Jackson looked as rough as I felt. Bleary eyes and a couple of days of stubble probably had our hosts thinking they were dealing with a pair of vagrants, rather than professionals at whatever it was we did.

We were being led to a meeting room but I asked for a washroom first where we could freshen up and one of van Druten's sidekicks said he would organize some sandwiches for us. At that point I realized just how famished I was, we hadn't eaten all day at DPD HQ, and how much I needed a shower and change of everything I was wearing. It would have to wait.

Ten minutes later we were all in the meeting room with Jackson taking immediate charge. He reviewed the entire case with no holds barred. From Jaeger being one or two parts removed from the torture and murder of security agents to, again, being one part removed from the setting up of Median Private Wealth. He then came to the fifty banks and the likelihood of funds being hijacked from UHNWI accounts and routed directly to them.

This drew no immediate reaction from the Swift guys apart from a cold stare from van Druten who, from the look of him, came out of a box marked 'Bureaucrats. Use once only.' "So… are you suggesting that this organisation, owned by 11,000 regulated financial institutions worldwide, is actually conspiring to relieve people of their money?" he sneered.

Jackson let out a loud exasperated and tired sigh. "Of course not..!" he snapped. In the pregnant pause that followed '…you prick' went unsaid. But everyone in the room heard it echoing around in their heads. "All I'm saying, or trying to say is that Swift *must* figure in this conspiracy simply because it keeps popping up. The purpose of our being here is to find out how and why. The first thing we need to do is get a proper handle on how and why these fifty banks were set up."

Beringer stepped in with a calming voice and hardly a trace of a German accent. "If I may just add a little to this discussion. We at Interpol have so far had feedback on the ID's behind eight more of the banks, in addition to the one researched by Detroit Police. They are all false and we expect the rest to be so, but we continue to investigate. So the start point for our discussion must surely be these banks."

Jackson explained that we were reasonably sure that this is where the stolen funds would be sent to, but we still had not worked out how GDWM was going to find their way into so many individual accounts in all these different banks to remove the funds. The discussion bounced around the table getting nowhere. Until van Druten eventually, and probably in an effort to appear more cooperative, suggested that he pass the list of all the banks to his cyber-fraud division for a data check on all of them. And we agreed to adjourn and re-commence the meeting the next morning.

Someone at Swift had fixed up a couple of rooms for us at the Chateau du Lac, a hotel about five miles away. We wrapped up the meeting, with van Druten showing some signs of being a little less defensive and more willing to cooperate.

When we got to the hotel we both fixed ourselves up with clean clothes from outlets in the lobby and arranged to meet for dinner at 8pm, after we had cleaned ourselves up.

+

After dinner we moved to the bar for some coffee. Maybe it was sheer exhaustion or the one glass of wine we'd had with dinner but he seemed to loosen up a bit. I got the impression he wanted to offload.

And offload he did. He told me all about 'wealth games'. I've wished ever since that he hadn't.

Twenty-One

Chateau du Lac, Belgium. July.
Wealth Games.

Jackson was looking at his tablet, and seemed to be getting his thoughts in order, so I didn't interrupt.

Eventually, still flipping through pages on his screen he looked up and explained that, after the 2008 crash the Bank of England, the Treasury and a few others started exploring different economic scenarios, in much same way that NATO explores endless battle scenarios with their war games.

The participants in the games grew over the following decade to include the U.S. Federal Reserve, CIA, a number of universities, the European Central Bank and other financial and economic bodies and institutions from Asia and South America.

Within the past year, Chancellors and Treasury Ministers from all the G20 countries and their national security agencies had joined the circulation for the monthly updates, all making their own contributions to the discussions. Also, to the online game-play which had been developed by the UK Treasury, U.S. Fed, an Australian university and a growing number of other contributors. A steering committee had been formed comprised of ten of the financial secretaries from the G20 countries.

The games were all conducted using computer modelling, or prediction. What has become known as 'game theory'.

The imposing title the grouping had given itself was the Committee for the Exploration of Economic Stimulators for Socio-Economic Breakdown, CEESSEB. Officially, it did not exist. It had started off quite informally, but as their game-play started to make it clear that the world's ultra-wealthy had been moving their trillions of dollars out of mainstream banks and into alternative depositories for over a decade, the games became known as 'wealth games'.

A direct consequence of this massive capital outflow from the world's mainstream banking network was that they were being left ever more weakened and exposed to unforeseen events. The computer modelling tried to predict and contain the weakest links as the stresses and strains on the global monetary and banking structures constantly fluctuated.

He explained that as far as he understood it while the Fed, the UK Treasury and ECB had managed to stabilize their banks after the

2008 crash, it would be verging on the impossible to ride to the rescue in the same way again as their economies and reserves had all been left vulnerable as a legacy. Even a decade after the event, they were still so destabilised that they would not be able to step in and control a crash again. Even if it came only halfway to the one trillion dollar sub-prime mortgage exposure which triggered the 2008 event.

He carried on swiping through the pages on his tablet, which he said showed the various levels of impact of any further economic upheavals. He was reading from some document, picking out the bits of the most interest.

Starting with a one trillion dollar exposure, as in 2008, governments and central banks would step in again, but national credit ratings would fall through the floor the more debt the affected countries took on to handle the crisis, meaning a downward spiral of ever growing cost for them to borrow funds on the markets.

For the populations, it would lead directly to widespread hardship, unemployment and decline that would take several decades to recover from, if ever. Sporadic civil unrest events could be expected along with great strains on social cohesion.

A few more swipes…

There was then a further, second level where all mainstream banks would need to be taken over by national or regional monetary authorities who would then assume responsibility for the loan books on all those banks, which would all be nationalized. Food coupons would need to be issued as there would be no value in currency and armed forces would need to work alongside police and other authorities in order to keep civil unrest under control.

The only way to recover from this would be for the banks to eventually write off all outstanding debt which, in effect, would leave them all bankrupt. Most G20 countries had contingency plans for a meltdown at this second level. Which would involve martial law in some form or another.

I asked "Where're you getting all this from? Some sort of circular?"

"I just get copied in," he said "someone at the Treasury added me to the list. Maybe they just thought I should know. I haven't really taken much notice of it before, but somehow or other this Jaeger case has made it seem all the more relevant. But I don't quite know how… Ripping off a few billionaires wouldn't cause these kind of problems…"

This was exactly what I'd been thinking. Thoughts that had now become firmly rooted in Jaeger's back-story.

He trailed off and was deep in thought for a while. For a few seconds it looked like he was going to drop off to sleep, before he carried on swiping and reading off his tablet.

He read through some pages a couple of times, before explaining that the third scenario would be where a sudden shock to the largest banks would reverberate down into the entire global banking network through the inter-bank lending markets. If the tier-1 banks somehow found themselves exposed to unsustainable debt, the inter-bank market would collapse leading to the implosion of the entire global banking system within a couple of days.

Essentially all banks, worldwide, from the top down would need to call in all outstanding loans and overdrafts, worldwide, and stop all banking provision to any individual or business with a banking facility of any sort. Billions of loans amounting to tens of trillions of dollars of largely unrecoverable debt. Global economic meltdown. The shutters would go up on every bank in the world.

At this point, there would not be any armed forces, police or anyone else available to keep the peace as no-one would be getting paid. No payrolls would be met, anywhere. Government, private sector or anyone else.

It would be every man for himself taking it upon themselves to leave whatever they were doing to protect their families. There would be uncontrolled looting and destruction of property on a biblical scale. It would take hold within a few days of people grasping what was really going on. Unimaginable anarchy unleashed across the world.

All utilities including energy, communications, water and sewage would cease to exist within days or weeks. Transport of any kind would no longer function. Telecommunications would progressively degrade and fail as maintenance ceased and power failures went unrepaired.

Underlying all that, widespread starvation as food supplies dried up.

Jackson let out a snort. "Probably the only place to escape it all would be North Korea! China would probably manage but even they would face social upheaval like they've never had to deal with before. For everyone else… unadulterated anarchy."

Whatever this was all about was really getting to him. Me too. But if any of this was somewhere in Jaeger's plans, how could it possibly be engineered? Until we understood that, we were working completely in the dark. He went back to his tablet.

The Committee, or someone on it, had allocated alert codes to each threat level which were to be used in the event that any one of them was forecast by their game play as being imminent. The first level was Roosevelt, the second Churchill and the third, the worst, Bretton Woods. He had no idea who had decided on these code words, or why.

He knew who Churchill and Roosevelt were, but he would have to Google this Bretton Woods character if he could ever get around to it.

He looked up at me, frowning. "Bretton Woods is the worst case scenario. Have you ever heard of him?" I knew all about Bretton Woods of course, but I didn't want to detract from what we were talking about. So I said nothing and let him carry on.

"Is that what we're involved in here..? Picture every street in every city in the entire world with no law and order… fires… looting… rape… shootings… killings… and no-one to keep the peace or uphold the law… every man, woman and even child for themselves.

I know we're getting a good handle now on this GDWM thing, but something tells me there's more to this case than pinching a few billion dollars from people who can probably afford it anyway."

A long silence ensued in which both of us got lost in our own thoughts and Jackson, cadaverous at the best of times, was looking worn to the bone with some secret, unnamed dread. Eventually and by unspoken mutual consent, we headed to our rooms.

Twenty-Two

Ashar was now increasingly worried about Mohammed. He was getting erratic and so far as he was aware, had eaten hardly anything in the past three or four days. There were now 77 GDWM client accounts with 133 billion dollars all set up to be moved into the fifty private capital banks. He had texted this, using their code, to Jaeger that morning. He did not think that Mohammed would be able to hold out much longer without doing something stupid that could endanger the whole project.

Ashar knew that it was only the thought of his parent's lives being at risk keeping him glued to his keyboard. He did not think he was that concerned about his own wellbeing.

He pushed all this to the back of his mind as he settled down to some more monitoring. He worked his way through those homes of the relationship managers, which he thought was a stupid name for salesmen, which all seemed to be hardly occupied until, by the end of the day, he had got back to Fox's house in London.

After a few moments Mohammed looked up across the desk in stunned surprise as Ashar gave a deep, primeval groan. He stood bolt upright knocking over his chair and then lurched backwards, crashing into the stud-walling behind him and forcing a dent into it.

He stared across the desk right through Mohammed, his breath coming in short panic-stricken gasps. His headphones had pulled out of the laptop as he had fallen back leaving it on loudspeaker. Mohammed heard the tail end of the conversation between Fox and Jackson, at Fox's mews house in London.

Mohammed watched as Ashar plugged the headset back in and started to type furiously for a few moments. Then stopped suddenly, and picking up his phone he started preparing a message on it. It was his own smartphone and not the burner.

Finally he was finished and, for a second, Mohammed thought he was going to lash out at him, but then he stormed out of the apartment onto the street.

The laptop was left unattended on his desk for the first time.

Twenty-Three

When we reassembled in the meeting room back at Swift the next morning, with neither of us having slept much, there were one page reports on each of the fifty banks waiting for us. Each page showed the name, jurisdiction, owner, date of registration and a whole host of other information on each bank with one line highlighted in yellow, 'Serial:' followed by a string of digits, which was the same for all the banks. The numbers now sat around the table had grown with the addition of Swift's cyber-fraud team.

Van Druten took charge. "The highlighted line you see is the serial number of the device used to apply for Swift registration for each of those banks. Any device used to access a Swift account has to be registered with the system, otherwise it won't be allowed access. We've modified the cookie process to make that happen. This is a Dell Vostro desktop PC. Millions of them, all over the world. And it was used to register all fifty of those banks."

Jackson took a note of the serial number and picked up his mobile.

Van Druten went onto explain that while it was highly unusual, even unique for one device to be authorised to set-up and access fifty different banks it was not something the system was ever programmed to pick up on, which would be rectified over the coming weeks.

Beringer was leaning back in his chair stroking his chin while everyone fell silent. The Swift technical and security guys were staring at each other as if passing telepathic messages between themselves.

I asked the room generally "So… just to clarify… we're working on the premise that the funds will be coming into these fifty banks from the GDWM client accounts which are all in different banks?"

Everyone nodded but remained silent until Jackson looked at me and said "Well, you're the inside man. Surely you can lay your hands on these GDWM client account details and then we'll know which accounts to intervene on."

I couldn't help myself. I snorted "Up yours, pal. If I asked for that kind of info I'd give everything away in a nanosecond, and don't even let it cross your mind to ask me to get it through some other means. And don't forget, Kelly's in easy reach of Jaeger. No. End of."

He stared at me hard, but eventually nodded his understanding. There was a further period of silence until one of the Swift technical guys spoke up. "We may not know where the funds are coming from, but we know where they're going to. It wouldn't be too difficult to intercept those funds on their way to those fifty banks, and re-route them to a holding account. Probably about a day of programming... coding... so that we can track exactly where the funds came from so they can be returned without delay."

Jackson's mobile sounded off. He looked up and told the room, "Ok... Just so everyone knows, the PC with the serial number you identified was purchased with cash in Malta a few months ago." He looked around the table questioningly "Is there anything special from a banking standpoint about Malta..?"

The response was bemused expression and shaking heads.

He continued "Okay then, all we've got by way of a lead is a PC bought on Malta that somehow was able to set-up all these banks' Swift accounts without raising any alarms. From where I sit, and I'm truly sorry to say it, but this looks like an inside job."

He shut down van Druten's objections before he could get started and asked one of the security team how many people were involved in Swift's cyber-security systems. The answer was fired straight back. 125 on the team, twelve with full access to the entire system with three of those on shift at any one time. Six different nationalities but all were fluent in English.

He looked across the table at Beringer "Klemens, we're going to need Interpol support on this. Can you rustle up a few really good interrogators and get to work on just these twelve to start?"

Beringer nodded and picked up his phone.

One of the cyber-fraud guys leaned across to his colleague, a French guy, Michel Brun, who van Druten had told me was Swift's Head of Cyber Counter-Measures, whatever that is, and said "It'd be great if Mo was still here. He would have got to the bottom of this in a few minutes."

For a second, I couldn't quite work out whether the expression that flitted across Brun's face was annoyance or fear. But emotions were running high and everybody was looking tense, scared or just downright confused.

Then Brun froze as Jackson fixed a laser stare on him. "Mo who?" Bumbling and uncoordinated as Jackson could sometimes be, when he needed to, he could command instant attention.

"Er… Mohammed Ibrahim, sir. He was head of network security till a few months ago."

Jackson's voice dropped a pitch. Focused. Threatening. "Why isn't he in this meeting?"

Van Druten stepped in, "Mo left us a few months back. He couldn't say where he was going. That's not unusual as many of our people move onto very senior and sensitive positions."

We could almost hear the cogs turning in Jackson's head "Do we have his phone number?"

Saying nothing, Brun looked through the contacts on his phone, wrote down the number on his notepad and slid it across the table to him.

Jackson pulled out his phone and within a few seconds had e-mailed the number to the MI6 desk at GCHQ, asking for a full report on the location and usage of the phone since Mohammed had left Swift four months before.

At one end of the room Beringer was talking to his people at Interpol while Jackson sat back and waited for the report on Ibrahim's phone to come back. In the middle, a hardly subdued argument was breaking out between the Swift people who were all playing the blame game. Jackson and me just looked at each other, nothing needed to be said.

It took just ten minutes for GCHQ to come back. He showed the reply only to me on his tablet. For the past four months the phone had been in Malta, switched on only once a week to make a regular call to a landline in Dartford, Kent which turned out to be Ibrahim's parents' number. This was not normal mobile phone usage.

Jackson stood up and started pacing around the room. "What was this Mo guy like?"

Van Druten answered for everyone. "He was a bit quiet… shy maybe but not anti-social. A very… uh… thoughtful man. We couldn't have had anyone better to rebuild our network security. It's called Dreadnought and took three years to build." He leaned back in his chair, hands clasped across his stomach. A big smile. "Swift is totally secure. We're completely impregna…"

His mouth hung open in mid-sentence as he was struck by the full-on realization of what he was about to say.

Jackson gave him a quick, pitying glance before asking the room generally. "Have we set up to re-route the funds going to those fifty banks to a holding account yet?"

As a speechless, open-mouthed van Druten was nodding confirmation, Jackson was on his phone ordering up a chopper to get us back to London. He looked across the table at Berringer. "Forget those interrogators."

Rather than go to Heathrow the chopper would take us directly to the old Croydon airport where cars would be waiting to take Jackson to his office and me home, so I could get myself sorted out. I desperately needed to talk to Kelly and tell her to look out for herself.

The chopper arrived about two hours later. As soon as we were aboard Jackson used the encrypted on-board system to call MI6 with instructions, the first was to get a SAS squad to Malta. As he hung up I pictured what would be happening, right now.

The scramble squad that was always on standby at Brize Norton would already be halfway across the tarmac to the waiting plane. They would be in the air by the time we landed in Croydon. In Malta, they'd await further instructions in the prep room set aside for them that all British Consulates and Embassies.

Twenty-Four

By the time I got back to Trinity Mews from La Hulpe I felt myself starting to cave in under a wave of exhaustion. I was able to stay awake just long enough to take a shower, throw everything into the washing machine and crash out on the bed. The house was steaming hot and I opened all the upstairs windows. The London noise was just a distant hum as I fell into a deep sleep. I surfaced 10 hours later at 8am and headed for another shower.

I had called Kelly as soon as the chopper had landed at Croydon but only got voicemail. I left a message asking her to call me, which she had but I had slept through her two attempts to return the call. I tried again but still got voicemail.

By 10am I had caught up on all my domestics and decided to go to the Red Lion and set myself up with one of their full-English breakfasts, after which I would head down to Croydon. I was halfway through breakfast when I spotted Jackson walking up the mews towards the house. I texted him 'Pub' and I saw him look at his phone, and steer a new course towards me.

At that time of the morning there was hardly anyone in the pub and he came over to my table after ordering a coffee at the bar. The expression on his face put me on instant alert.

Without saying a word he took out his tablet and passed it to me. I was struck dumb to see the two of us sitting in my lounge just a few yards away up the mews. He clicked the 'play' button for me and I watched the entire conversation we'd had the day after I moved in. When it had finished I had my head in my hands.

You pillock, Fox. Yes, it was *all too bloody good to be true!*

"How..?" I started to ask, but then "I need to get hold of Kelly."

"We've got Kelly covered. Obviously, these bugs were put in while the house was being made ready for you. That was my stupid mistake. We knew GDWM was leasing the house for you and it should have been bloody obvious that it could well have been bugged. My rotten bad I'm afraid. Jaeger's probably got all his people's homes and phones bugged, we know Ted Larkin's phone was, but we don't know about his apartment in Singapore.

"That was also set up for him by GDWM so it most likely is, but the procedure was to communicate with us through the SASR guys while he was in Oz and through other contacts we've got placed around the world for him. Nothing ever through his phone or e-mail... Anyway, he was notified about this video when he got into Sydney so he won't be going back to work for Jaeger. I came to tell you directly about it 'cos I didn't want to risk any chance of being intercepted."

He went onto explain that GCHQ had been monitoring Jaeger's known e-mail addresses for the past few years but nothing of any real significance had come out of it. Not that they had ever expected it to. But this recording was a link in an e-mail sent from a mobile from a previously unknown Gmail address, which had been tracked back to Malta. Obviously sent by someone who had reacted out of panic when they saw the footage and forgot to observe whatever security protocols were in place.

My mind was racing in all directions. My first priority was Kelly's safety as I knew that Jaeger had some kind of fixation on her, but at the same time I knew that Ted would be on her case, along with the Aussie SASR guys who were already assigned. I was looking at my breakfast, which was now stone cold, when my phone sounded off.

"Are you ok?" She asked

I felt a surge of relief at hearing her voice. "Has Ted been in touch yet? Are you safe?"

She gave a reassuring laugh as if she were talking to a frightened child, "Don't you worry about me, bless you! I've never had so much attention from so many fine, handsome and kinda sexy men in all my life! I couldn't get myself into any trouble even if I wanted to. It would be nice if someone would tell me what all this is about though. Is it anything to do with the reptile..? That Jaeger chappie?"

I told her it was best not to say any more about it on the phone but to make sure she did exactly what her security detail told her to do.

But just hearing her voice had lifted a huge weight from my shoulders. I explained that I was with someone and I'd come back to her with my plan of action later, but that I'd prefer to get to Sydney to be with her more than anything else. She told me she was now in Canberra, which I was half expecting after our last call.

When I'd hung up, Jackson pulled a phone and charger out of his briefcase and gave it to me. It had his, Ted's, Kelly's and the Croydon outstation centre numbers in it and told me to use it in preference to my own. I decided that it would be best to switch mine off in case Jaeger had found some way to track my movements through it. The burner was prehistoric with just phone and text, nothing that would come with a smart phone, like e-mail.

Jackson left the icing on the cake till the very last. GCHQ had monitored Mohammed's weekly call to his parents the day before, and the stress analysis on his voice showed beyond any doubt that he was under duress. Meaning there was probably someone else involved and keeping him under control, most likely whoever it was with that mobile. That was as far as they had got but, for me, it was equally possible that it was just the stress of being directly involved in the conspiracy, whatever that might be.

They had managed to track down the mobile which was operating through a mast at the southern end of Malta, but they had not been able to narrow it down any further than that. The small local police force, some in plain clothes, was working the area and would be able to spot anything out of order as they all knew their turf well. The

SAS squad had been sent to the area concealed in a tourist bus ready to be deployed as soon as they knew where to go.

By the time Jackson headed back to Croydon we had both agreed that Mohammed Ibrahim had somehow been inserted into Swift so that he could provide the access Jaeger and his conspirators needed. It was becoming ever more apparent that this was a massive conspiracy that had taken time and money, lots of both, to put together.

Jaeger was very serious about whatever it was he was planning. And, like Jackson, I'd become convinced it was more than just ripping off a few billionaires.

From what we now knew of this man's history vengeance, on an unfathomable scale, was the motive.

Twenty-Five

Ashar's e-mail arrived halfway through the second day of Jaeger's winery tour, which he had undertaken on a whim. He only ever carried his burner with him and had left his smartphone at the hotel and it was the afternoon of the second day of his tour before he got back to the hotel and logged into his e-mail. He opened the attachment, standing stock still in the middle of the room while he watched the whole conversation between Fox and Jackson.

When the video had finished he continued to stare at his screen for a few seconds but then felt his legs buckle beneath him as he sat down heavily on the bed.

At first, he was paralyzed with shock, but then he felt his whole being consumed by raw fury.

From Ashar's failure to monitor the bugs properly, and his utter stupidity with the unauthorized killing of the Davey's on Antigua, to Fox's deceit in asking for an update on progress. That treacherous creep would have been fully aware of what was really going on when he had asked for it. Heads would need to roll. Fox's especially. He, above all others, would pay.

He knew the meaning of betrayal. He had watched his father work himself to death just to put him through the education that would guarantee him the career he needed to exact the revenge his father had craved. His beautiful mother, who had given up her budding modelling career for his father had been taken to an unknown fate, which he had never dared let himself think about, for no other reason than she was married to someone who was merely, and wrongly, suspected of spying for the Israelis. He did not even have a photo of his parents as the escape from Egypt had been so fast and chaotic.

There was no other family for Jaeger outside of his mother and father. He had never been sure if he had imagined it or if, at his graduation, it really was the ghost of his father standing in the centre of the aisle, alone amongst all the audience smiling at him when he collected his degree.

But it was in that instant that he realized his father had not only had to sell their lovely home in London, but also work himself to the bone to put him through university. He had never been quite sure why he had caught his father quietly sobbing in his kitchen in that grubby little flat in London when he went home unexpectedly one weekend. Now he knew. And he had a debt to repay.

That bank, along with the entire global banking firmament that had destroyed his family was going to pay. No-one on this earth was going to stop him from exacting his revenge. Especially Fox. And if he couldn't have Fox…

He quickly packed and checked out, running to his Humvee and headed for the compound, doing his best to avoid drawing attention to himself by keeping within state speed limits on the hour long drive north. All the while itching to ram his foot down and go full pelt.

At the last count, Ashar had told him 77 GDWM client accounts were compromised with 133 billion dollars ready to be moved, and that would have grown even in the past few days. He needed to bring his plans forward and send an advisory to his tenants group on Whatsapp, telling them things could well be happening sooner than anticipated and to relocate to the compound.

By the time he got into his office he knew exactly what needed doing. The priority was to take control of events. He picked up his burner and called Ashar.

On answering he sounded nervous, like he did not know what to expect and the sigh of relief was clearly audible as Jaeger said, polite and calm as ever, "Thank you for the e-mail, Ashar. What's the current position on Mohammed's task?" There was no point alienating Ashar. Right now he needed him onside but somewhere deep inside he knew that it was his stupid escapade on Antigua that had alerted the authorities.

"82/202." Was all Ashar needed to say. 82 GDWM client accounts with a total 202 billion dollars in removable funds.

Jaeger gave this a couple of seconds thought. Then "How's your task progressing? The MT799's?"

"All set to go. Once logged in I only need to key 'enter' to set it all off."

There was no preamble from Jaeger. "Good. Task Mohammed with preparation for removal of funds from all the GDWM client accounts. I'll be sending full instructions by close of play today. Seven."

He hung up without a further word, and Ashar immediately passed on Jaeger's instructions to Mohammed who seemed pleased that, at long last, perhaps his torment was coming to an end. He had been confined to the apartment for over a week and was now fast approaching a real and genuine nervous breakdown, even if he did not know it. He was a shadow of his former self having lost two stone in just a few months, with pinched features and deep shadows under his eyes betraying his inner torment.

Rage, fear and impotence do not make for a contented soul.

Ashar took out burner number seven and put it on charge, then put his laptop and phone into his backpack and headed down to the quayside cafe where he would have a coffee and think things through. Whilst there, he summoned his friend who arrived on his scooter within five minutes.

+

In Margaret River Jaeger had more calls to make, one in particular to the jihadi cell based just south of Sydney. He gave full and explicit instructions finishing with Kelly's current location at the Hyatt hotel in Canberra.

He stood and thought for a few seconds and then picked up his phone again. Always best to have a contingency in place.

A few moments later, one of his goons knocked at his office door.

Twenty-Six

Policewoman Lela Rossi was born and had lived in Marsaxlokk all her life. She knew everyone, everyone knew her and she was trusted and popular with the locals. For the past week she had been working in plain clothes and quietly asking around if anyone had seen anything suspicious or noticed anyone not quite fitting in. A tough call in a fishing village constantly overrun with tourists.

Her unobtrusive yet persistent enquiries had prompted her to take up station at this popular café from where she could look all the way down past the many cafés and bistro's which all had tables out on the sunlit quayside to the market and, beyond that, the town square about half a mile distant.

The proprietor, Vittor, had mentioned that he had a new regular customer who was definitely not a tourist. He would sit at a table with a coffee for half an hour, and always had a backpack with him, from which he would sometimes pull out a laptop. He would speak if spoken to but, otherwise, kept himself to himself. He had become a regular at the café over the past three or four months.

He did not read a paper or book but just sat there for half an hour or so, sometimes working on his laptop, before leaving and walking up the street, Triq Il Luzu, that ran adjacent to Vittor's café. On a few occasions he had been joined by another man who arrived on a scooter.

A couple of times he had walked over to the quayside and stood there for a while, apparently just gazing out across the harbour. Plenty of people did that, especially the tourists. But usually no more than once.

Two hours into her surveillance and after her third reading of the *Times of Malta* from which she could by now recite almost its entire contents, she saw 'backpack man' emerge from Triq Il Luzu. She looked across to Vittor who gave her a nod in confirmation. Folding her paper she strolled off towards the market tapping her colleague's shoulder, another cop, sitting in plain clothes at one of the other café's as she walked past. He stood up and set himself up to replace her at her table after ordering a coffee, eyes constantly on backpack man.

Ashar was now under full surveillance.

Lela concealed herself in the market but could not get a picture of Ashar without him clearly seeing her doing it if he happened to glance up, so she wandered about the stalls keeping a constant eye on him. Eventually she saw him finish his coffee and stroll over to the edge of the quay. She could not be sure but she thought she saw him throw something into the water, making her grimace at yet another tourist dropping their litter where they shouldn't.

She watched him turn around and go back into the side street, and her colleague get up to follow him. She was halfway across the square to the police station before she stopped, thought for a moment and turned back.

+

Kelly had been in Canberra for the past few days working hard to get her business dealt with so that she could get back home. This was her first time in Canberra and had not had the time or inclination to explore the city. She had been working on the funding of a massive railway project for New South Wales, and the Australian Treasury bureaucrats were showing complete ignorance of the massive array of financing options that were now available, through the sheer weight of private capital entering the market. Trillions of dollars of capital, 'dry powder', looking for opportunities to invest in major projects.

She had spent several months assembling all the funding required from hedge funds, family offices, wealth managers and other sources. Now, to her intense annoyance Australian Treasury bureaucrats were treating her funding structure with downright suspicion, just because there were none of the usual banks involved. They simply did not understand that the banks no longer had the liquidity to lend into these projects, and that the primary source for major projects was now private capital.

She had been forced to go way beyond her original brief and actually give lessons on the new project financing structures that had emerged since the 2008 crash, powered by private capital coming direct from the world's UHNWI's. For a while all this quite legitimate capital, and the structures it used to find its way into the market had been referred to by the financial establishment as 'shadow banking'. Tainting her entire market and making life needlessly difficult for her.

But if what she was doing bore no relation to what these little darlings had learned at uni, then as far as they were concerned her financing structure was at best fanciful or, at worst, fraudulent.

This implication, openly voiced to her, when someone had mentioned 'dirty money' had been the last straw. On top of that she had suddenly found herself at the centre of some sort of security scare, which she neither wanted nor understood, and surrounded by men who she did not find 'fine, handsome' or even 'kinda sexy' as she had told Dez, for no other reason than to put his mind at rest.

In fact, she was royally hacked off at the constant intrusion all this security was making into her life, and the concern it was raising at the Treasury, where her job was becoming more challenging by the day. She could take a joke, but enough was enough.

After getting back to the Hyatt at the end of her third day, she called her client in Sydney and told them that she was at the end of her tether, that she was being asked to go far beyond her original brief and that as far as she was concerned the financing structure was perfectly sound and that she was going home. So, send some other mug to replace her.

This was met with dismay by her client, but only because they did not want all the hassle that goes with dealing with careerist treasury bureaucrats trembling at the thought of anything new. They had thought they could leave all that crap to Kelly. How wrong can you be?

Not her problem. Kelly Murchison was going home. She called Ted Larkin and told him as much and refused to listen to his pleas to hold fire until they had got proper security in place for her journey.

Twenty-Seven

Since the Brits had invaded a few weeks ago, the awkward gangly one and the nice one with the limp, Arlene's police career had taken on a life of its own. Whenever there was mind-numbing liaison required with either the FBI or foreign police forces, she had found it being 'dumped' on her. But the truth was, she enjoyed it.

She was seeing what life was all about not just outside Detroit, but outside the USA. She had even got herself a passport in hopeful anticipation of actually going to visit some of the places she was now dealing with.

She had now completed her probation and was a fully-fledged police officer with what looked like a bright career in front of her. She was loving her job and, on top of all that, she had even got her own small apartment in a nice part of town, with a little help from the bank of mum and dad.

Eric Day had introduced her to a brilliant mortgage broker. She was becoming a proficient networker.

After some delay, the Antigua police had finally managed to get their press release out to the local newspapers and tv stations. It showed the pictures of Valiece and Daphne as two separate images, cropped and lifted from the photograph she had found. But even on out of the way Caribbean islands there are plenty of people who like to make a nuisance of themselves and calls were coming in from all over the region. Even other parts of the world that happened across the images on the web.

Thankfully, these could be immediately discounted as one thing they could be sure of was that the Davey's had come directly to Antigua from Detroit and gone nowhere else. Two weeks later and after the flood of calls had eased, everything had been sifted through. There were just two worthwhile sightings reported. A call from a waitress at Catherine's Café in English Harbour to say she had served the couple, which the police confirmed by tracking Valiece's card.

The second was from a jeweller in St John's who had a very clear recording of them on his CCTV looking in through his shop window, which he sent to the police. Who forwarded it to Arlene, who forwarded it to Drew Fallon at the FBI, which would be an excuse for them to have yet another long phone conversation, in which they would both dance around what was really on both their minds.

When the video from the jeweller's shop had first arrived it had finished with the Davey's looking off to their left for a split second, giving Arlene the uneasy feeling that something had been deleted or edited out of the recording. She called Antigua to query this and they told her that they had been having a conversation with someone off camera, and then walked off out of the picture. They had just pulled out the section of them looking into the window so that she could see the time stamp as a further indicator of their movements.

Whoever they had been talking to did not appear in the recording, so they had just sent the part showing them stopping to look in the window until they moved off. She asked for the full recording which was sent to her within hours.

This time, she saw the full sequence of events and was cursing Antigua police for the delay they had caused. As with many jewellers the window display was brightly lit, with mirrors everywhere to enhance the lights and sparkling products on offer. While the person the Davey's were talking to had remained out of shot, his reflection could be seen in one of the side mirrors in the window.

She had pointed this out when she forwarded it onto Drew who replied, "I sent it down to the image lab and they're working on it now, the guy's face is quite small as a proportion of the entire image, so it'll be heavily pixelated. It's going to take a lot of work to pull anything meaningful out of it."

"Ok. There was also a car in the background." she said "A Merc C120 from what I could see… could we pull the tag off it?"

"Nah. The angle's too sharp and there's also that wooden bench in the way. Street furniture can be such a pain sometimes."

Then the conversation moved on. It would edge towards the mutual attraction they felt, but it had never actually been said out loud. She had dropped as many hints as she could about having a meal or doing something together rather than just the occasional work meeting. But, typical man, he just would not bite.

Ask me the hell out will you?! She gave it one more try. "Maybe we'd get more done if we could actually get more than just grabbing the odd five or ten minutes to go through everything."

She could almost hear him thinking through his reply "How about I get this image sorted out with the lab and then come over to you and work through everything we've got…" and then, after clearing his throat and in a tremulous tone he said nervously "…er, we could have lunch… after… um, maybe?"

At last, he's grown a pair! "That would be *really* nice. Look forward to it."

There was a stunned silence from the other end of the line before he replied, in what sounded like genuine surprise "Oh. Good… I should have it in the next day or two. I'll call you then."

Twenty-Eight

It would be another week before Kelly was due home and I decided that I wasn't going to put myself through a whole week of worrying about her. I managed to find a business class seat on a Malaysian Airlines flight out of Heathrow for the following morning. My leg was settling down a bit after all the travelling but I was not going to set everything off again by sitting for nearly an entire day in cattle class. I was still having to use my walking stick, but I travelled with cabin bag only so I wouldn't have to hang around the carousel in Sydney.

When I got to Heathrow I texted her from the burner Jackson had given me that I was on my way and would be arriving in Sydney at 6pm her time and asked which hotel she was staying at either there or in Canberra. I settled in for the journey slightly more relaxed than I had been, knowing that I'd be seeing Kelly and putting my own brand of protection on her very soon.

Jackson had briefed me on the action in Marsaxlokk. The local cop who had followed the guy they had branded 'backpack man' to his front door, revealing the exact location of the target apartment, had been shown a picture of Mohammed, who he had not recognised. So this was obviously someone new in the equation and probably the owner of the mobile that had sent the message with the recorded conversation to Jaeger. The ground floor apartment was being kept under observation. Difficult, as the street was so narrow that anyone watching it would have been easily spotted.

For the time being it was drive-, walk- or cycle-by's and cops posing either as couples or solo customers at the café on the quayside and, occasionally, walking round the block and trying to get a look inside the apartment as they strolled by. But, even then, it was a quiet street and any undue activity would be quickly picked up. It was pointless anyway, the blinds were closed all the time.

The café owner had also offered the cops a back room that gave them a partial view of the apartment's front door. But the angle made it impossible to get a camera or laser mic targeted on it. Checks with the landlord showed that it was leased by some obscure company hidden behind proxy directors in Peru, and paid up for a full three years. So that got us nowhere, but it fitted the pattern.

I also heard how one of the local cops, working on instinct, had seen a small collection of burner phones in the shallow water off the quayside that had been thrown there by backpack man, after first thinking he had thrown litter into the water.

There was no way those burners could be recovered either by day or night without backpack man realizing what was going on. If they suddenly disappeared he would get himself out of town in a flash. Most likely, after all that time in the water there would be no worthwhile retrievable data on them anyway.

The SAS squad had already done a recce of the location and would be able to do a forced entry within seconds of piling out of their tourist bus. But we did not want to kick off any action yet as it needed to be coordinated with nailing Jaeger at his compound, his 'fortress'.

On top of everything else we still had no idea why it had been built, its existence bore no relation to the fraud we had already exposed and hopefully, if Swift had done their job, thwarted. It was something we needed to understand before moving forward, we did not want any unintended consequences.

The consensus was that Mohammed was there under duress, maybe with his own and his parents' lives at risk, but there was no actual proof of that. From where I sat though, he was right in the thick of it. Everyone also agreed that he would have to be collateral damage if the platoon had to make a forced entry and there was a firefight.

All this was going round my head as the drone of the plane's engines began sending me off to sleep. Then, I was jolted wide awake, adrenaline pumping, heart thumping and looking around the cabin. I dredged through the thought process that had, in the end, sent me off to sleep.

It was all to do with backpack man. Where did he fit into the equation? Was he just a minder for Mohammed or did he have other roles to play? And why were my thoughts constantly coming back to MT799's? *What was I missing?!* Something intangible was nagging at me and, whatever it was, prompted me to pull Van Druten's business card out of my wallet. I used the airline phone to call his direct line.

Thankfully he answered on the third ring and I wasted no time "Hello, Dick. Hope you remember me, it's Dez Fox. We were with you last week..."

He remembered and was very receptive, maybe trying to make up for his obstructive attitude at the meeting. "Dick, if you've got a minute, I'm trying to get a handle on MT799's. I mean, how many are in use at any one time? Is it possible in any way at all to remove them without authorization? How are they lifted?"

I heard him clicking away at his keyboard before he came back. "Of course... um... from the dashboard here there are 38,932 MT799's currently active. There's absolutely no way they can be lifted without authorization. It's an inter-bank transaction between the two banks concerned and executed by codes known only to those two banks. They can either time out or be removed if the pre-agreed release code is exchanged between the banks."

Somehow, his explanation was not making me breathe easy. And I was completely thrown by that number of MT799's currently active, but he explained that they are used on a huge range of transactions, blocking anything from a thousand to a billion dollars or more.

I asked him about funds blocked as collateral against loans for PPP's. Was there any way to separate these from other MT799's other than that they would always be for amounts of one hundred million dollars and upwards?

"What are PPP's?" he asked.

Best not to push it, so I just thanked him for his time. After a moment's thought I took a risk, fished my own phone out of my cabin bag and switched it on just long enough to find and write down the number of the CSA client who had first told me about PPP's, Pat Wheeler. The one who had told me the little nugget about the 'gift' the Americans had supposedly made to Europe after the war which, actually, had cost them nothing at all.

He was close to the market, knew many of the traders and had done a couple of programs himself. He was a billionaire six or seven times over and as straight as the day is long.

I hadn't spoken to him for more than two years, and had no idea if I would be waking him up at silly o'clock somewhere on the planet. I used the plane's phone again and I was really gratified when he answered and immediately recognised my name.

"Hey, Dez! Good to hear from you. What've you been up to?"

I didn't want to be associated with GDWM in any way so told him that I'd been doing some freelance PR. I jumped straight in and told him I was trying to get a handle on how many PPP's would be in progress at any one time, and what the total amount of deposits would be in play and what the total loan exposure for the host banks would be.

Pat was as close to the market as anyone I knew. But he sounded thrown by my questions and asked why I wanted to know. I told him it was just a bit of research I was doing for a client.

"Oh… Okay… Well… Strange you should ask, I actually had a conversation about this with a couple of bank treasurers at Davos back in January. Seems they're getting a bit concerned about the whole PPP thing. The trouble is, as you know, it's all very… opaque…almost impossible to put numbers on it. But their best guess was that exposure at any one time's probably around the five trillion mark. But I know of family offices and foundations that can sometimes place as much as five or even ten bill into a program, so I think that five trillion as ten times leverage on, I dunno, 500 programs on the go at any one time could be a bit on the low side."

My head was spinning. I looked down and saw my knuckles turning white as I gripped the armrest ever tighter. That OCD sixth sense of mine setting off a primal, fearful ache in my gut.

I asked him what would happen if the MT799's blocking the placements were cancelled before time-out or release codes were exchanged. I don't know what prompted me to ask the question. That bloody sixth sense of mine again.

He was emphatic, "Well, that can't happen."

That's when I felt an inexplicable cold rush of fear. There's nothing wrong with fear, when you know what you're fearful of. But I didn't know. This wasn't like soldiering, where you knew what you were dealing with and could work out how to handle a situation, and its likely outcomes. This was the unknown. Unknown to anyone except, it seemed… me.

The drone of the engines was fading into the background. I was in my own little bubble. I persisted. "But, just… *what if* MT799's being used on all current trades were somehow over-ridden or cancelled? Any thoughts..?"

"Well. It's quite simple really. If the collateral is no longer there, because the 799's have been lifted, then the loan to the traders would have to move to the balance sheet as unsecured… uncollateralized… debt."

He went quiet. Then "Um… These banks are at the apex of the inter-bank lending market". Another pause. "But with that kind of unsecured debt moved to the balance sheet, because there's no um… *apparent* collateral to leverage against, they would all become insolvent... bankrupt…"

He stopped to think some more. "The logical conclusion would be that all inter-bank loans between themselves and onward down through the global banking system would have to be recalled. The whole system would implode from the top down. First step would be for all those banks to call in all personal and business loans, overdrafts and the rest of it. Millions… no, no… of course, *billions* of private and business customers all over the world. That'd be trillions of dollars. But it won't happen, 'cos it can't."

A short pause, with only the hollow sound of the ether on the line. "Or is there something you want to share with me, Dez?"

He asked the question like he was expecting an answer." *Oh crap.* I could hardly think straight.

"…Dez? Are you there?"

The plane seemed to evaporate around me. I was sitting there alone in my speck of a business class cubicle, eight miles up, white knuckles clasped onto the arm rest, staring out at an endless blue sky. Alone.

"Pat… I just don't know." My voice sounded muffled. "It'd take too long to explain what I think I know. I don't even know if I'm right."

No reply. He was waiting.

I went out on a limb. "Okay… you might want to think about a short term 'liquidate and consolidate' approach. Tell your friends. Quietly."

He knew exactly what I meant. Liquidate all shareholdings and other tradeable assets and consolidate the proceeds into private bank accounts, or private capital banks for those who have them. Out of reach of the mainstream banking network and its febrile inter-bank capital markets.

"Thank you for that, Dez. If ever you need anything, just call."

If nothing else I had either just cemented a priceless friendship, or set myself up to be the world's most monumental idiot.

But I now knew that the CEESSEB outfit Jackson had told me about would never have factored in the failure of the MT799 system into their Wealth Games.

Something more than ripping off a few billionaires was going on. And, if I was right, Wheeler had just spelled it all out for me.

Eight miles up. Alone. Looking down on a world that, *if* I was right, was poised on the edge of the abyss.

But, even if I was right, who could I tell? And who would believe me?

I called Jackson.

Twenty-Nine

Sydney, Australia. August.

Ted Larkin had fit straight in with the Aussie SASR guys who had been assigned to protect Kelly and who were now joined by an inspector from the Australian Federal Police. He was a wiry little Scotsman called Josh Miller, who took immediate control of the meeting. He was one of those that just took command assuming that everyone understood that was his role in life.

He was setting things out, as he saw them, in an almost comical blend of heavy Glaswegian tempered only slightly by an Australian accent, a challenge for those straining to understand him.

"Now this Jaeger bloke knows we're onto him, we have to assume he's going to be out for blood. From what I see from this briefing," he waived a sheaf of papers over his head "the numbers are big. But *big*. We're talking tens or maybe hundreds of billions. He's going to take any steps necessary to protect his wee turf."

Jackson was looking down on the meeting from a screen up on the wall at the end of the small room in Canberra police headquarters, through an encrypted link to the MI6 outstation in Croydon. He introduced himself and gave a rundown of how the case was progressing at his end. Josh thanked Jackson and turned to Ted.

"You're the one who's been closest to him lately, what's your take?"

It took Ted a while to organize his thoughts after hearing the input from Jackson about Swift and the GDWM accounts, which was all new to him. "Alright. Here goes. I'm no head doctor but from what I've seen of this guy he's a borderline psychopath. Definitely some element of paranoia… He rates himself above all others and I know he's been directly involved in torture and murder, or at least associated with it." He looked around the room, "I guess we've all seen those pictures..?"

Those pictures were not easy to forget and drew sober nods from everyone. "Right now he knows he's been exposed. If Swift is able to intercept all those funds he wants to steal it's going to cause him a whole heap of problems we can only speculate on. But he has a lot of people to call on who'll be delighted to offer their services by way of getting even for him. They have cells all over the planet, no doubt including here in Oz. And I'm pretty sure he can call on others if he needs to. I think we can safely say that we need to get eyes on Dez as quickly as possible."

He looked up at the screen "Tony, can you organize that?"

Jackson came straight back "Right now he's on his way to Sydney, I've just taken a call from him. He just wants to be with Kelly to make sure she's safe. Getting in at 6pm tomorrow. I'll e-mail his flight number to you." He did not want to get the discussion bogged down in what Dez had told him about his conversation with Pat Wheeler.

Josh interrupted saying that Kelly had said she was planning to leave Canberra tomorrow and was quite prepared to hire a car herself to get to Sydney airport, a three or four hour drive. She was starting to kick up against all the security and it seemed she was having some problems on the work front. She had made it clear she had had enough of the whole thing.

The meeting broke up with agreement that it was fine being all feisty and independent but she was putting herself, and possibly others, at risk. They knew that Jaeger would beyond doubt have the means to do real harm to Kelly, just to get at Dez.

The first priority was to get Kelly safely to Sydney airport and on a plane back to the UK with Dez, with an escort if it could be arranged in time. They would reassemble when that had been done, with the objective of seeing how to directly deal with Jaeger and his 'fortress'.

Thirty

Jaeger was working his keyboard furiously after receiving the final position from Ashar on Mohammed's work. He had a spreadsheet showing how much would be paid into each of the fifty private capital banks the unfortunate Valiece Davey had set up. Then, the instant those funds were received, the coordinates of all the banks with accounts held by his terrorist and crime syndicate 'clients', and how much would be paid onto each of them

This would see, at the last count, 202 billion dollars taken from 82 GDWM client accounts evaporate into the global banking network. Once the funds arrived at the fifty banks, it would all happen in seconds and be impossible to recover. As soon as it was ready he e-mailed the spreadsheet to Ashar with instructions for Mohammed to load up the data so that everything could be executed within seconds of the funds being removed from the GDWM client accounts.

Even though he had had to bring the completion forward, his partners-cum-clients in the project would still do very nicely out of it and would have nothing to complain about. They would have enough funds for them to set up the super-jihadi group, global mafia or whatever they wanted to call themselves and wage all the chaos they wanted.

There was nothing he had seen in the conversation between Jackson and Fox to show that they had any notion of what he was preparing.

He then checked with the cell in Sydney to make sure everything was set up for Ms Kelly Murchison. He smiled to himself for the first time in a whole day when he thought about how much pain he was going to cause Mr Fox. So. Much. Pain.

He checked and re-checked that everything was set to go. Then texted Ashar with one word: 'Execute'.

+

In Marsaxlokk, Mohammed needed only to log into Swift and access the program he had set up to remove the funds from the GDWM accounts and review where those funds were to go. He would then re-check that everything was set up at the receiving fifty private capital banks for instant onward payments to the banking co-ordinates provided by all the groups, all listed on the spreadsheet sent through by Jaeger.

With feelings of relief but, again, mixed with the same feeling of guilt and despair as he had when keying in the laptop and PC serial numbers back at Swift all those weeks ago, he keyed 'Enter'.

Deep in 'the hole' at Swift headquarters, a screen at the control desk flashed red. The shift supervisor called Dick van Druten.

He had the control desk monitor switched through to his office, where he was joined by his heads of cyber-fraud and network security. So that everyone could see what was going on, he put it all up onto the large screen on his office wall. Heads nodded in satisfaction after they had studied its contents closely.

All the funds headed for the fifty private capital banks had been successfully intercepted and routed to the new holding account set up by Swift. It took just an hour for the funds to be tracked back to their origins, and set up to be returned. But Jackson had told van Druten to hold fire on that, and check with him first.

Everyone was itching to return the funds because as they saw it their loss, even if they were ultimately returned, would be a major hit to Swift's reputation. They were a long-established and trusted monopoly within the global banking industry, but that could change in the blink of an eye if 82 influential, capable and very angry billionaires decided to do something about it and set up their own alternative.

Van Druten wanted to get these funds returned and wasted no time in calling Jackson and telling him what was going on. He also mentioned the conversation he had had with Dez Fox and his strange query regarding MT799's.

The line went suddenly silent for a few seconds. Then "Dick, please hold fire on returning those funds. We need a… a pause.

There's something much bigger going on here that we need to get a proper handle on."

Every instinct was telling him that there were aspects to this case that were still unknown but the MT799, till now so much of an enigma was slowly starting to take on some form.

It was a big step, but this now had to be shared with people above his pay grade.

He sat at his screen and spent an hour arranging the history of the Jaeger case into a series of bullet-points. No mean feat when there was five years to condense into just three sheets of A4. Taking a deep breath, knowing that what he was about to do could well be career damaging, or terminating, he sent his summary to the head of security at the Treasury.

It did not go by e-mail. He printed it off and walked into his PA's office, adjoining his, and asked her to log it into the Whitehall pneumatic tube system. Ultimate security.

Within half an hour his opposite number at the Treasury called him over for an immediate meeting with the Chancellor who, it seemed, had not changed in any way since Jackson had last met him at yet another boring cyber-fraud briefing a couple of years before.

A gaunt and humourless man, exuding as much charm and charisma as his position demanded. None. They spent just ten minutes discussing Jackson's summary of events, after which there was a short call between the Chancellor and someone whose name Jackson did not catch.

He started to feel he was losing control of events. He was led to an elevator which took the three men down to somewhere below ground level where they emerged into a white-tiled tunnel, with worn green painted concrete flooring lit by an endless line of fluorescent strip lighting curving away into the distance before them. It had obviously been built many decades before and could even have been used during both world wars.

Wordlessly, each lost in their own thoughts, they strode along the tunnel, lined with pipes and wires carrying information and contents that Jackson could only guess at. But he did catch the long-forgotten sound of pneumatic tubes, propelling their pods between people who did not want to commit the messages they carried to any kind of electronic transmission. He had lost all sense of direction and had no idea where he was as another elevator took them upwards and they emerged into what looked like a storeroom of some sort.

He followed both men up a service stairwell, until they went through a door which led out into a large meeting room which, from all the photographs he had seen, Jackson immediately recognised as the Cabinet Room in number ten Downing Street. As they entered at one end the Prime Minister, his private secretary and Head of MI6 entered from the other.

The Chancellor made quick introductions and the small gathering sat around the end of the table. Jackson was asked, once again, to repeat his concerns.

He went through the whole Jaeger case and how, working with Swift, they had managed to intercept and divert over 200 billion dollars into a holding account. They now knew, from the onward payment instructions awaiting the arrival of funds in the fifty private capital banks, these billions would have been routed into the coffers of a whole range of terrorist groups and crime syndicates.

He finished his short presentation with "The only reason I was prompted to contact the Treasury was something telling me that… maybe somewhere in all this… this MT799 is going to be far more significant than we currently think it is. But we don't yet know how…"

When he had finished the Chancellor then went onto explain CEESSEB and how it came about to the Prime Minister. Although he had heard about it, had never really followed the proceedings and updates but knew that it was some kind of early-warning network that was set up to anticipate financial crises.

But he did recall a briefing on CEESSEB and its 'wealth games' by the Treasury Secretary when he first became Prime Minister. And its alert codes, the origins of which were as much a mystery to him as they were to everyone else.

The Chancellor reminded him of those codes and sat back to wait for him to process the deluge of information that had rained down upon him over the past hour. He had seen Jackson's bullet point presentation only a few minutes before the meeting.

"So, to summarise," he said, looking hard at Jackson "we know there's something going on, but we don't know what. We can't put a value or outcomes of any sort on this conspiracy, if that's what it is. All we have is your gut feeling, Tony, which revolves around this, er…" he took a look at his notes "…this MT799 thing."

He fixed his gaze on him, as if willing a response out of him. This was make or break time for Jackson. Answering 'yes' or 'no' were both potentially career ending.

'Yes' could see him perceived as a grandstanding *prima donna*, and 'no' could pre-empt the opportunity to thwart global economic desolation. All those in the room watched him agonize over his answer.

He looked to the chancellor, sat statue-like and expressionless next to the prime minister. He then looked at his boss, the Head of MI6 and could see straight away he was going to get no help from that direction. If he was not careful, any blame from making the wrong call was going to fall on himself alone. But that is how Whitehall works.

He qualified his answer. "What's driving this gut instinct which is very important in my job, Prime Minister, is the fact that we have Jaeger with his 'fortress' down there in Margaret River, and the – as yet undefined – involvement of North Korea. Also, his family history, which I consider very meaningful and which I summarized on my presentation."

He nodded towards the three sheets of paper showing his bullet points. "This MT799 thing that, we're told, is absolutely secure and can't be interfered with. Really? You would have thought that all those billions of dollars that we have just intercepted would have been secure enough with all those firewalls and whatnot that these geeks produce. It's the North Korea thing that's really nagging at me. Why are they involved in all this? And don't forget, we have an insider, this Mohammed Ibrahim at the helm, or the keyboard, in all this. Under duress or not, the outcome is the same."

He paused and looked down at his briefcase and then glanced back at the Prime Minister. "I was hoping I wasn't going to have to show you these. Robert Jaeger is linked to all these pictures."

He pulled the images of torture, agony and death out of his briefcase and fanned them out on the table in front of the Prime Minister whose blood drained from his face as he sat bolt upright against the back of her chair. He recovered himself quickly.

Looking at the chancellor with glazed eyes he gave his instructions. "Order a… what was it..?" he looked down again at the briefing notes. "…that's right, order a code Bretton Woods, whoever he is. I'll leave it with you. Thank you, Mr Jackson… Tony"

With that, he got up and hurriedly left the room, probably to find the nearest washroom to throw up in, private secretary trailing closely in his wake.

A Bretton Woods alert requires the Finance or Treasury Secretaries from all G20 member countries to assemble for an emergency, top secret meeting. HM Treasury would host and it would take place in two days.

Van Druten was not happy, and protested loudly, when Jackson instructed him to be at the meeting and to hold up returning the intercepted funds that had been taken from the GDWM client accounts. He kicked up so much that Jackson called Beringer at Interpol and asked him to take whatever steps were necessary to ensure he complied.

Code Bretton Woods means that delegates are to arrive with no fanfare. Quietly on private jets, scheduled flights or their own air force transports bringing them unnoticed into airports all over the UK with onward travel to London arranged by their own embassies and consulates, where they would stay while in London.

Thirty-One

The first thought Jaeger had after receiving the call telling him no funds had arrived was that it must be a glitch of some sort at Swift. Or more likely the group that had called him, a cell in Sweden which he was sure was something to do with the Russian mafia, had provided the wrong banking co-ordinates to forward the money onto from the private capital bank. There were a lot of account identity numbers, all in different formats and strings, and with that many funds transfer instructions there was plenty of room for something to go wrong, probably a keyboarding error.

Also, Mohammed's coding had allowed for the funds to be moved to all fifty banks over a full 24 hours to avoid flagging up any unusual spike in activity on the Swift network. Nothing to worry about.

He knew that Mohammed would not have made any mistakes or, even more stupid, made some attempt at sabotage. Either way for him and his family, the consequences would have been too dire to contemplate.

A smile appeared as he recalled the meeting with him at his small apartment in La Hulpe. The little guy was a gibbering wreck by the time he had finished with him.

He decided to give it a day or two just to be sure that network delays or some obscure compliance issue had not got in the way of the movement of funds. It would not be the first time, he had experienced it throughout his long banking career. He knew what he was doing.

Whoever it was on the other end of the line, he had forgotten the name, was told to be patient and let the system do what it had to do. The funds would turn up within the coming couple of days.

The next day, there were half a dozen more calls and e-mails, all saying that no funds had arrived. These were from cells and groups all over the world so he had no choice but to start thinking through all the options that could lead to this kind of failure.

All his member groups across a whole range of terrorist movements and crime syndicates, some well-known to police and security agencies around the world, and others with no profile at all, had paid 'commitment' deposits to benefit from his scheme. All in the millions of dollars.

The North Koreans had paid significantly more than everyone else to get what they wanted, but he knew that would still happen for them. He decided to give it one more day, but he did not sleep well that night.

He woke up to a whole string of e-mails and voicemails which meant that no-one, absolutely no-one, anywhere, had received any funds. He could not delude himself any longer and a hunted look appeared in his eyes as he realized that he would be the target of a dozen different terrorist and serious crime groups who would want more than just their money back.

Each of them would have had their own plans on how to use their billions, and now they would not only be out of pocket but, worst of all, especially for the jihadists, they will have lost face. Even worse for them than the loss of funds. They would be out for blood. His blood. But of course, there just had to be a simple explanation. This was not meant to happen.

As he texted Ashar he noticed his fingers were shaking ever so slightly.

Thirty-Two

London, August

The meeting room was set up in a U-shape format in a magnolia painted basement room of the Treasury. A lectern at the centre-front of the 'U', with a 70-inch screen behind completed the scene in the austere room. There were no plush leather boardroom seats, only office chairs that would maybe satisfy the boss of a small business. The walls were bare. The tables were the basic range from any office furniture catalogue.

Some delegates, all finance secretaries or ministers representing their governments, looked around in confusion as they entered, wondering if they had come into the right room. But most just headed for a chair and settled down for business, even if none of them were too sure what that business was going to be.

There was only coffee and sandwiches available on a side table, with none of the drinks and socializing that the delegates would normally expect at such an august gathering.

At the front of the room the Chancellor, impassive as ever, a fidgeting and impatient Dick van Druten and a pensive Jackson sat in a row behind a table facing the delegates. Once everyone was in the room, doors locked and translation headphones on for those who needed them, the Chancellor stood and walked the few steps to the lectern.

"Good morning, lady and gentlemen… delegates." This was met with slight nods of acknowledgement and expectant, curious stares. "This is the first proper meeting of CEESSEB, which at the moment is simply an informal body. So there are no set procedures, minutes to review or other matters to get in the way so we can get straight down to business. This meeting was called by the CEESSEB Steering Committee, elected by everyone here which is made up of myself and my counterparts from South Africa, Saudi Arabia, Russia and South Korea."

He paused to look around the room, trying to assess if he had everyone's attention. For some reason he was feeling nervous as hell.

"We are also joined by the CEESSEB representatives from the Development Committee of the IMF and World Bank. I understand that they wish to work with us to formalize our status as an Inter-Governmental Organisation… an IGO." This generated a murmur of approval from around the room.

He cleared his throat. "Ahem. Our apologies for the, um, basic surroundings. All our other meeting rooms were booked and we didn't want to draw any attention to ourselves by changing existing arrangements."

Expressions ranged between perplexed and just plain baffled, as the delegates looked through the bullet points that Jackson had produced just a few days before. To which he had added a few notes for clarification.

After a short pause and a deep intake of breath he went on to review his report, now with additions from Swift, the latter of which had reported a conversation with someone who was to remain unidentified embedded within the conspiracy. He had queried a Swift instrument called an MT… message type… MT799 with van Druten.

At this point van Druten looked down at the floor and exhaled loudly, slowly shaking his head – if only, if *only* he had not mentioned his brief conversation with Fox to Jackson, this meeting might not even be happening, and all would be right with his world.

He did not know about Dez's separate conversation with Jackson when he called from his plane to relate the input from Pat Wheeler. And expressed his real, dreadful fears about what the consequences of compromising the MT799 process could be. So dreadful, so incomprehensive, that Dez himself could hardly believe it.

But it was this conversation, and not his one with van Druten that had prompted Jackson to alert his security contact at the Treasury, from where everything had accelerated at a pace he could hardly keep up with, towards this meeting.

Swift was already taking urgent calls from member banks querying the whereabouts of countless billions of dollars which had disappeared from client accounts. To which the stock answer being given was that it was a cyber-fraud countermeasure and the funds would be returned as soon as possible, at the same time asking for discretion as the investigation continued.

That would not hold water for long, even though a screen grab of the holding account had been sent with the replies. There were some very wealthy and influential people who were starting to make ominous noises.

The meeting was now gaining pace with Jackson trying to answer questions being thrown at him by all the delegates. His tall, rangy frame was at odds with his deep tenor and he knew he did not cut an overly impressive figure at the lectern. If he was ever giving any kind of a presentation it was usually to his peers on obscure intelligence matters in the bowels of some Whitehall building. Where appearance and accomplished public speaking were irrelevant.

He was having trouble keeping back Fox's or Jaeger's identities as, once these people left the meeting there was no telling how much of what had been said would find its way into the public domain. He dared not even contemplate what would happen if anything discussed here leaked into the media.

He managed to give reasonably coherent answers to all the questions being fired at him until the Russian Finance Secretary, who Jackson was sure had direct links to their mafia asked, in perfect English, "What exactly *is* the concern in the matter of this, er… MT799 instrument?"

Everyone was looking directly at him. Eyebrows raised. Expectant. "That's the problem. We simply don't know other than that it's figured in the investigation and that it's critical to the PPP program, which is described in brief in your notes. But no-one can work out how it might be compromised. If it *were* ever compromised the consequences would be catastrophic. From what I understand after talking to, er… our man inside the conspiracy… There is a potential for some of the world's top banks to be exposed to *at least* five trillion dollars of unsecured debt, a figure he in turn got from someone very close to the PPP market… and who actually believes it could be higher than that.

"This is precisely the kind of scenario this group… CEESSEB… was set up to anticipate and counteract. We simply have to take this seriously."

Jackson looked over his shoulder towards van Druten and invited him to the lectern. He got a nod in return as van Druten stepped up to the lectern and, after a loud sigh, gave a summary of what the MT799's function was and how it worked.

The room fell silent until the Russian asked. "So, really, we're all here because of Mr Jackson's, er, what do you call it… 'gut instinct'..? And to say that the world's top banks could find themselves liable without warning to… what was it..? five trillion dollars of unsecured debt? …is, shall we say, fanciful in the least!" A snort of derision, somehow emphasised by the Russian accent. "I doubt they even have that much money between all of them! How could they possibly be so stupid as to leave themselves open to such risk?"

He did not try to hide his scepticism. All the other delegates were looking between the Russian and Jackson with expectant or bewildered expressions.

It was clear Jackson was not getting his message across to these people. All politicians and few of which had ever lived in the real world. Should he attempt to explain what a PPP is in more detail, and how the banks leverage loans against massive deposits from the world's insignificant number of UHNWI's?

If he did, he would start down a slippery slope with every answer to every question simply generating more questions which eventually he would be unable to answer. He stood up and tapped van Druten on the shoulder, who went back to his seat.

While the room looked on silently, he opened his laptop on the lectern, which was linked to the large screen behind him.

"The reason we asked CEESSEB to issue the Bretton Woods alert was because, by sheer chance, and at the cost of two innocent lives, Valiece and Daphne Davey, as we have already explained, we only just managed to prevent what would have been the biggest cyber-fraud… crime… theft… call it what you will… in all history."

He paused while he did a few things on his laptop keyboard. "Now then, an MT799 might sound like a boring way of managing a certain kind of financial transaction, but because it's figured so much in the investigation, and because of the unexplained involvement of people we know to be members of the North Korean military and ruling family… and aside from the attempted fraud on all those billionaires," said with a lingering glance at the Russian who was giving him so much grief "…we're asking for your assistance and support."

He could see the Russian getting his hackles up. He gave him a half smile which, he hoped, would lift the tension that was building in the room.

"North Korea might be many things, but it's not a hotbed of terrorism. So why are they involved? We're asking if the members of G20 gathered here might be able to share their knowledge and see if we can identify how it might trigger the kind of event that CEESSEB… this committee… the people in *this* room… was set up *specifically* to prevent."

Blank looks with no-one seeming to engage, or even wanting to have any involvement in what was happening.

Desperate times, desperate measures. He needed to shake these people out of their complacency. He took a deep breath.

"Ok… so you already know that two lives that we know of, the Davey's in Antigua, have already been lost in a failed attempt to prevent us even knowing about any of this… In fact, those murders were what exposed this entire conspiracy in the first place. Aside from those two lives, if you will bear with me… I just want to show you something that illustrates the real magnitude of what we're trying to deal with here."

Without any further comment from Jackson, the images of the tortured agents appeared on the screen behind him. He started to scroll through them.

"These are agents from a number of countries," and then, looking around the room accusingly, "some of which are represented *here*, in *this* room! What did they know that caused them to be tortured… tortured to death like this? What were their captors trying to find out? Why would they go to such lengths to ensure their secrets would stay just that… secrets?"

There were quiet gasps, whimpers and barely suppressed groans as he progressed through the images. The expressions of shock and disbelief were almost a pleasure for Jackson to behold as he worked through the images. *Finally, maybe now they'll take this seriously.*

He left the Mossad agent till last. He was still alive when the picture had been taken. He was naked, arms and legs strung taught between some piping in a filthy basement somewhere. The skin had been taken off across his upper chest, arms and legs and hung in strips exposing muscle and blood vessels, glistening in the dim light.

There was a tight gag around his mouth holding in an oil-stained rag. His head was tied back and wedged between two wooden blocks so he could not move it. No-one had the words to describe the expression on his face dominated by bulging, petrified, agony-filled eyes.

His tormentors stood each side of him facing the camera with arms crossed, hands holding upward pointing cut-throat razors, with the same self-satisfied expressions on their faces as you might find on fishermen on a quayside showing off a good catch.

There was only one woman in the room, from South Korea. With a faint squeal she slid off her chair as she fainted, but he left the image on the screen while other delegates tended to her. This was a 'closed' session which was to be maintained under any and all circumstances. Even the two translators who helped the MI6 agent standing by the door who tended to the woman, were cleared to 'Cosmic Top Secret', the highest NATO security level.

When everyone had settled down, he explained who the victims were and that whoever was behind the conspiracy that had set off his gut instincts, were the same people who had committed the mayhem on the screen behind him.

He finished with "These poor men, who worked for *us* don't forget," he said pointing at the room generally "discovered what was really going on, and what you see is the price they paid. These images demonstrate quite clearly to what lengths this conspiracy will go to maintain secrecy, which tells us how massive the conspiracy itself is."

He paused to give time for what he was showing on the screen, and what he had said, to sink in.

"We know, from the murder of the Davey's in Antigua, to those fifty banks, the extent of the strategy to get direct access to the Swift network and other information I cannot disclose at this meeting and what you see on the screen behind me, that this is an unprecedented conspiracy. And we *still* don't fully understand the extent of it – but we're 99 per cent sure that whatever it is will be catastrophic at the macro-economic level if it is ever executed."

There was a long, overpowering silence broken eventually by the Russian.

He spoke quietly. Measured. "Yes, Mr Jackson. Quite a show and you're 99 per cent certain. But you don't actually have any *evidence* showing that there is any kind of conspiracy or fraud being perpetrated other than the one you have already intercepted and, um, stopped… foiled. Or do you?" He paused for a second, offering Jackson the chance to respond. No answer.

"Also, Mr Jackson, you seem to forget that our deliberations took on the pseudonym of 'wealth games' because we were using game theory… computer prediction to anticipate possible shocks to the global economic system, the impact of private wealth and to track capital flows across the world and their socio-economic impact.

That's all. Nothing else. We're not interested in your cloak and dagger spy stories."

Jackson could not help himself. His whole lanky body sagged as he gave a resigned shake of his head and almost whispered "No. But with a little help from you, the people in this room, maybe we could find out exactly what it is. Fill in the other one per cent. At the very least, we can say that you've been warned and not to be surprised when something comes at you out of left field. Because it will, believe me. We're absolutely sure that whatever it is will not be 'if' but 'when'."

The Russian came straight back. Sneering. Patronizing.

"As far as I… and Russia is concerned you solved the matter when you… Swift… intercepted all those funds. Congratulations… well done… hats off to you, old boy…" the last few words said in a mocking upper-class English accent. "Again, there is no evidence of any further conspiracy beyond the failed attempt to hijack those funds from all those billionaire accounts. I think you've wasted our time when we all have far more important matters to be dealing with."

Jackson could hear the blood pumping in his ears. He was stunned. Speechless.

After a few moments the US Treasury Secretary said, "Thank you for your presentation, Mr Jackson… and you, Mr van Druten. I've been advised that the FBI was marginally involved in this investigation with the Davey's homicides on Antigua, but that nothing of any consequence has been flagged up since. Until now. The USA for one will be taking your warning seriously, and we'll be following through."

Nobody else had anything more to say. Some of them were looking at Jackson as if embarrassed for him. Or that he should be seeking help from some sort of counsellor. Others could not tear their eyes away from the image of the tortured Mossad agent still up on the screen behind him, and which he had forgotten about.

Within a few minutes everyone had packed up and gone, phones clasped to their ears as they arranged homeward travel. Within minutes the room was left empty except for the Chancellor, Jackson and van Druten sitting alone in their chairs, staring into the empty room.

Finally, the Chancellor stood and muttered something incomprehensible before scuttling out of the room. It was his job to report the outcome of this surreal meeting to the Prime Minister and somehow he had to do that without implicating himself in its negative results. He would see to it that that would fall squarely on Jackson. When you are ostracized in Whitehall, it is not subtle. Only the thought of your pension entitlement will keep you there, despite the pain.

But Jackson knew he was right about this MT799 thing. If Jaeger had found some way to get round them… Van Druten was the first to speak "Can we please now return those funds to their rightful owners?"

He decided that it would have taken no time at all for Jaeger to realise that no funds had arrived in his fifty banks and that his operation had been stopped in its tracks, at least that part of it. So there was nothing to hold up the return of the funds to the GDWM client accounts from where they'd come.

"Yes, of course. And thank you for coming, Dick. I know it's put a real strain on you. It might be worthwhile blocking the PC that gave all the instructions for moving those funds. At least then we'll have shut down that part of the operation."

Are you kidding? That PC was blocked the instant we intercepted the funds. He left the room, already on the phone. The people waiting in his office in La Hulpe gave a loud cheer as the instruction to return the funds was executed.

Jackson was still lost in thought and, by the time he looked up he realized he was on his own in the room, with the image of the Mossad agent still up on the screen behind him. He quickly switched it off, hoping that no Treasury staff had looked around the door while he had been sitting there lost in thought. That would be sure to have ruined their day.

He was down, but not out. The focus now was on trying to find out what Jaeger and his 'Fortress' was all about. Maybe in doing that some further information might come to light that will explain where the mysterious MT799 fits into all this.

Thirty-Three

Ashar was waiting for confirmation from Jaeger that the payments execution had all gone through but, with nothing heard from Jaeger, he was starting to get jittery. When the text came in he eagerly picked up the burner. And froze.

'No funds arrived. Check execution.'

Hs blood ran suddenly ice-cold through his veins as he stared across the desk at Mohammed, who had now been waiting for three days to be told that all was clear for him to pack up and go home.

"No funds have arrived anywhere, Mohammed…" he heard himself say. Quite calmly, and sounding as if he was in another room. "Can you check that everything went through ok?"

Mohammed stared back, dumbfounded. His mouth opened and closed but no words came out. He was overcome by a sudden dreadful weakness that almost opened his bowels.

Dreading what he was about to see he cut and pasted the long and complex URL to his 'back door' into his browser, keyed 'enter', and instantly got the heart-stopping response: *Error 403. Access Forbidden.*

He did not need to say anything, he could see Ashar looking up at the large screen on the wall behind him where he could see for himself. His face an expressionless mask as he tried to absorb what was happening. He seemed to have stopped breathing. Then, with trembling hands, he cut and pasted his own backdoor into the browser on his laptop.

He replied to Jaeger's text:

'Mohammed Swift access blocked. Mine still working.'

Through the maelstrom of emotions going through his mind, Ashar was thinking that this had to be down to either Mohammed trying to be clever or, more likely, that conversation the bug had picked up at Fox's house. But there was no hint that either of the men in that video had any idea of what was really going on.

No matter what, it looked like a decade of planning and preparation had come to nothing and there was every chance he was, right now, under surveillance. He knew that, for Jaeger, the planning and preparation had been going on for much, much longer.

He needed to put things in place for a rapid exit. This was well prepared, and it took only a text and a few online confirmations to make final arrangements.

As an afterthought he started searching for any news items that might relate to the biggest cyber-fraud in history, more than $200 billion disappearing from over 80 bank accounts around the world, but there was nothing. Mohammed had executed his program three days ago and, by now, something would surely have leaked out.

+

At his compound In Australia Jaeger was doing exactly the same, and getting the same result. He sat back in his chair, suspended in shock. His world stopped for a few long seconds as the self-image his ego had built over fifty years was dissembled in an instant.

The tectonic plates underpinning the world he had built for himself shifted from master of his universe, to hunted prey. And he knew that, if caught, those in pursuit would not go for a quick kill. They would take the greatest pleasure in making him pay, in spades.

Without warning, the image of the Mossad agent being skinned alive jumped from his subconscious to consume his entire being. He had seen the full two hour long video, and found himself strangely excited by it. Everyone else had only seen a screen grab. A dread beyond description began to engulf him.

He replied to Ashar:

'Evacuate. Leave nothing. Come home. 8.'

On those instructions Ashar would leave nothing behind in Malta, head for the compound and change to his last burner, number eight.

+

Kelly had not expected to end up in Canberra and had not come prepared for it. She could hardly wait to be on her way to Sydney and find a flight back to the UK with Dez. She was also getting worn out with living in hotels, craved her own bed and was missing

Dez more than she ever thought she would. She also had not seen their new home in London yet which, Dez had told her, was perfect for them.

A rapid exchange of texts with Dez who, strangely, was now on a new mobile number, had ended up with them agreeing to meet at Sydney airport that evening when he got in from Kuala Lumpur, and they would find a flight they could come back together on to the UK. Maybe, just maybe, this whole sorry trip was coming to an end. Both she and Dez deserved a really good holiday after all this.

She had arranged a hire car which had been delivered last night and she was drying herself after her morning shower when the hotel phone rang. It was Ted Larkin

"'morning, Kelly. Are you decent? Do you mind if I pop up to your room?"

Her eyes rolled. *Not more 'security briefings'!*

"Sure, gimme ten."

When Ted arrived at her door he had one of the Aussie SASR team with him along with a Sydney policewoman, Linda Petersen, who Kelly thought was far too pretty and petite to make a difference to the mindset of any criminal. Her career should have been on the catwalk.

+

Mohammed was watching Ashar move around the apartment preparing to leave. After a few minutes of this he paused and told Mohammed to start sorting himself out and get ready to go. Not that there was much for him to pack. He allowed himself the luxury of looking forward to getting home and seeing his parents, safe and sound. Ashar was focusing on piling old newspapers and every other scrap of paper he could find under the desks.

Almost as an afterthought, he told Mohammed to run an Fdisk (format disk) on his hard drive to wipe it clean. As he turned to his keyboard to do as he was told he noticed Ashar reaching for his backpack. He turned back to see him pull something out of it and, for a second, was staring down the barrel of a silenced .22 Beretta. No time to react. No discussion. Oblivion.

Ashar gazed down at Mohammed's body, with the neat hole through its forehead and the look of surprise still on its face slumped in the corner beside the overturned chair. He then fired two more shots directly into the hard drive through the PC casing. Much quicker than an Fdisk.

He looked around to make sure everything was prepared and then went out to the utility room and heaved out a gallon can of petrol that had been hidden inside a cupboard. He pulled the desks apart just far enough to be able to pour the petrol over the pile of paper and some bedding underneath, then checked his watch. He messaged his friend. He went into the kitchen and turned on all the gas taps.

Five minutes later he heard the scooter pull up outside and looked out the window just to check it was him. He gave a satisfied smile as he made sure the timing would be perfect and settled his backpack comfortably onto his shoulders. With the scooter ticking over outside he emptied some of the petrol into the kitchen and then most of it onto the pile of paper and bedding under the desks and, as an afterthought, what was left over Mohammed's body.

He opened the door and gave his friend a nod, then turning back he flicked three matches at once into the apartment, waiting just a few seconds to confirm that the fire had caught.

Then he was on the back of the scooter and heading out of Marsaxlokk, up the hill to the main road, as the blaze surged through the apartment. They both laughed as they passed fire engines and police cars, sirens blasting, going the other way as the scooter sped towards the Malta-Sicily ferry terminal in Grand Harbour. They were last over the ramp, just two minutes before it was lifted as the hydrofoil prepared to cast off. Ninety minutes later they were among the first off the ferry in Sicily.

His friend continued on up-country on his scooter after dropping Ashar off to pick up a hire car at the ferry port, which he would drop off at Rome airport. He would then board a Qatar Airways flight for the first leg of his journey from Rome to Perth the next day.

He smiled grimly to himself. Despite Mohammed's complete and utter failure, his mission was still on track.

Soon after, the SAS team packed up their gear and were back at Brize Norton as the UK sun was rising. They had been taken completely by surprise.

When they got back to Hereford, it was a very short de-brief.

Thirty-Four

The three men in the Toyota Land Cruiser parked opposite the Canberra Hyatt kept quiet as they listened to Hit 104.7 FM while keeping a constant eye on the main entrance. Eventually they saw the hired white Holden Commodore brought round from the car park and Kelly's distinctive blond bob emerge from the lobby, trying to hide herself within a group of people leaving the hotel.

They saw one of the security detail open the back door of the car for her and then get in beside her. His colleague was at the wheel and both of them were clearly looking around the area outside the hotel for anything suspicious. It was unlikely they had picked up the Toyota in their sweep, parked anonymously among the many other cars around the hotel.

A police car emerged from the service area on the other side of the hotel and took up position in front. Another came from the road and placed itself behind the Commodore. After just 30 seconds testing radios and making other preparations, the small convoy headed out of town on Commonwealth Avenue to pick up the M23 highway for Sydney.

The observers looked on. How stupid can these people be, making themselves so conspicuous? No matter, it just made life easier for them. There was no need for the Toyota to follow closely, they could maintain their position three or four cars behind the convoy for now.

After a call from the Toyota, a white Mercedes van pulled out of a lay-by half a mile ahead of the convoy. In the Toyota, now they were under way and moving away from Canberra's CCTV cameras, weapons were passed from behind the rear seat. Checked, loaded and cocked.

Jaeger's instructions had been clear. Bring Kelly Murchison to him, alive, in Margaret River, where he would deal with her himself. It did not matter what condition she was in, so long as she was alive enough to know and understand the hell she was going to be put through.

The convoy was cruising in close formation on the M23 just 20 miles outside Canberra at the Bywong junction. The van had dropped back to position itself directly in front of the lead police car, and the Toyota was now immediately behind the tail car.

At 50mph and with no warning the van braked and swerved violently across the highway, forcing the police car behind onto the hard shoulder by the Bywong slip road. Two men threw themselves out of the van's cab rolling free and, in one fluid movement settled into the classic kneeling position to hose the lead police car with an unremitting hail of fire from their AK47's.

Seconds later, with their magazines emptied and the car smouldering with its two dead occupants inside they re-loaded, ready for the next phase.

At the same time the Toyota had back-ended the following police car and shunted it forward into the Commodore, pounding it with more AK47 fire from one of its crew standing up through the car's sunroof, killing both cops in the car.

The two SASR escorts had rolled out of the Commodore and were by this time shooting back, quickly taking out the two from the van, and wounding the one firing from the sun roof in the arm, but the other two from the Toyota were now out on the road and quickly outflanked them. They were torn to shreds with sustained fire in seconds.

The whole action had taken less than two minutes and left a haze of smoke and the distinctive reek of cordite floating back down the highway on the light breeze.

One of the Toyota crew reached into the back of the Commodore to haul Kelly out but was shot in the gut, with another round to the head before he hit the ground. She swung round to respond to the door opening on the other side of the car but slumped into instant oblivion as the butt of an AK47 was smashed into the back of her head.

Even though wounded and bleeding, the remaining terrorist from the Toyota was still giving back-up to his comrades.

Her reaction had taken the attackers completely by surprise and they were not about to show any mercy to this woman who they thought would be a walkover. She was lifted bodily out from the car and thrown into the back of the Toyota where she was tightly zip-tied at the wrists, knees and ankles. Heavy duty Gaffa tape, secured firmly across her mouth finished the job.

It pulled away, passing the smoking hulks of the cars and motionless bodies lying in their pools of blood across the tarmac in the aftermath of the vicious slaughter. It powered up the slip road towards Bywong.

Behind them the carnage of bodies, blood, shell casings, abandoned weapons and the hardly recognisable remains of smoking, demolished cars blocked the road. Traffic had pulled up creating a long tailback.

People had got out from their cars and were looking around for the cameras that were filming all the action. It was a full minute before someone, who recognised the smell of spent cordite, realized that what they had seen was for real, and called 000.

At a lay-by five miles on, she was starting to come around, catching a glimpse of the Toyota bursting into flames as she was thrown into the back of a pick-up and covered with a heavy tarpaulin. The pain from the blow to the back of her head felt like a hammer-drill trying to break through her skull.

Sweltering under the heavy tarpaulin, magnifying the heat from the glaring Australian sun, she bounced around in the well of the pick-up as it headed west towards the coast. She was trying not to choke behind the Gaffa tape and sobbing in agony as the zip-ties cut into her wrists, knees and ankles with every movement. The blood from the back of her head caked itself down her face.

Six hours later after a long slow drive, she was delirious and hardly noticed the vehicle coming to a halt on the dirt road leading to a small jetty, away from the main harbour in Bateman's Bay.

She felt the tarpaulin being lifted off and the rush of fresh, early evening air made a weak attempt at reviving her. She noticed that the daylight was fading and felt rather than saw the two men standing each side of the pick-up staring down at her, and tensed as she waited helplessly for whatever might come next.

Then, with no warning, she felt herself being lifted by her trouser belt and hair out of the truck, but the blond wig came away leaving her head to crash back down onto the ridged metal bed of the pick-up. She was lifted again, semi-conscious and hauled out, this time by her belt and her own brunette hair and tossed to the ground as if she were no more than a sack of grain.

At seven stone she was no more than a rag-doll to these men. All she could see through the tears and dirt in her eyes was the men's boots and one of the tyres on the pick-up.

She heard one of them standing just feet away from her shouting hysterically, and saw her wig being stamped under his heavy boot before he walked away to make a call. She could not make out the language. Maybe some sort of Arabic…

Now that he had moved away she could see that he had a bandage around his upper arm with a patch of blood showing through. It did not seem to bother him and she could see that the bandaging had been done almost professionally.

Even in her terrified and weakened state she could work out that these men were pro's and knew how to look after themselves.

Thirty-Five

When he hung up on the call Jaeger could hardly think straight from the rage that was consuming him. But he managed a grimacing smile. This pathetic attempt at foiling his plot to take revenge on Fox by using some no-count police whore doubling for Kelly Murchison was laughable. It seemed the bitch was still alive so he had told them to do whatever they wanted with her, and then dispose of her in any way they chose but so that the body was never recovered.

But he would still have his revenge, he had already heard from his back-up team that everything was still on track and, in a few hours, he would have Ms Kelly Murchison at his disposal. He had already decided how she would die. With any luck, it would take days.

Mr Fox would never recover once he knew the agonies she endured before the blessed release of death came. Knowing that it was all his fault would be the icing on his life-shattered cake.

But, even so, he knew his world was starting to unravel. For as long as he could remember it had revolved around his life mission to exact revenge for what that bank had done to his family. His father forced into a life spent as a bottom feeder insurance salesman, and his mother disappeared into things he could never bring himself to imagine. Even now he could feel his whole being consumed with loathing of the entire global financial firmament.

He had spent decades working from his first job as a trainee corporate banker through careful relationship building and moving jobs always into more senior positions where he could learn ever more about the world's capital markets.

He quickly understood that if he could penetrate Swift he would be half way to achieving his objective. But it would never be permanent. No, he had thought long and hard and spent years in the planning and execution of every step of his scheming. The plot to defraud those billionaires of their wealth was nothing more than a front, a camouflage to conceal his real intent. But still a necessary first step to achieving his ultimate aim.

And now, because of Fox's treachery he knew that his one-time clients were, even now, preparing to hunt him down. There would be no mercy. There was no choice but to abandon this part of the project. Those who were once, if not friends, were at least trusting clients now regarded him as nothing less than a scam artist. Someone who had taken their money, and lots of it, under false pretences. These were not people you conned, even if it was unintentional.

His 'defence force' was made up of just half a dozen maintenance crew on-site and with the rest made up of his 'guests', when they arrived, who would stand no chance against a determined attack by rampant terrorists intent on rape, torture and slaughter.

His three goons had made it very clear that they would be long gone if there was any sign of real trouble coming their way. It would be him they were after, but anyone else close to him would be regarded as fair game. They would have a ball, especially with the classy women his UHNWI guests would be bringing with them.

He needed to clear his head and did a walk of the fence making sure it was fully secure. There was only one main entrance to the compound, made up of two separate gates set in the first and second fences. But they would not hold up against a sustained attack by anyone determined to get through them. He went into the armoury and gave himself some comfort by standing and staring at the vast array of weaponry stored in there. Great, but who was going to use it?

Ashar would be here tomorrow. And cold and heartless as he was, which is why he felt such an affinity towards him despite his stupid escapade on Antigua, he was no universal soldier. Ten billionaires and their women would be disposed of out of hand by those who were now already no doubt on their way to deal with him.

With hands in pockets and a mind that seemed to be progressively seizing up, he stood staring down at his phone on the desk. As if on cue, it began to ring with one of his 'guests' showing on the screen.

A Latin American accent. "Hello, Jaeger. Thank you for your alert. So things are now heading in the direction we have been anticipating I see. We have arrived in Perth and will be with you in a few hours. I believe you will be hearing from some more of your guests soon."

Jaeger put the phone down carefully, picked up his walkie-talkie and instructed his head of staff to start preparing for arrivals. Then he called what he called his 'first lieutenant', who headed up his small team of special operatives, his goons.

He confirmed that his back-up plan had worked and Kelly Murchison would be arriving at Margaret River airfield in seven hours, about 3am. He said he would be there to meet her. He had one of the SUV's fully gassed up, and made sure there were a few rolls of heavy duty Gaffa tape on board.

Thirty-Six

Mum and dad would be wondering where she was by now. Probably calling her police station in Sydney where she had received the call this morning asking if she would agree to act as a decoy on a special mission. She had eagerly accepted. She had taken self-defence and weapons training in readiness for the break she had been waiting for which would get her into the anti-terror branch, which she coveted.

Her dog, a mongrel called Muppet which her parents had bought for her 13th birthday, now a lively ten years old, would be sniffing at the front door wagging his tail waiting for her to come home.

The zip-ties were giving her unremitting, excruciating pain as they bit ever deeper into her flesh, drawing more blood with every move she made. She was trying desperately not to move for fear of inflicting more pain on herself. She could hear the men talking, louder and more excitable now, in their strange language.

Occasionally one or other of them would look over to her as she lay helpless and in quiet agony on the ground in the failing light. Cold, empty stares that made her innards go weak with terror. If she had been able to understand their language she would have known that their plans had changed.

They were supposed to take her 120 miles up the coast to Wollongong and load her onto a waiting King Air 350 twin-prop at the small airfield that would take them across Australia to the airfield at Margaret River. Jaeger would be waiting for her, with who knew what in mind. That was not their concern. In the dark and on these quiet airfields, it would have been easy enough to do.

Now, things had changed. A second call had come in from their cell to tell them Jaeger had failed them, stolen their money, and that he was now their sole objective. They were still to go up the coast to Wollongong, but they would now be joined there by two more from their cell, who were already on their way from Sydney. At their refuelling stop, a farm half way across the continent in South Australia, they would take on more than just fuel. Additional weapons and ammunition would be waiting for them to take onto Margaret River, where they would join others equipped with even more weapons and trucks.

They knew all about Jaeger's compound and how difficult it could be to breach. Their intelligence was that there was a small army defending it which they would need to overcome to get control, and seize Jaeger.

She had drifted deeper into delirium and hardly noticed as she was lifted up, again by her belt and hair and carried down some steps onto a floating jetty and swung bodily into the bottom of a scruffy,

30 foot motor cruiser. It stank of fish and diesel and was no different to scores of others moving up and down the coast at all times of the day and night.

She did not feel any sensation, aside from a vague curiosity as a rusty chain was wrapped several times around her waist, pushed between her tightly bound legs, wound round her body and eventually locked tight with a shackle on the back of her neck. She was almost totally encased, unable to move, with her head lolling to one side out of the coil of rusty, foul smelling chain. It was now dark. The ocean was mirror calm.

Under low cloud hiding what little light there was from a quarter moon, she lay in the oily bilge water. Lit only by the pale yellow tint of the jetty's solitary light, its glow dispersed through a heavy drizzle. Through her torment, as she slipped back into semi-consciousness, she heard a distant throbbing and felt the vibration through the boat as the engine started up.

Police Constable Linda Petersen was mercifully unconscious and did not hear the grunts of the two men when, ten minutes later, they lifted her over the side to drop soundlessly into the still, black, anonymous deep of the South Pacific Ocean.

They turned the boat around and headed back to the jetty. It would be a three hour drive up the coast on the empty roads to Wollongong airfield.

+

Jaeger wondered if he was on a watch-list somewhere, or if he had been promoted to 'world's most wanted'. He always planned for contingencies and, far from having nowhere to hide, he had a bolt-hole to run to. But he had never thought for a second that he would have to use it.

Hunted not only by the authorities, but the most evil men and some women on the planet he felt an alien sensation, fear, as he realized he had absolutely no choice but to run to that bolt-hole.

He called Ashar and they arranged for him to change plans and, instead of coming to the compound once he arrived in Perth, to organize a private jet from Perth International.

It would take them to Jacksons International airport at Port Moresby in Papua New Guinea, from where they would take scheduled flights to Belize. Once there, Jaeger would join *The World*, an ultra-luxurious floating hotel with suites owned exclusively by the world's wealthiest.

Every one of the 165 luxury apartments on board is worth between three and fifteen million dollars, owned by residents who must prove a net worth of at least ten million, which Jaeger could do many times over. He kept an apartment permanently on stand-by. He would join the ship when it dropped its massive anchor off Belize City the day after he got there.

He would stay aboard, safe from the hounds of hell that he knew were now seeking him out, and the global economic carnage that would be triggered once Ashar hit his 'enter' key.

Ashar would carry onto Antigua where he would execute the program buried deep within Swift that he had been working so diligently on these past few of months. Jaeger drew some comfort from the knowledge that his master plan, which would set off global economic Armageddon, the vengeance he would wreak on behalf of his whole family, was still on track.

He psyched himself up and reluctantly went to greet his guests who were now starting to arrive.

+

The orders went out over the dark web. Brainwashed fighters-in-waiting from all over Australia began their journeys to the seafront car park at Yallingup, a small beach community of just 1,000 residents, ten miles north of Jaeger's compound.

Some arrived with their vehicles covered in the distinctive red dust of the outback. Others, coming over from the East, flew in. On the first day a dozen had assembled in the beachfront car park. By the end of the third day, almost 100 of them and their vehicles were there. The majority were no-hopers looking for a cause and a good time. The worst kind of people to be armed to the teeth.

Among them were a few who had already killed, in many ways, and believed in their hearts that their mission was justified in the eyes of their god.

+

I got into Sydney on time a half hour after sunset and was the first off the plane. At the immigration desk I watched the officer press a barely concealed button under his counter when he saw my passport.

Within seconds two airport security guys had arrived at the desk and I was hustled at a brisk walk towards an anonymous door set in the wall of the immigration hall. I had to tell them to ease up as my leg was only just coming back to life after almost 22 hours sat on my backside. I was still having to use the walking stick which was making no impression at all on these two dumbo's. Inside an interview room I was confronted with Ted and two other guys, stood in a small triangle looking at each other. Their expressions put me on immediate alert.

Dumbo's one and two took a look at this tableau and left quickly, shutting the door discreetly behind them. Ted took charge and waved his hand over the room generally, a signal for all of us to find a seat. His look telling me there was seriously bad stuff going on.

He introduced me to the two others in the room, both Aussie SASR, and then fell silent. He stared at the floor. I looked around the white painted immigration interview room. One fluorescent tube, with more than its fair share of fly droppings on it putting out relentless white light, and no windows. Bare white walls and an alert strip around the whole room that your hosts could press at any time to summon reinforcements if you started to kick up.

Warm and welcoming it wasn't.

I broke the awkward silence and asked the obvious question. "Where's Kelly?" I wasn't sure that I wanted to hear the answer.

Ted and the two guys, Bill and Jack, with no surnames given and even the first names probably false, had received a full account of the attack on the police decoy on the road out of Canberra which they relayed to me in graphic detail. Bill let slip his thoughts with "I don't give much for Petersen's chances once they find out it's not Kelly."

I asked again. "Where's Kelly?"

Ted explained that Police Constable Linda Petersen was the nearest thing Sydney police could find to a lookalike with anything near the necessary training to act as decoy for Kelly in the time they had.

No-one had actually said it, but if Kelly had not been so impulsive, understandable from what I could make of the people she had been trying to deal with at the Aussie Treasury, there would have been more time to set things up properly, with fully trained and seasoned people.

Ten minutes after the decoy convoy had set off from Canberra, Kelly was meant to leave the hotel by a back service entrance and driven to the helipad at the Treasury. She was to have been flown direct to Sydney airport to meet me.

I asked again. "Where's Kelly?"

Ted looked at me with a pitiful expression on his face. "We lost her."

My mind seized up. I felt myself flailing around for a chair, before Ted stepped over and helped me towards one.

Thirty-Seven

Ashar was well set up. Half a dozen passports and a cash reserve that was far out of proportion to his appearance and demeanour.

The first serious hacking program he had unleashed five years ago had been inserted into hundreds of banks and identified unused accounts all over the world. If the account remained unused for two years it was emptied of half its contents, which were then sent to any one of his three private bank accounts around the world, under three different identities. Two years later he would come back and take the rest.

Once he had secured access to the banks, a walk in the park for him most of the time, his program would automatically search out his targets and then remove the funds without leaving any trace of where they had been sent. In total, he had liberated some one hundred and fifty million dollars which he could access at any time across his three private bank accounts.

While he had been in Antigua, he had taken time out to set up his own private capital bank, which took just three days. He had completed the final part of the process just an hour before he had watched Valiece Davey walk into the same regulator's office in St John's. Since then, he had bought himself a luxury penthouse apartment on the outskirts of the town, overlooking the Caribbean. While in Malta, he had all but cleared out his three private bank accounts and moved the funds to his own bank in Antigua. No matter what happened, he was all set. Untouchable.

His other program, the one he was most proud of, was now sitting on a hidden file buried deep in the Swift system, which he could execute simply by logging in and keying 'enter' on his laptop. There had been a frustrating three hour stopover at Dubai on his flight from Rome to Perth, and he had used a bit of the time to make sure that he still had access to Swift and that his program was still there waiting to be executed.

His finger had hovered over the 'enter' key for a few seconds and he did not know how he resisted the temptation to set it all off. But he needed to be safely hidden away before the consequences of doing that could interfere with his own plans.

They had re-scheduled their travel plans after they had found out where *The World* would be so Jaeger could meet it and get aboard. Their jet would be ready for them at Perth International for 7am the next day. He had re-boarded the plane for the last leg to Perth with his mind racing, and self-preservation now at the top of his agenda.

Right now, only those working with Fox knew of his existence. But, so far as he knew, they had no images of him so facial recognition, now being rapidly deployed at airports across the world, would not catch him out. And he still had a couple of passports that had not been used.

He arrived at Perth International on time, at 5.30pm. He had travelled with only a cabin bag and, once through immigration found a small hotel near the airport to lie low for the night. He would be up at 4am to give himself plenty of time to be at Perth International to meet Jaeger and board their jet in the morning.

+

Within half a minute of Petersen, wearing her blond wig, and her two escorts leaving the room there was a knock at the door. Kelly picked up her bag and, after checking through the spyhole to see two men looking up and down the corridor, answered it. They were both wearing smart suits with no tie, the unofficial 'uniform' of SASR troops when wearing civvies. This was obviously her escort. They would take her to the car park and then over to the Treasury where a helicopter would be waiting.

They led her to the elevator and stood either side of her, silent, as it descended to the basement level. They led her to a car and pulled out of the hotel car park. Not a word was spoken. One of the men was sat in the back with her and she turned to speak to him.

She hardly registered the massive balled-up fist flying into her face, before waking up tied and gagged lying across the back seat of what she quickly worked out was a twin-prop plane. She did not know that she had been out cold for four hours, helped along by small doses of chloroform whenever she had showed signs of regaining consciousness.

She had been driven from the hotel to Wagga Wagga airfield, almost three hours to the west of Canberra, and lifted into the plane parked behind a hanger, out of sight of anyone. When she came round they had been half an hour in the air and she lay still, on the back seat of the plane as it droned on.

Confused, terrified and seething with cold fury she tried to work out what was happening, and why. Her face was a volcano of pain and she felt sure that bones had been broken.

What had she… or maybe Dez done to set all this off? She didn't think it was any kind of misunderstanding. For two more hours she lay bound in the back of the plane, her face throbbing with pain, as it droned on. She could not see the land below only, from where she was, the bright sky above. Then she felt the engines throttle back as the plane descended to land.

As it taxied to a stop she was expecting to be lifted out, but as soon as she smelt the aviation gas she knew that this was just a refuelling stop. She couldn't help herself. "HELP! HELP! I'm being kidnapped!!" she screamed.

She stopped short as soon as she heard the guffaws of laughter from outside the plane. One of the men leaned into the cockpit and she heard the sound of a zip on a bag being opened. He leaned over the seat. Again the distinctive odour of chloroform. It does not act instantly but takes several seconds, during which his huge hand held tight onto face so hard she wanted to scream the pain out of her.

Her face was already swollen and bruised from the punch meted out by her kidnapper and the agony now was unbearable. Falling back into unconsciousness was a relief.

She came round again as the sky was darkening and the plane still flying steadily on. Then, she felt it descending again. This time, she knew that they had reached their destination, wherever it was. And somehow she also knew that Jaeger would be waiting for her.

+

There was no point in throwing a fit or trying to find someone to blame. But I had to work bloody hard to keep my feelings in check. It took me a good while to start thinking clearly again and began ticking off options for what I was going to do to Jaeger when I got my hands on him. While I was sat there Bill, who seemed to be the senior of the two SASR guys, took a call then looked around the room. A hard glint in his eye.

"Someone's phoned in two bodies, shot through the head, in a car in the Hyatt car park. Those were our guys, meant to pick up and escort Kelly. I think we can figure out what's happened now. But we still don't know where Kelly is."

I asked if anyone had heard from Tony Jackson, to which Ted related the briefing they had had with him and Josh Miller. Last they heard he was preparing for some meeting or other… people from some obscure G20 committee. He had sounded quite stressed about it. But nothing since. My mind flew back to our 'wealth games' talk when we were at Swift and worked out that he must be trying to sort something out with the CEESSEB people. Okay, but for now we were on our own.

Through the turmoil going on in my mind I heard myself say "We know where Kelly is. She's in Margaret River. That shitfest Jaeger has her."

Bill piped up with "There's nowhere else she can be. I've spoken to our CO and he's told us… and this is direct from our Prime Minister, guys, that we're to return to Campbell Barracks over in Perth and work up a plan from there. I've organised a plane. Jaeger is clearly on Australian soil doing whatever it is he's doing and, from what we can make of what intelligence we've got, and after Constable Petersen's kidnapping this morning and… of course… Kelly, there could be danger to the civil population in that area. So, guys, we're taking charge. Josh Miller's been advised that this is now strictly an Australian Defence Department matter and police involvement will be to keep civilian traffic away from our operations area, and to look after the clean-up operation."

He gave me a long, cool stare followed by an awkward smile.

"Ted's coming with us, and he'll be acting as liaison between us and any UK, USA or other countries that'll be staying involved. No offence, Dez. Really… we know your track record… but you're staying here, we'll bring… hopefully bring Kelly back to you. You're an invalid and not on active service. We're not taking responsibility for you."

I was as tactful as circumstances would allow.

"Fuck you, Bill. I can take responsibility for myself and I'm coming with you. If I don't come with you I'll find my own bloody way over there and deal with that slimy little maggot myself."

There was no argument. Better to have me on the inside pissing out than the outside pissing in.

Thirty-Eight

Arlene was no longer hot-desking. She now had her own cubicle and was running three screens on her desk, one for whatever document she was working on in the middle, Google on the left for all her research and e-mail on the right. She was no empire builder, she just liked to do things right and Beth Haydon, who had always seen the need for someone to handle inter-agency relations, had told her to get on and do things in her own way. But not to forget that she was still part of a team. She needed no reminding about that.

Drew arrived as arranged and looked over the screen into her cubicle. "Knock, knock."

"Who's there?" she answered, looking up and giving him a smile that took his breath away.

"This is the FBI. You're obliged under federal law not to refuse my advances."

I know you can do better than that, but it'll do for now. "You'd better come on in then. Take a load off."

Drew slipped into the small cubicle and sat alongside her. Their knees touched and she felt a bolt of electricity shoot through her. She became acutely aware of his aftershave or whatever it was giving off that irresistible scent, or was it just him..? She had to avoid saying anything until she was sure her voice would not shake when she spoke. *Oh yes, bring it on!*

She wanted to enjoy these sensations as long as possible, so she took her time over bringing up the image of the man in the mirror that Drew's FBI lab had managed to pull out of the CCTV recording. It was not too bad, just a bit too grainy to circulate in the media to try and pull an identity. But they could work with it in-house.

"So, what do you think?" he asked in what, she thought, was a slightly higher-pitch voice than usual.

She pulled up her notes onto the documents screen and scrolled through it. "Ok, well we have Valiece at the regulators office at 1pm… Looking into the jewellers window here at 2.10pm and then at Catherine's Café between around 7pm and 10pm-ish. They didn't return to their hotel. Whatever happened, it happened after 10pm. And I have a notion that our mystery man here, the man in the mirror… has all the answers."

They both loved their jobs and became deeply immersed in their work, distracting them from the feelings and emotions surging through both of them. The mirror in the jeweller's CCTV had also shown the Davey's getting into the car and driving off. It was common practice for cab drivers to approach tourists and offer personal tours of the island, drop them off at a restaurant, which would pay the driver a little bit of commission, and then return to pick them up and take them back to their hotels. There was nothing unusual in any of that.

Many of the cab firms on the island used Mercedes C120's, invariably silver, and it is also popular among car hire firms. This stranger, frustratingly fuzzy but the best the FBI image lab could produce, could well be the missing link in all this.

They decided to produce a full report and send it the line to Drew's boss, with a copy sent to Tony Jackson at MI6. Protocol dictates that any contacts made through Interpol must be kept in the loop of the ongoing investigation.

Drew surprised Arlene when he told her that he had taken a call from someone at the Fed saying that the Treasury Secretary had attended the first ever meeting, in London, of some secret G20 committee that tries to anticipate upcoming financial crises.

The Davey homicides had been mentioned at the meeting and, as they were American citizens, the message was passed on as a matter of process to the FBI. So their report, which they agreed should be produced within the next 24 hours to include the image of the cab driver, would be passed back to the Fed as well.

All this was followed by a pregnant silence, each waiting for the other to say it was time to move onto lunch.

In the end she grasped the nettle "Ok… look… I'll produce a first draft of the report and send it over for you to play around with. Once we're agreed on the final draft we'll decide where it's going to go and get it away. Best it comes from you. I'll get on with that this afternoon, after we've had lunch."

Why should this be so hard? But she knew why. Sitting in such close proximity, the unspoken chemistry was crackling between them. And, until now, despite endless exploratory and nervous phone conversations they had hardly seen, let alone touched each other.

As they left the DPD building she said "Actually, why don't we just pick up a bite and go to my apartment and have a cwawffee? More comfortable and we can talk everything through there in private."

Arlene became pre-occupied that afternoon, and had to go back into the office in the evening to write her report.

Thirty-Nine

Over the past two days all Jaeger's 'guests' had arrived. Ten men aged between 30 and 50 who obviously went out of their way to keep themselves fit. All brought their wives or partners. Jaeger spent some time in the reception area as they were arriving and spoke with all of them, giving away no sign of the growing fear gnawing away inside and noticed that these women were stunningly good looking, and a few even showed signs of real character and intelligence. Others, not.

But he knew that none of this would take away from the diabolical suffering that he knew, even now, was headed their way.

All had taken cabs from Perth airport for the 150 mile trip to the compound and Jaeger had noticed the questioning looks on the drivers faces as they drove into this strange 'resort' with its high wire fencing and surrounding open area full of tree stumps to drop off their fares.

They had been told to travel light but that did not stop some of them arriving loaded down with suitcases crammed mostly with the women's wardrobes. Jaeger wondered what his guests had told them in order to get them to come along. Most of them seemed to think they were going to be spending a while at some luxury boutique resort.

He had covered all this stuff in his terms of tenancy along with personal security through to the use of the communal laundromat and waste disposal. But these people being who and what they were would no doubt have their own ideas, although none of that would count for anything for much longer.

If everything went the way it looked like it was now going, all their lives were about to descend into the deepest pit of despair, with not the slightest hope of escape. The men would be a bit luckier. They would all be killed, although how long that would take would be anyone's guess. The people that were surely now coming after him would view his wealthy guests as filthy, capitalist infidel and deserving of whatever they decided to mete out to them.

Others would see them as just objects that could satisfy their more basic cravings. Fair game, and playthings for any kind of torment they judged appropriate. That torment would be even more brutal once they realized that their main target, Jaeger himself, had made his escape.

Ashar would be executing his Swift program within the coming days and, within a few weeks of that, there would be no law and order anywhere in Australia, or most other parts of the world. Their tormentors will have free rein and be able to do whatever they wanted with all of them in their own time, once they had breached the compound's defences. And while he was relaxing in carefree luxury on *The World.*

Everything was set. It was time for him to go. It was 2.30am before the last of his guests were in their rooms and getting themselves sorted out.

He called his head of staff to tell him he had to go into Busselton to clear a few things up, and gave him a briefing on how to handle the guests. With just one cabin bag as luggage, he got into the Toyota SUV that had four rolls of Gaffa tape laying on the front passenger seat, and pulled out of the compound.

He noticed the senior manager and a couple of the other staff in his rear view mirror staring after him curiously. 2.30am is a strange time of day to be leaving to sort out some business in Busselton, a small town where nothing happened just half an hour away.

No matter. He had plans for Robert Jaeger's survival. In the meantime, he had to go and meet Ms Kelly Murchison at the Margaret River airfield. He got there just a few minutes before the plane touched down and taxied to the end of the last in a small row of hangars.

He was standing just inside the hangar door, Gaffa tape in hand, as the plane taxied into it. There was an overwhelming silence as the engines were switched off and stopped echoing around inside the large, metal shed. Only the ticking sound of cooling engine parts broke the stillness.

He smiled with satisfaction when he saw Kelly lifted out of the plane. Her face was a swollen mass of black, purple and yellow as she was held upright between two of his goons, hands zip-tied behind her back.

He wrapped the tape over her mouth and around her head. Then, saying nothing and starting at her upper arms he began to wind it tightly around her body, ensuring there was no give anywhere. He kept this up all the way down to her waist. Then he spoke.

"So, Ms Murchison, it's an absolute pleasure to meet you again. It's a shame we didn't have the opportunity to get to know each other better. If it weren't for the fact I have some imminent travel plans… I can assure you we would have."

For good measure he wound the tape twice, tight around her midriff before cutting it with a carpet knife. Her upper torso was cocooned in tape leaving her completely immobile. He nodded towards a workbench and the two men lifted her up and laid her down on it.

They lifted her legs and he began winding the tape tight around her thighs. "You see, Ms Murchison, your lover-boy has caused me a great many problems. So, if I can't put things right with him, then you have to be his proxy. I hope you understand, it's just the way it is. For every action there's a reaction and I'm afraid, Ms Murchison, you're it."

She was slowly coming out of the grogginess and headache that comes after too much chloroform and was taking in her surroundings. Panic and paralyzing fear overcame her as she realized what was happening to her. Her instinct was to scream, but this only increased the terror as it was blocked by the uncompromising Gaffa tape.

"I'll tell you what's going to happen now Ms Murchison. I'm leaving on a journey, and my car will be left in the airport car park with a month's parking on the ticket. It'll be there amongst hundreds of other cars. No-one'll notice it."

She felt tape being wound tight around her legs, ankles and even her feet, and the all-consuming horror which now overwhelmed her was even more acute now it was confined within the body-constricting sheath of unyielding Gaffa tape. He nodded at the two men, who lifted her up and threw her into the back of the Toyota. She stared up at Jaeger. Silent. With wide, tear-filled, pleading eyes.

He was leaning on the opened rear door. "I think current daytime temperatures are hanging around 25 to 30 degrees… Average for the time of year?" He looked questioningly at his goons, as if in casual conversation, who both nodded their agreement.

"Hmmm… So, let's see, inside the car..? what…? 40, 50, 60 degrees..? So there we are then. Slow roasted Murchison. Two, maybe three days… It'll be your stench, or the flies hanging around the car that'll get you noticed. But you won't care by then."

He stood back while one of his men put the luggage compartment cover back in place, then stepped back to watch the door click back shut after pressing the 'close' button.

As he did this they all heard another plane start its engines and strolled out to the perimeter tarmac to see what was happening. It was a twin-prop plane taxiing to the far end of the runway. The smell of aviation gas in the air told them that it had just finished refuelling. The engines were turned off, and they saw the pilot get out and walk across the tarmac to the crew room. They could see the red glow from the lights in the cockpit, indicating it was on 'standby', with pre-flight checks completed, ready to depart.

"King Air 350. Nothing to worry about," one of the goons said, "They're used a lot to haul light freight around the country. Probably just dropped some cargo off and waiting for his return load."

The goons got into their car as Jaeger drove off in his SUV. Kelly gagged, immobilized and petrified in the rear.

Forty

Yallingup, Western Australia. August.

The operation was being led by Kenny Kassab, a second generation Syrian with a homeopathy practice in Sydney. He had flown straight to Perth as soon as he had received word of Jaeger's failings, and the orders sent to him from his cell south of Sydney. He was waiting to meet the plane when it landed at 1am at Margaret River's small airstrip.

The four men jumped out of the King Air and lifted the weapon and ammunition boxes they had loaded at the half-way stop from the hold straight into Kassab's pick-up. The pilot, who had been fully briefed as to what was going on, was told to refuel and stand by for further instructions.

An hour later the pick-up arrived in Yallingup to join the many others in the beachfront car park. There were few lights on in the town and the car park had its lights turned off at midnight. There were shadowy figures lit only by the cloud-obscured moonlight, moving around between SUV's and pick-ups and the sound of boxes being loaded into vehicles was carried on the light breeze coming off the sea.

Kassab briefed his force and the advance party of eight men in two SUV's. Two of the men in the second vehicle were the seasoned killers that had come in on the King Air and who seemed more determined than anyone to get their hands on Jaeger. This advance force was dispatched to keep watch on the compound and its surrounding area. They left at 3am and would be positioned on the main road opposite the compound within half an hour.

Jaeger's compound was set alongside a road that led to what was once a group of small houses alongside a meteorological research station, on which Jaeger had sought planning permission to build a luxury hotel. This had been quickly approved by the local government district, which was always keen to see new developments that would attract tourists and their money to what was quite a remote area. It was set some half a mile off the main road but could be clearly seen, as most of the scrubland had been cleared.

The SASR snipers had built themselves a hide high in a Karri tree on the landward side of the main road, disguised as a fire look-out. It was painted green but was easily spotted and did not try to conceal itself in any way. The snipers would come along and relieve each other posing as volunteer firewatchers quite openly, avoiding any suspicion from the compound.

Kassab's advance party was silently observed from the Karri tree as the second vehicle slowed down and turned off the road, almost directly beneath the hide, to conceal itself in the roadside bush opposite the turn off for the compound. The lead car carried on another thirty yards before turning into the dense undergrowth. A few moments later men moving and taking up positions from where the compound could be observed could be clearly heard. Followed by the unmistakable metallic 'schlucks' of a variety of weapons being cocked.

At the same time the motley collection of so-called terrorists were moving out of Yallingup with instructions to disperse themselves in their vehicles over a couple of miles north of the compound among lay-by's, parking and picnic areas off the main road and await further instructions.

Several of Yallingup's 1,000 residents had called the police station in Busselton through the day expressing concern at these strange goings on in their little settlement. The patrol car passed the convoy on its regular nightly tour of the district and called it in to HQ. Probably just a surfer's club off to some beach party or other, but they made a note of it anyway.

+

Bill had fixed up a Royal Australian Air Force Boeing business jet which had the range to get us across to Perth in one hop. It wasn't done out to anything like the luxurious standards of a commercial configuration. But it was spacious and comfortable enough for all of us to put our feet up, lay back and catch up on some shut-eye for the five hour hop across to the SASR base at Swansbourne, just south of Perth.

If nothing else, I knew I was getting closer to Kelly.

The SASR's Campbell Barracks has its own runway and, as soon as we had disembarked we were all loaded onto a bus and taken straight to the ops room.

The CO, a Lieutenant Colonel Steve Hayward, reminded me immediately of Frank Sinatra in his heyday, all he needed was the fedora. Jack told me that he was well aware of this and that his Regiment had nicknamed him 'Frankie', which didn't bother him as everyone had a nickname. Not always complimentary. There were quick introductions all round.

The room was much larger than I had expected and lit entirely in red, so that eyes were already adjusted to the night time dark outside. The only other light was coming from the many computer screens around the room. In the centre was a large table displaying this south west corner of Australia which Frankie demonstrated could be zoomed in to any location by focusing in on a three mile radius around Jaeger's compound.

He was not going to waste any time on niceties. The welcome was brief and to the point. He spoke to me directly. "I know you're ex-Regiment but I'm going to ask you to remain quiet at all times. You're here as an observer only and…" nodding towards Ted "you and Ted here have some knowledge of this Robert Jaeger bloke and what he's been up to."

I had no problem with any of this. He had to lay down the law because if things kicked off he would have no time to waste being sociable or explaining himself. And neither he nor we had any idea what was coming down the pipe.

He unfolded a large sheet of paper on top of the table-top display and switched on a desk light so it could be seen clearly. He called Ted over to look at the set of architect's drawings. "What can you tell us?" he asked.

Ted looked over the drawings for a few seconds and then pointed at the top floor. He explained that it showed six, spacious one-bedroom apartments with a large lounge and each with a sizeable kitchen-cum-diner and large en-suite bathroom, which were also safe rooms. It also showed Jaeger's office and private apartment which was set in the middle of the floor. There were stairs and elevators at each end of the passageway which ran along one side of the top floor at the back of the building, providing access to each of the apartments.

The ground floor had a huge entrance lobby at one end which Ted explained was fitted out like a top class hotel. The opulent gleaming marble, chandeliers, mirrors, original artworks and lush furnishings gave the illusion of a full service hotel, but with one significant difference. If you wanted a coffee or snack, you went into a communal kitchen and made it yourself. And left it as you found it.

Next to the lobby, through an open archway, there was a common area with snooker and ping-pong tables, sofas, chairs, tv screens and a self-service bar with every drink imaginable available to the 'guests'. At the very end of the ground floor, and next to the furthest apartment was the laundromat for which each apartment was given an allotted time in the week to use.

Frankie pulled out another large sheet of paper from under the first which showed the outbuildings with four garages, each easily able to accommodate two or three cars with the top floor split into eight, large one-bedroom apartments for the maintenance staff.

Ted explained that one of the garages was actually a well-stocked armoury, with a separate control or operations room of some sort, which he couldn't describe in any detail, next to it. Frankie asked him what it was meant to be used for.

"I really couldn't tell you, sir. It was Jaeger's little sanctum and, like the armoury, I wasn't given any access to it. I think that he had someone else looking after the really heavy security… or defence. I was just the grunt, pretty much there to look after the vanilla end of things. I wasn't allowed to get too close to the real action."

An operator at one of the desks raised his hands and shouted "SIR! Incoming from Watchtower."

Frankie replied instantly. "Speaker!"

Ted looked questioningly at Bill who explained in hushed words "Watchtower. The hide observing Jaeger's compound."

The silence dragged on until it was broken by the incoming message from Watchtower. "Two vehicles arrived… They've set up concealed positions opposite the road to the compound. One directly under me. Heard weapons being cocked…"

His radio was on 'whisper' setting. He could whisper into his mic, so that he could not be heard by the terrorists thirty feet below him, but it was being amplified here in the control room.

The operator at the desk clicked his mic to let Watchtower know he had been heard.

We waited in silence.

Forty-One

After leaving the airstrip on his way to Perth International, Jaeger drove slowly as he passed by the junction to the compound and looked back down the road. There was no sound or movement from the back of the car, and his lips curled into a scowl as he envisaged Ms Murchison completely helpless in the python-like constraint of the Gaffa tape in the back of the car.

For a moment he tried to envisage the diabolical, degrading, despairing state she would be in the moment before the suffocating heat and her claustrophobic confinement finally took her. He was hoping it would take days on end.

It was now coming up to 4.30am but he wanted just one last look at what he had built. Then, he needed to check one more time with Ashar that everything was set with the private jet and their onward travel arrangements.

Ashar had called down to the desk to make sure there were cabs outside and, if not, to get one there in the next few minutes. He was throwing a few things into his travel bag as Jaeger's call came in.

"All good to go?" was all Jaeger asked.

"Yep. We've got a Gulfstream G280. A bit big for the two of us but it has to be something like that for the range."

"My favourite jet." Jaeger replied. "Do you think we've forgotten anything?"

There was a few seconds silence from Ashar as he thought everything through before answering "The only thing I haven't done is confirm your arrival on *The World*. I was assuming you'd do that yourself."

"Yes, all done." Jaeger replied. "See you in a couple of hours at Perth. Let's get ourselves up and away ASAP."

"No argument there. Seeya."

The call ended, with Jaeger's face clearly illuminated by the blue light from his phone. And observed in open mouthed astonishment by the advance party hidden in the bush just ten yards across the road.

+

The speaker whispered "Stand by…"

In the dim red light of the ops room everyone glanced at each other with expectant frowns on their faces

"Okay. Er… stand by… A car… red SUV… Toyota… stopped at the junction into the compound. Driver's making a phone call… *Strewth*! It's Jaeger… bloody Jaeger… still talking… activity in the bush below me… three men running low across the road, can hardly see them… moon's gone… cloud… hold on…"

The speaker went quiet again, then a loudly whispered "FUCK ME! Driver and passenger door windows smashed in… doors open, Jaeger hauled out. AK butt to head… yep, out cold… dragging him across the road."

From the speaker came the sound of car doors slamming and an engine starting and revving before screeching onto the road. The sound faded away and then a whispered "Shit shoot! These blokes are good… but *good*. They've got Jaeger. Took a few seconds. Car went south… stand by."

There was the sound of another car engine and we could all hear it manoeuvring.

"Ok… the lead car has reversed back to the position directly below me, opposite the junction. Hold on… No. Engine switched off. I can't tell from here where the other car went. Hang on… ok… someone's run across the road and driven off Jaeger's car. Straight into the bush. Well hidden. Engine's switched off."

Frankie was stood by the situation desk, with its light casting menacing upward shadows on his features.

"Right-oh. Mount up. Ten squads."

Four men to a squad, forty SASR should cover most anything.

I grabbed Bill by his sleeve. "Get me a car and a weapon, I'll be tail end Charlie and stay by the junction out of the way. I won't interfere in the operation. I just need to be there."

He looked furtively across the room towards Frankie and then unbuckled his sidearm belt with the pistol and spare magazines and gave it to me. "Just make sure you stay out of the way. I'll replace this at the armoury. There's a row of Humvees outside to the right of the building… you'll see a Land Rover at the end of the row. Take that. Key's in ignition."

I didn't know how to thank him. So I just nodded and buckled up, and picked up a camouflage jacket I saw hanging on a hook, which no-one seemed to own. Their sidearm issue was the same as ours. It felt safe, familiar. And I knew from the weight in the holster it was my sidearm of choice, a SIG P228. Perfect for close quarters packing its 9mm punch. The frustration that I wasn't going to be able to dish out the punishment I wanted to Jaeger was offset by the overpowering need to find Kelly.

If Jaeger had been abducted, and she hadn't been with him, then she just had to be somewhere on his compound. The instant the action was over, Bill would call me to help search for her. Till then I was going to be stuck at the end of the access road twiddling my bloody thumbs.

+

Jaeger came to as he was being lifted out of the car. He was hoisted upright with his hands tightly zip-tied behind his back. Then, another tie was pulled excruciatingly taught above his elbows so his shoulder blades almost touched. He leaned over backwards, forced to stare up into the sky as stars showed through gaps in the cloud.

He sank to his knees with a gasp. The smell in the air told him that he was back at the airfield where he had been just half an hour before, preparing Kelly Murchison for her final hours on Earth.

One of his captors who, Jaeger noticed, had a bloodstained bandage round one arm, came and stood over him. He looked down and spoke in English, with only a hint of his obvious North African origins. Jaeger was starting to shiver uncontrollably when he spoke. Quiet. Gracious. Ominous.

"Mr Jaeger, sir. So pleased to meet you. I've had a long day so I'm not going to waste any time on this. I'm told that we paid you ten million dollars on your promise of significantly more sums being paid back to us." A pause. "If you don't have our... er... profit... Perhaps you are able to refund our deposit?"

Jaeger looked back into the eyes of his inquisitor. There was nothing there. He had met an equal.

"Yes..." he gasped as the uncompromising zip-ties sent pain shooting through his arms and back "Yes... of course... I can do that. You can have your money back within a couple of days. Yes... let me go and I can set it all up." At the end his voice was just a groaning sigh as he tried to speak through the pain.

Staring directly into his eyes his captor leaned down, smiled and spoke deliberately. "That's most considerate of you, Mr Jaeger, but there's really no need. The money, you see, is not the issue."

He shook his head thoughtfully. "We have plenty of it, as you well know. The problem we have, unfortunately, is that... You. Have. *Betrayed*. Us. And really, *that's* all that matters." As if explaining some basic mathematics to a ten year old... "Not just us... oh no...

all the groups in our movement… we trusted you. We had great plans for all those billions you promised us."

By now Jaeger had rolled onto his side trying to find some way to ease the agonizing torment going through his arms and back.

"But it is *we* who have you… own you… you are our property so it's *our* responsibility to ensure that you are punished for all of us. So that *your* suffering is shared equitably between all our groups. You are their proxy, so to speak…" A questioning look. "You do understand… do you? That's all that matters now. Please just accept it, Mr Jaeger. It is what it is. Nothing can change it."

He paused, continuing to stare unblinkingly into Jaegers eyes, now beginning to sting with something unfamiliar. Tears.

"And now, Mr Jaeger, we're going on a journey. We hope you enjoy it."

His captor looked across him as one of his men raised the butt of his rifle ready to lay it into the back of Jaegers head. He raised his hand.

"Oh no… no... We want our honoured guest to remain conscious and alert, so he can enjoy every moment of his journey. Every... Last... Moment…"

He felt himself hoisted back to his feet and ties pulled tight around his ankles and above his knees. A rag was stuffed into his mouth and a rough rope bound excruciatingly tight round his mouth and back of his head, ensuring he would be silent for the journey.

He felt the warm rush of urine released from his terror stricken bladder as he was lifted bodily into the bare, aluminium panelled luggage hold of the plane. The door slammed shut, leaving him in pitch black darkness. The tears flowed freely as he heard and felt the plane's engines start up.

He was supposed to be meeting Ashar. Would *The World* wait for him or just sail on? How could these people possibly do this to him?

Forty-Two

Kassab could hardly believe his ears and stood silent after hearing the report from the advance party. So, he had missed out on the pleasure of capturing Jaeger, but there was still pleasure to be had. He pulled himself together. Each car and truck in his convoy heard his instruction over the walkie-talkies.

"Return to the road and line up behind me."

The first rays of the sun were bringing on the ethereal early morning mist in the forest to the east as, along a half mile stretch of the main Perth to Margaret River highway pick-ups and SUV's emerged from their lay-by's and picnic stops onto the road. They lined up behind each other, engines ticking over, awaiting instructions.

They saw one of the advance party cars return. Only they and Kassab were aware of what had happened to Jaeger. They were just a quarter mile from the turn-off to the compound.

Everyone dismounted from their vehicles and stood around talking and smoking while the remaining advance party leader, with the lead crew now in the air somewhere with Jaeger, was talking to Kassab. He instructed them to return to where they were and get themselves well concealed in the bush, and to stay there to watch the road and report any activity. Then the walkie-talkies came alive throughout the convoy.

"We're going in. Prepare weapons. But no shooting unless you see it from me first."

Everyone rushed back to their vehicles and the sound of weapons and ammunition boxes being levered open, magazines being loaded and weapons being cocked and readied echoed on the still morning air. It carried down the road to Watchtower on the slight breeze.

No-one noticed or cared that no civilian traffic was on the road, which would usually be getting busy at this time of the morning. All traffic had been diverted onto the old coast road between Busselton and Margaret River, with local and federal police planted every 500 yards along the road along with mobile patrols ensuring no-one made their way into the area on foot or through the many tracks that crisscrossed the forest.

The Federal Police Chief, Josh Millar, had been thorough if nothing else. An entire battle-zone had been cordoned off with police cars, ambulances and fire engines on stand-by both in Busselton and Margaret River, ready to go in and clean up whatever mess came out of all this.

+

In the ops room the speaker whispered again "The car below has turned back north up the highway. Maybe they got what they came for and are going home."

I don't think so glances were exchanged between everybody in the ops room.

There was silence for fifteen minutes, then the speaker again "There's something going on… Some sort of noise up the road… yes, it's engines ticking over… hard to say how many… slamming… creaking… sort of mechanical noises. The vehicle that headed north has returned… it's back in the bush opposite the junction. Two men on board. Right under Watchtower."

Silence again. Then "Frankie… er… sir… there's a whole bloody convoy coming down the road… pick-ups, SUV's… all sorts… stand by…"

A short pause while the sniper took a closer look at the convoy through his 'scope. A gasp "Strewth! Every one of these vehicles is tooled up to the gunwales… shit shoot… RPG's… uh… AK's seem to be the weapon of choice but there's SMG's and all kinds of other hardware. It all looks a bit rag-tag though, I don't see any sign of any training… discipline… more like a bunch of bloody pirates…"

With the noise of all the vehicles going by the sniper was now talking in an almost normal voice, coming over loudly on the amplified receiver. "It looks like we have about a hundred armed… fully tooled up men about to invade the compound. About 20 vehicles. SUV's, pick-ups and stuff. No uniform, just a bunch of blokes looking to satisfy some bloodlust I reckon… I've seen ten cabs arriving with passengers since yesterday afternoon, all couples, with the cabs returning north to Perth after drop-off. Watchtower still secure and on point. Out."

Frankie looked across the situation table to his deputy. "Bloody hell… where did that lot come from? Are we mounted up?"

"Of course, sir. On your orders."

"Thank you. Send the relief to Watchtower, but add another so we've two snipers up there now. Do we have a spare weapon up there?"

He was told there were two L115A3 long range rifles, the sniper's weapon of choice in many armies, with a good supply of ammunition.

The Watchtower sniper was told to descend and await the arrival of his two replacements who turned up in the old Land Rover they had been using as cover to deliver their relief fire watch teams. As usual, they should act relaxed and ignorant of what was going on around them. He would return to give Frankie and his ops room team a full face-to-face briefing.

+

Jaeger's phone had landed in the footwell of his car where Kelly, in fear and shock, concealed and immovably encased in Gaffa tape, had heard it sound off three times. She was now breathing the fetid stench of her own released faeces and urine, which it had been impossible to contain. The Toyota had been driven straight into the bush and was now well concealed, dumped behind undergrowth and trees.

She had heard the windows being smashed as Jaeger was abducted, but had no idea of what was actually happening. There was no other sound made throughout the whole episode, which had taken no more than ten seconds. She had no idea where the car, or she, was. The overwhelming sense of despair was pushing her into a state of shock and delirium.

+

Ashar had started getting worried when Jaeger had not shown up at 6.45, when he called the first time. By 6.50 he was aboard the plane and still waiting for him. After another failed call at 6.55 he had no choice but to tell the crew they could take off. If he did not, there was every chance there would be problems with the control tower which could draw attention to himself.

He had the whole ten seater aircraft to himself for the almost six hour flight to Port Moresby. From there, he had set up the flights to Belize, which had stopovers at Brisbane and Los Angeles. With fake ID and an obscure flight itinerary, he had done everything it was possible to do to cover his tracks.

The plane had phone and internet and, once again, he tried calling Jaeger's burner with no answer. Then, he tried his regular phone and got an answer, in a voice he did not recognise.

"Hello, who is this please?"

He felt an uncontrollable tremor surge through him. But played along. "Hi, Robert. Tom here…" *think fast* "Just calling to confirm our meeting today."

The accent was Arab. "You know this is not Robert, and I think we can be sure you're not Tom. Mr Jaeger is currently indisposed…"

By then Ashar had opened the back of the burner and removed the battery and SIM card. He did the same with his regular phone and then, overcome with cold shock, sat back in his seat to take stock. He was sure he had heard the sound of propellers in the background. Wherever Jaeger was, he was in a prop aircraft with every chance he did not want to be there.

He could not imagine what had happened that would compromise Jaeger, although he was quite sure it was nothing to do with him. He had sounded perfectly fine when they had their call a couple of hours ago.

The only reason they had agreed to head to Belize was because that was where Jaeger could meet *The World*, on which he was planning to slip off into obscurity, and they were going to have a parting meal together. Now, he would not even leave the airport when he got to Belize but organize another jet to take him on down to Antigua as soon as his scheduled flight had arrived.

He called the flight attendant to get that set up. He would be on Antigua, safe and sound, within 48 hours.

After an hour he was thinking straight again, and congratulated himself on being such a resourceful guy. Dealing with the situation in Malta and, now, having everything set up to see things through to their planned conclusion with no help from anybody. He thought about checking into Swift again to make sure everything was still in place, but then thought that too many visits without actually doing anything might set off an alarm somewhere in the system. He knew how these things worked.

From when he had first got to know Mohammed, he knew that he could use him in some way with his ultimate plan to compromise or sabotage Swift. It was not until he met Jaeger, at one of the 'movement's' irregular meetings, who explained the PPP process to him that he fully grasped the utter devastation that could be unleashed. By cancelling all the MT799's blocking PPP deposits the host banks would be exposed to trillions of uncollateralized debt in an instant.

Then, Jaeger told him about a conversation he had had with one of his clients, a group of North Koreans, at his private bank, and how they would willingly pay if someone could find a way to create this havoc. All done without firing a single shot or nuclear-tipped missile. Economically the world would descend to their level almost overnight which, for them, would put them on a level playing field.

At least that was their take, and they were probably not too far off the truth.

It had taken a lot of working out, with him planning a strategy and Jaeger using his high level connections to have Mohammed recruited first into Euroclear, and then Swift. Ashar, who was well known in the global banking technology community, played his part by talking up Mohammed's network security credentials at every opportunity.

For Jaeger, Ashar with his peerless coding and programming skills, along with his direct access to Mohammed, who was on his way towards banking security guru status, was the final piece in his jigsaw of retribution.

The moment they both realized how they could benefit each other, a firm and unholy alliance was forged.

Ashar knew that, once he had gotten inside Swift, he would be able to deliver what Pyongyang wanted, and for which they were paying handsomely. They had already added to Jaeger's significant bank balance, and some of that had been added to Ashar's considerable bank balance.

A further sum, ten times what had already been paid, would be paid out the moment Ashar told them that the program had been activated. And now, it seemed, it would all be coming to him.

Setting up GDWM and arranging the MT799 placement blocking with his senior contacts at the bank had taken no time at all for Robert. The scam to relieve all those billionaires of their fortunes was just a very useful by-product of the ultimate strategy. They needed real live PPP's to work with to be able to target and compromise real accounts and compromise the MT799 system. And Jaeger had the resources behind him to get it all done properly.

Ashar knew that, just to be sure, one of Jaeger's contacts inside Swift who had been a part of the movement from the beginning, had Mohammed under constant observation throughout his three years on the job. Making sure he did not do anything stupid.

Someone senior in the cyber-fraud section at Swift was doing the observing, from what Ashar could understand from Jaeger. But he had never actually given him a name.

The program he needed to write to cancel the MT799's was simplicity itself. All he needed to do was find his way to the root of the MT799 process and set things up so that he could enter a new date to override all the thousands of time-out dates that were already stored. The real life GDWM PPP's provided all the data he needed on which to build his program. The challenge came in picking out only those that were blocking sums of $100 million or more for PPP's. But he enjoyed a challenge.

Now, all he had to do was log-in, enter the current date into his program, click 'enter' and there would be nothing to stop total global economic meltdown. He could do no more. He settled back in his seat and wished away the next 48 hours until he landed on Antigua.

He said a little prayer for Robert before drifting off to sleep.

Forty-Three

When he got back to the control room, the Watchtower sniper reported that after he had watched Jaeger being kidnapped, he had seen a few other cars leave the compound and head both north and south on the main road, driving fast. These were mostly older cars and he could only guess that they were the maintenance and other staff who had read the runes, sensed something wrong and decided to bail out.

Before he left the hide, he could see one other car still on the compound behind the garage block. It now looked like, aside from just one staff, the ten guests and their wives and partners were in the huge compound all on their own.

+

As far as putting a battle plan together, everything came down to the fact that the compound had been sited so that it overlooked the surrounding terrain in all directions and, where there had been any trees or other obstructions, they had been cleared to create a lethal kill-zone. Seaward, there was an unassailable cliff.

Any attack in daylight looked like a non-starter. But this would leave twenty or so civilians, men and women but it seemed, mercifully, no children, at the helpless mercy of what looked like a hundred apparently amateur terrorists, with more weapons than they knew what to do with. A lethal mix.

Something needed to be done, otherwise they would have a whole free and clear day to satisfy their most basic blood and other lusts if we waited for nightfall.

One rule about battle plans is that they invariably need to be changed on first contact. We did not want that to happen here.

Special Forces around the world are not democracies, but battle plans are worked up with input from everybody with the CO taking final decisions and setting tactics and strategy. At the end of the day it was agreed that, while any attack in daylight would be at the enemy's tactical advantage we had no choice but to go in, if only to distract the terrorists from all the fun they would now be planning to have with their captives.

It was decided to deploy two of the SASR Black Hawk choppers to support a full-on incursion through the main gate from the landward side. If necessary firing RPG's at the gates to bring them down as they drove towards them. Watchtower would pick off tactical targets at will.

+

The plan was decided and confirmed within five minutes and everyone doubled back to their quarters to get kitted-up and then go to the armoury to draw weapons. I began to limp after Bill, Jack and Ted but then heard Frankie shouting at me.

"Where d'ya think *you're* going, Fox?"

Oh crap! He was right. I'd automatically fallen back into soldier mode and completely ignored the fact that I would only be a liability. I was going to have to live with being tail end Charlie.

Ten minutes later I stood by my Land Rover watching as the SASR troop, codenamed Blue Force, left the base for the two hour high speed drive on the traffic-free road down to Jaeger's 'fortress'. Ted was in the back of the second truck and we gave each other a nod as our eyes met. I joined the end of the convoy in the Land Rover.

Two hours later the two Black Hawks would lift off and head towards the coast, staying so low they'd skirt the few buildings higher than four stories. All this activity would mean nothing to the locals who let their beloved SASR get up to whatever they wanted around their base. So, to them, this was just another training exercise. And those Black Hawk birds were almost silent. No-one knew they were there till they'd passed overhead and thudded on their way.

I was really, I mean *really* hacked off that I wasn't going to be a part of the action. After all, it was what I'd trained for. But, after his kidnapping, it looked like Jaeger was going to be dealt with anyway, and I didn't care to think what shape that would take. He would be 'dealt with' far more thoroughly than I'd have had the guts for. I wondered if I'd ever see or hear anything of him again.

I felt a vibration in my pocket and it took me a second or two to remember I still had Jackson's burner in there.

It was a long call and I had to concentrate hard while I was keeping up with the Blue Force convoy. I got the full Monty on everything that had been going on these past few days. Especially the abortive CEESSEB meeting which appeared to have set things right back. But now Jackson was taking great pleasure in preparing an update, which included a high level briefing on the action that was now going on in this corner of Australia and the kidnapping by terrorists of the main suspect, Robert Jaeger.

On top of that, the FBI guy we'd met in Detroit had managed to get an image of a possible suspect in the Davey's killing. With more than just a little help from the young cop, Arlene Smith, it seemed. I wondered if he'd plucked up the nerve to make a move on her yet.

Jackson had passed the image onto the Malta cops and, even though it was fuzzy, they had quickly confirmed that this was the guy that Vittor, the café owner, had put them onto, backpack man, and who was the other suspect in the Malta apartment. So this was definitely the one with the mobile, but impossible to tell if he was in any way linked to the MT799 enigma.

The CCTV on the Malta-Sicily hydrofoil had picked him up with another guy on a scooter, but there was no trace of where he went after they landed in Sicily.

Finally, the U.S. Treasury Secretary who had attended the CEESSEB meeting had given the heads up to the FBI that there was some connection between this suspect and a possible major financial fraud, although no-one was too sure what exactly it might be.

This was quite an update and things were now all starting to drop into place for me. I told Jackson that I would flash up my own phone again, as whatever Jaeger had been up to was unravelling fast and we could safely use proper phones again rather that the ancient burner he'd given me.

+

By the end of the call our convoy had come to a halt about a quarter mile north of the compound. I saw the line of Humvees in front of me, wishing like crazy I was going to be there and amongst it instead of hiding in the bush like a spare part.

I took the Land Rover alongside the row of Humvees and picked a spot off the road about twenty yards north of Watchtower.

As I was building myself a hide, about five yards away from the vehicle, my phone sounded off. I didn't get many calls or e-mails, and there were only half a dozen of each waiting to be dealt with when I flashed up my phone. I was looking through the waiting voicemails while the convoy was parked up, when there was an incoming from Pat Wheeler. Not a call to decline.

He had always been bluff, but only as a means of getting accurate information, quickly. There was no beating around the bushes.

"What's going on, Dez? I'm hearing all kinds of things."

"Erm… Hi, Pat… hard for me to say really." I whispered, "bit awkward to say anything right now…It's difficult for me to talk right now."

"Don't bullshit me, Dez. I've got friends who had billions taken from their accounts which mysteriously reappeared a few days later. They all got e-mails from their banks giving them some bull about it being all to do with Swift preventing some cyber-fraud or other. I don't believe a word of it and after that call from you on the MT799 thing I have a feeling in my water that you know more than you're letting on. And what's all this about some secret hidey-hole for rich folk down in kangaroo-ville, somewhere near Perth… and again, Dez… don't bullshit me 'cos I know that's where you are *right now*."

It would have been easy enough for him to track me down, and it would take no brains at all to make the connection with the missing billions after my call with him from the plane. He was no idiot and I wasn't about to treat him like one.

I was still whispering into my phone. "Pat, I'm sorry, but I simply *cannot* say anything. Please accept that. Yes, I do know what's been going on, and I think there's more to come. I'll be back in the UK hopefully in the next week or so and I'll tell you what I can. I don't *think* there's anything for you to worry about provided you've got your funds out of the mainstream banking system. And for all I know, I'm completely wrong about the whole bloody thing. This MT799 thing is still bugging the bejeezus out of me… Besides that, that shit Jaeger kidnapped Kelly… and now he's been abducted we don't have a fuckin' clue where she is…" My voice was starting to crack and I realised my fears for Kelly were starting to surface. Without thinking I was venting and offloading all my fears onto the poor guy. I finished with "Sorry, Pat. Just a bit pissed off right now."

Silence. Then, "Oh… shit… sorry, didn't know… You get on with what you gotta do. Call me when you can. There are many people who are very grateful for the heads-up you gave me."

I was about to hang up but then, suddenly, it came to me… *Luck is being prepared for opportunity…*

"Thanks, Pat… don't hang up! Er… do you know a really good corporate lawyer in Singapore who's well connected to the regulators there? And can move fast, *very* fast if necessary?"

Yet another long silence. "Dez, my friend, you're asking some very weird questions lately… but the answer's yes and I'll send you contact details by e-mail. You can trust him. I'll let him know that he might be hearing from you."

He hung up.

Forty-Four

The call from Drew was short and very sweet. "We're going to Antigua. Leaving tomorrow. All cleared with your sergeant... Beth Haydon was it..? Meet you at Detroit Metro tomorrow morning. Flight leaves 10am. FBI jet as there's no direct flights this time of year. Get all relevant files onto your laptop. Will brief you on the plane. Catch up tomorrow."

He was obviously in a hurry and hung up with no further comment as Arlene nearly fell off her chair. She stood up, surprised face framed by her dark curly hair appearing over her cubicle screen to survey the rest of the office. Yep. It was not a dream.

Everything as it should be. People sitting by desks being interviewed, uniforms and plain clothes milling around on whatever mission they were on and someone kicking the drinks machine, which had not worked properly since she had joined the department.

And Beth Haydon looking up from her office across the expanse of people and cubicles to give her a nod and a small wave confirming she knew what was going on. Yes, this was real.

As Drew had instructed, she copied her complete Davey homicide file onto her laptop and put it into the old floppy leather briefcase her grandpa had given her, which she had used until now mostly to bring her own cwawffee and sandwiches into work. If DPD fell down on anything, it was on the low grade cwawffee it served up. She powered down, tidied her desk and left the office at a steady walk then, once outside, ran to her car. Antigua. With Drew!

No matter how hard she tried, she could not wipe the big wide grin off her face all the way home.

She spent more time than usual making herself look good the next morning, and took a cab to the airport to arrive at 8.00. Well ahead of time, but it passed quickly as she indulged in some people watching. Eventually she spotted Drew coming across the concourse. Casually dressed, expressionless, with a backpack and carrying a cabin bag. She realized then just how stand-out handsome this guy she had fallen for really was. He gave her a wink and said quietly, "We're colleagues, nothing else. Play the part."

She took on the same, dispassionate and professional attitude as him as they walked to the ramp where their jet was waiting. Anyone looking would have seen two young professionals setting out on some mission or other. Nothing to see here.

They were the only two passengers in the five-seater Lear Jet. Soon after take-off, and making a start on the coffee and sandwiches that had been provided for the four hour flight, they sat opposite each other with a table between them and got down to business. There was CCTV in the cabin and they needed to act the part all the way to their hotel rooms, two of which she had reserved for them, stuff like that was now part of her job, at the Caribbean Inn in St John's.

Drew told Arlene that someone high up in the FBI had taken a call from the Treasury Secretary with instructions to get people to Antigua and follow through on the Davey's homicide. It looked like CEESSEB, or at least MI6, was trying to expose something major after all and, right now, there was some kind of action brewing in Australia between their special forces and a group of almost 100 terrorists. No further information had been provided other than that the ringleader, a guy called Robert Jaeger who Arlene and Drew already knew about, had been kidnapped and whose whereabouts were completely unknown. But no-one was giving much for his chances.

Apparently, whatever fraud he was working on had been intercepted and dealt with by MI6 and the Swift outfit they had been talking about when they first met. But MI6 still thought there was something else waiting in the wings and, if at all possible, they needed to track down the Davey's killer who appeared to be the missing link in the whole case.

They talked through the whole scenario and then Arlene moved to a separate seat and took a book out of her briefcase and settled back to read, remembering to hold it the right way up and turn the pages occasionally for the benefit of the camera. She had other things on her mind.

They hardly looked at each other for the rest of the flight. At Antigua immigration Arlene's virgin passport got its first stamp and they both got into a cab to the hotel, both of them already feeling the relaxed ambience of the island. It would be difficult to get motivated to actually get any work done tomorrow.

At the hotel they picked up the key-cards to their (*oh, yessss!*) adjoining rooms.

+

The King Air was flying on fumes by the time it landed on hard red earth in the Northern Territory after a bumpy almost five-hour flight. It had flown at 7,000 feet to ensure all on board had sufficient oxygen but Jaeger, confined in unremitting agony in the luggage hold, did not have the luxury of heating.

Through the never-ending misery of his heavily restrained arms causing unbearable, deadening back pain and the relentless pressure of the gag secured tight around his mouth, he felt the planc land and the engines stop. There was then a lot of activity as he heard the plane's tanks being refuelled using a noisy pump, against a background of people moving around and casual conversation.

Then the hatch flew open and he was dragged out and dropped face first to the ground five feet below. His eyes squinted hard as they tried to adjust to the light, and he felt the mid-morning sun start to warm his body. He was sobbing through the unforgiving gag with the agony of his viciously constrained arms.

He felt the cable ties around his ankles and knees cut. Then, mercifully, those around his wrists and above his elbows. His arms flopped to his side. No matter how hard he tried to move them, they lay numb and lifeless.

He lay face down, helpless as he felt his shoes and socks removed, and his leather belt cut as if it were paper at the back of his waist, followed by the same knife slicing through his trousers and briefs which were then torn off. The same treatment followed for his jacket and shirt and he was lifted up while these were all removed and discarded. He was dropped back to the ground to lay flat, face down and still unable to make any part of his body move.

People were moving around going about whatever it was they were doing, as if they were ignoring his naked, helpless body. The bindings had left him completely paralyzed and, for the first time in his life he knew what it was to be totally defenceless and vulnerable. He heard a truck or pick-up moving around somewhere ahead of him. He managed a soft grunt.

This bought someone closer to him and they pulled at his gag, he sighed in relief as he felt it being loosened, but then pulled even tighter. So tight that he felt his jawbone dislocate on the left side. His arms were pulled forward, crossed at the wrists and tied tight with coarse rope.

He heard more people moving around and then the plane starting up. He heard it turn around and rev its engines, blasting him with stones and sand, before fading into the distance as it took off from the packed earth of the Australian outback. The distant sound of the engines diminished until he could almost hear the silence it left behind.

Then, what he guessed was the fuel truck started its loud, clacking diesel engine and drove off to somewhere on his left. Then utter silence again broken only by the sound of occasional distant birdsong.

He smelt cigarette smoke as his captors stood around him, looking at their helpless victim and talking in what he recognised as Arabic. He figured nowhere in their conversation and he quickly realized they were talking about a cricket match between Australia and the West Indies, and something about a woman being dropped into the sea.

He was nothing more than a job to them. An irrelevance. Something they had to deal with, and then move on.

They stubbed the cigarettes out on his back and legs, with one pushed between his buttocks until it went out as it was forced into his anus. He jerked around on the ground and his suppressed squeals drew only disinterested laughs.

The gag bringing unbearable force on his dislocated jaw stopped him moving his head to see what was happening but he heard the vehicle ahead of him start up again.

Then, after hearing the revving of an engine and with no warning he was hurtling along the ground over scrub and rocks for what seemed to him like miles before being hauled upward, almost ripping his arms out of their sockets and left swinging by his wrists under the thick, solid bough of a Eucalyptus tree. The vehicle switched off its engine and he heard people walking from the car towards him. Three of them.

They stood in front of him, expressionless as they threw what they were carrying onto the ground in front of them. A crowbar, an outsize wrench and a baseball bat. A camera was set up on a tripod facing him, carefully focused and left ready. They disappeared again as he slowly swung round under the bough, toes barely touching the ground.

Through a haze of merciless pain wracking his entire body, he could see them set up some cooking gear on the back of a pick-up, looking at him occasionally as they talked, laughed, ate and drank coffee. The sun was now high in the sky and he could feel his skin starting to burn and felt the flies crawling over him. He picked up the aroma of spicy North African food cooking on the camping stove.

Then, replete with food and drink, the three walked towards him. A blindfold was tied tight around his head and he heard the metallic sounds of the men picking up the items they had dropped on the ground earlier. They stood and watched in amused silence as his terror-stricken body began to shake uncontrollably.

Faeces ran down his legs and his breathing started to come in short, uncontrolled bursts.

Forty-Five

Antigua. August.

Arlene went back to her own room in the morning to shower and get ready for the day ahead. There had been nothing to change the plans she had made. They had four visits scheduled. The first to the local police to introduce themselves, then the financial regulator, then the jeweller where they had asked to have free access to the entire CCTV file.

Finally, Catherine's Café where they were going to view the full CCTV of the Davey's visit and talk to the waitress who had flagged up that they were there on the day they were murdered. Once all that was done, they would have dinner.

She had arranged all of it. It was now part of her job.

They walked the mile into St John's to the police station where they did everything that visiting law officers are meant to do. Arlene had been told that she should not take her weapon with her to Antigua as that would conflict with local firearms law, but Drew could take his FBI issue 9mm Glock, which he carried in a leather holster clipped to the back of his belt, under a treaty the U.S. had with the island. But it meant wearing a jacket in the ever growing heat to conceal it from the curious eyes of the locals and tourists.

They were asked to complete a couple of forms and told that they could carry on their investigation unaccompanied but were not allowed to make any arrests. If an arrest were needed, they were given a number to call and the local police would be there as quickly as possible. Neither of them expected anything major to happen during their visit and the whole meeting was very relaxed.

The perp had done what he had come to do and would by now be somewhere far away from Antigua. The visit by these two American law officers was only a matter of process and to gather any more information they could.

The regulator's office was just a ten minute walk from the police HQ. The regulator himself, David Samuels, a morbidly obese man had pulled out the entire file on the private capital bank that Valiece Davey had registered. It was sitting on his desk waiting for them when they arrived.

After they had both looked through it, with not a word being spoken, Drew had already decided on what his first question would be.

"I see there's all these proof of ID's… passports, utility bills and all that… but don't you guys check and verify any of this? If you did, and all those other regulators did, then all these banks wouldn't have been able to register."

Samuels stared back at Drew for a moment before explaining patiently "It's not our job to check that kind of information. As you can see, the bank is registered by a company, not an individual. The company is registered on Antigua, usually by a local law firm so we simply assume that all documentation on the individuals behind the company have been validated either by the lawyer or the company registration department. Our job is simply to register the bank as a point of reference for anyone who might enquire."

Samuels had not been fully briefed as to why the FBI and DPD had asked for this meeting and this was all explained to him, including the Davey's homicide and the world-wide hunt for people behind the biggest cyber fraud in history. Samuels, whose world view was limited to processing bank registration application forms was dumbstruck. Arlene thought she might have to remind him to breathe.

He added that his office assumed any background checking was done by the law firm registering the company. No-one really knew if they did or not. *Or even cared*, Drew thought.

Calling people in to put a 'wet signature' on documents was standard procedure on Antigua, whereas many other jurisdictions were happy with electronic signatures and e-mail attachments. It was a way of getting people to come to the island and spend some money. But he had no idea who was actually behind the registrations and he did not bother trying to check because the whole idea of registering in offshore jurisdictions was to conceal or mask identities.

But then he asked what Drew had meant by '…all these banks…'.

Drew explained. "There were fifty banks registered all over the world, we believe all under fake ID's by Collins, Day in Detroit, who Mr Davey worked for, and that was done on behalf of a wealth management firm in Gibraltar, which is now de-registered…. Collins, Day were not aware of the false ID's. Interpol has so far confirmed half of them had false ID's and we expect the other half to go that way too."

Samuels gasped. "Interpol? Is Antigua… am *I* implicated in any way?"

Arlene saw her chance. "You'll hear directly from them if you are, after we send them our report on this meeting." That should scare him into cooperating properly.

There was an awkward silence and, after a few seconds, Arlene and Drew started to prepare to go which, for Drew, was returning the case folder to his smart new briefcase and putting on his jacket. When he had taken it off he had draped it over the back of his chair in a way that Samuels would not see the weapon on his belt. Now, he let him see it which brought a deeply concerned frown out of Samuels.

For Arlene, she just picked up her granddad's old floppy leather briefcase. The meeting was ended and they both headed for the door but, as Arlene was about to follow Drew out she stopped and walked back to Samuels' desk. He looked at her curiously.

"I'm sorry…" Arlene explained opening her briefcase again on Samuel's desk "it's just a long shot but we have a POI… a person of interest, that's a part of all this. There's a strong chance he was involved in the Davey's homicide. Just a second..."

She pulled a print-out of the image of the suspect picked up in the jeweller's mirror. "As I say, a really long shot… but do you recognise this man."

Samuels was already preparing to give the stock 'no' answer but, on seeing the image, stopped short. He took it off Arlene and held it away from him, looking over his glasses and then squinting through them. Arlene and Drew looked quickly at each other then back at Samuels.

"It's a bit fuzzy… Hmmm… hard to say…"

After hearing the word 'Interpol' he was on high alert and keen to assist in any way possible. Yes, it was a reach, but, "I think this gentleman may have been in the office here just an hour or so before Mr Davey."

Drew came fully back into the room, took his jacket off, the air conditioning wasn't up to much, and sat down again. Both of them looked at Samuels expectantly.

"Er… One moment…"

Podgy fingers clattered away on his keyboard for a few seconds and then wrote something down on a notepad. He left the room, the departing of his bulk leaving it seeming much larger, and came back five minutes later with a folder. He looked at it for a moment, nodding to himself. "Yes, I remember him now. A very polite gentleman with a British accent…"

He pulled a sheet of paper out of the file, a copy of a company registration document which showed the name of the company and its sole director, Jeremy Hitchens. Most important was a copy of Hitchens' passport attached to the sheet with the photograph showing a much clearer image of the one they already had. There was no doubt it was the same man.

Samuels said nothing while the two law officers looked closely at both images. The likeness was too close to ignore and, for Arlene, when she took every cop's mantra of 'there are no coincidences' into account, this just had to be an epic lead.

Hitchens, if that was his name, had registered a private capital bank on the island, with the registered address being in a building where hundreds of similar banks were already registered. He had used a British passport which they would check out when they got back to the hotel, but they could be pretty sure that it would be fake. If they had learned one thing in this investigation, these perps were past masters at ID theft.

They had the name of Hitchens' bank, Revbay Capital Bank, obviously an off-the-shelf name, and its registered address. If it was going to function properly it would need to register with Swift.

Hopefully they would be able to pull up some more information for them. Samuels offered to scan the documents and send them all to Drew's FBI e-mail address.

They thanked him, this time shaking his hand with genuine gratitude and then paced it out towards the jeweller's where they would be spending some time reviewing the CCTV footage. After that was done, they went outside and positioned themselves where the Davey's had stood, imagining themselves in their position. And then walking the few yards towards the kerb where they would have got into the Mercedes.

All this did was give them a 'feel' for what happened but, in some supernatural way, this helps on crime scene investigations. On reviewing the footage in the shop, they had also seen the Mercedes drive off with the Davey's inside past the shop window, smiling while they talked to the driver, indistinct on the video, but who she was pretty sure by now was the killer. Two innocents in complete ignorance that they were being driven off to their deaths. Arlene could not help herself welling up when she saw this.

Back at the hotel they compiled a joint report to send to both Drew's boss at the FBI and Beth Haydon. They would also copy in the Fed and Jackson at MI6, who would ensure it was passed onto whoever else needed to see it.

They asked MI6 to push Swift for a quick response on any further information they could offer on Hitchens' Revbay Capital Bank.

They both looked through the report one more time before adding the attachments. Drew clicked the 'send' button and sat back with a sigh. This had been a far more eventful day than either of them had anticipated and were surprised to see it was coming up to 6pm. Their next meeting was with the full CCTV footage at Catherine's Café.

+

At the café, in fact an up-market beach-themed restaurant, they were taken into the proprietor's upstairs apartment where the CCTV, with none of the usual poor reproduction, was all set up for them to view on a large tv screen in the lounge.

They could see the Davey's arrive with a setting sun casting long shadows as they walked towards the café after getting out of the cab. They were looking around the patio area but then a waitress, the same one who had reported the sighting, appeared and could be seen showing them to a table, mostly hidden behind a trelliswork screen covered with foliage.

After that, it was what you would expect other than it was obvious they were enjoying their meal, and making the most of their vacation. They fast forwarded to when they paid and could be seen chatting to the waitress before leaving the restaurant and walking hand-in-hand off and out of the left of the picture on the far side of the patio area.

They continued watching, expecting to see them walk back to meet their cab. Instead the Mercedes pulled up and after half a minute the driver, their suspect now clearly identifiable on the screen, got out and looked into the restaurant, before walking in and looking around.

The waitress walked up to him and there was a short conversation, at the end of which she pointed in the direction the Davey's had walked off in. They kept looking, not knowing what to expect until ten minutes later the Merc, they were sure it was the same one, drove back the other way with a different man at the wheel. A big guy and nothing like the suspect they now knew as Jeremy Hitchens.

Without realizing it both of them had slowly been leaning further and further forward on the sofa, engrossed. At the end of this last segment they sank back into the sofa with loud sighs.

Arlene was the first to speak. "We need to see where they went."

They left the restaurant and walked off in the same direction the Davey's had taken. To their right was the marina with its extensive collection of boats ranging from small dinghies to a couple of large private yachts overshadowing everything else. A couple of hundred boats of all shapes and sizes in various states of repair. From barely afloat to fresh out of the boat-builders.

Their walk took them away from the marina to an old floating jetty that jutted its way out some forty feet into the harbour. Upright stanchions giving off the distinctive smell of ageing waterlogged timber, seaweed and barnacles either side, holding large metal pontoons in place as they floated up and down with the tide. This must have been where Valiece and Daphne had come.

They walked to the end, holding hands. It was now dark, with the marina lit only by the half moon and the rows of lights on the walkways they had left two hundred yards in the distance behind them. They felt completely alone. There was only the sound of water lapping, small boats bumping against the pontoons and the occasional distant car or scooter.

They could have been on a romantic holiday or, Arlene secretly thought, their honeymoon. She looked down into one of the boats tied up to the end of the jetty and leaned towards Drew, "This is where it happened. I know it… They were taken out onto the water where no-one would hear the gunshots. Any one of these boats tied up here could have been the one they used."

Drew nodded and pulled her closer to him. They kissed gently, but both their minds were on the business in hand. "I think you're right. We'll get a copy of that CCTV and send it on when we get back to the hotel tonight. At least it'll give us a clear image of Hitchens we can work with. Right now, I think we better eat."

The two young professionals, no longer holding hands, walked pensively back to Catherine's Café to re-join the real world.

Forty-six

Margaret River, Western Australia. September.

Kassab's instructions had been to take Robert Jaeger alive, and ensure that his departure from this mortal coil was as long and as agonizing as he could possibly devise. But that was now well in hand and being looked after by the crew who had flown over from some cancelled mission south of Sydney. They were by far the most professional out of all the motley force he was now commanding, and probably doing a far better job on Jaeger than he would. Shame they were not still here.

But now they were gone, and having all the fun he should be having with Jaeger. He had been told where the compound was and given some basic description of its layout. One of the maintenance staff, who he knew from the Australian cell, was there and would be able to give him fuller details of the compound when he got there.

But as he drove up to the main gate at the head of his convoy, it was hanging wide open. This is not how it was meant to be. Where were all the heavily armed guards, some of them the people who were resident here, defending the place? The fence, which he could see quite clearly now as he drove towards it, with the gates swinging wide open, was supposed to be electrified and impenetrable.

Through the open gates he could see a carefully mown grassed courtyard, half a football pitch. He was standing in the back of his pick-up at the front of the convoy and he raised his hand to bring it to a halt. Some of the courtyard, over by the fence facing out to the sea, had been tarmac'd over as a large parking area.

He pulled out his walkie-talkie and issued his orders. "Everyone except drivers dismount from your vehicles. Keep a constant look-out and take your weapons. Leave ammo boxes in your vehicles for now…"

He saw someone leave the garage block and walk across the courtyard towards him. He was not carrying any weapon as far as he could see. He came up to the side of the pick-up.

"Kassab. Good to see you. Been a while." Kassab grunted acknowledgement as he continued looking around the compound.

The man shook his head and spread his arms wide. "Well, I don't know quite how to tell you this, mate, but Jaeger's gone and the guests are still in bed in their apartments. Ten men and," with a menace-laden smile, "ten women. Ten very hot women. We have completely free run of the place. All the staff have abandoned ship."

He held up a large bunch of keys. "Keys to everywhere. I've already opened up the armoury for you." He continued looking at Kassab, expectantly.

"Thank you." And then into his walkie-talkie "As before, everyone except drivers dismount. Keep your weapons with you, carry spare ammo and assemble – QUIETLY – in the centre of the courtyard. Drivers take your vehicles into the compound and park facing the fence on the tarmac, no heavy revving."

Everyone did as they were told. The force, some dressed in clothes resembling combat gear, others wearing what they would wear on the street. Some with a bit of self-discipline about them but all here for nothing other than the fun they had been promised, assembled in the centre of the courtyard. Kassab and his deputy walked into the main building on their own.

+

In the control room and on the radios in all the Blue Force vehicles and Black Hawks they heard Watchtower's commentary. "Convoy's pulled up at the gate... someone coming across the courtyard... now speaking to what looks like the leader... ok... everyone's getting out of their vehicles, all carrying weapons... vehicles moving off... um... eighteen vehicles... parking in a line two-deep along the fence facing the sea, I s'pose 'cos that's where the tarmac is... all grass otherwise. Leader's gone off with one other guy into the main building... Stand by... Stand by..."

Frankie and his Blue Force were listening simultaneously on the same frequency as they approached the compound. They came to a halt a quarter mile up the road from Watchtower, the closest they could get without being seen from the compound.

The Black Hawks had now landed on the beach at the foot of the cliff, menacingly quiet with rotors spinning ready to lift off at a second's notice. Frankie issued a few short, sharp orders.

Everyone knew what they had to do when the time came.

+

Kassab looked around the lobby in disbelief. What kind of place was this? The opulence was overwhelming. Chandeliers, marble, antique furniture and what looked like genuine art hanging on the walls and open common rooms stretching away into the distance along the ground floor. He walked quietly through the entire ground floor with the maintenance man who had met him, until he came to a door that he could see led to further doors, he was told that these were the four ground floor apartments.

It looked like the guests were all still in bed.

Forty-Seven

Ashar looked down as the plane banked for its approach into Belize. It had been a lot of flying but he was sure he had successfully lost himself among the millions of travellers in the air at any one time. He could see two mid-range airliners on the ramps of the small terminal and about a dozen private planes parked on the apron.

A large minority of passengers arriving and departing from Belize came on private aircraft from all over North and South America, to visit the offshore branches of their banks. They were mostly larger single- or twin-prop aircraft but there were three or four jets among them one of which, he assumed, was waiting for him.

Everything was going to plan. As he went through the transit lounge he visited the washroom and wrapped up the two SIMS, both broken in half, from his phones in toilet paper and flushed them away. He wiped his burners clean and dropped them into a bag on the front of a passing waste collection trolley on the concourse. The batteries went into separate waste bins around the concourse.

He bought a new phone from one of the shops on the concourse. It would only be used to contact his friend who had helped him escape from Malta who, by now, would be settled somewhere in the Czech Republic to wait out the coming storm.

Maybe, also, he would one day use it to talk to Robert Jaeger. He was a resourceful guy and had probably managed to negotiate his way out of whatever situation he was in. He would find some other way to get to Belize and join *The World*, which would be arriving tomorrow.

But, once he had keyed 'enter' it would not be long before the world's telecoms systems failed due either to lack of power or non-maintenance anyway. So there was every chance the phone would turn out to be useless in the end anyway.

He checked the flight number for his private jet and headed for the gate leading out onto the apron where someone from airport security, such as it was, was waiting to lead him to the plane. Another Gulfstream G280. Big, but necessary for the almost 1,800 mile flight to Antigua. He thought that Robert would have been disappointed to miss two flights on his favourite jet.

+

As the jet taxied for take-off, he opened his laptop and logged into YouTube where he could usually find some fun stuff to keep him occupied. He looked under 'trending'.

The video he selected had gone viral within minutes. By the end of the first day it had taken over 12 million views. Ashar, as he downloaded it while the jet was turning onto the runway, probably came in at around number three million.

It showed a gagged and blindfolded man hanging by his wrists from what had been quickly identified as a Eucalyptus tree. Some of the comments speculated that it was somewhere in Australia's Northern Territory.

The hour and a half movie started at mid-day with hardly any shadow showing beneath the hanging body. The face was disfigured by a dislocated jaw and it was easy to see that the gag was not just there to keep him quiet, but to add to his unending torture. The blindfold had been tied tight and was not going to go anywhere.

Ashar's guts churned at the dreadful realization that he was looking at Robert Jaeger.

Three men appeared and picked up some items from an indistinct pile on the ground. But as they were picked up they became more defined. A crowbar, a baseball bat and a large wrench. They walked over to the hanging man, circling him slowly.

The first swing was at the man's right knee followed quickly by another to his left. The men kept swinging until both knees were unrecognizable masses of bleeding flesh and bone. Before the assault, his toes had been barely touching the ground. His feet were now flat on the ground. Robert's whole body was convulsing with the indescribably agony he was suffering.

The picture faded out and then back in again with the time stamp moved forward three hours. The same men came into frame and moved purposefully towards him.

More blows, this time to the chest, back and sides, hammering relentlessly for several minutes until a broken rib could be seen protruding through the skin on his back. The soundtrack gave out only the thudding blows, and Robert's suppressed squeals. Enough to severely maim and inflict dreadful pain. But not enough to kill.

Again, the picture faded out and back again with the time stamp moved on another two hours and the men returning once again to pick up tools from the pile on the ground. The gag was removed showing the disfigured face with the dislocated jaw.

Ashar felt himself recoil into the back of his seat as each man took a long, targeted swing direct at Robert's genitals.

The unending, high-pitched primeval howl that came from the man made most viewers turn off the sound, including Ashar. Jaeger could scream all he liked. Aside from his tormentors there wasn't a soul within a hundred miles to hear him. The film faded.

Then fading back in with the cameraman walking around Jaeger in the moonlight, showing their forlorn and pain-wracked victim hanging silently from the tree. The time-stamp showed 3am before fading out.

Then, fading back in again at dawn, with the shadows showing long on the ground. Again, the three men came into frame this time carrying something in their hands which one of them showed up to the camera, a surgeon's scalpel. He went back to the hanging man and cut off the blindfold off. It was easy to see that he was barely conscious, but there was no intention of letting him die, just yet.

The men began working from Robert's forehead downwards, carefully and methodically carving two or three-inch incisions into the skin across his entire body. Front, back and sides, down his torso to legs and feet. This part was time-lapsed and the hours it took to move from his head to his feet, including what looked like taking time off for a few refreshment breaks, took until late-afternoon, when the shadow was starting to stretch the other way.

These endless hours of suffering were condensed into 20 minutes of fast-forward. It showed Jaeger mostly as a blur as his whole body constantly contorted, convulsed and jerked with the unbearable pain that came with each incision the scalpels made. Arms, torso and legs with nothing omitted, except arteries.

The movie alternated between real time and time lapse, but the viewer saw everything that was going on and no-one who saw it could comprehend the torment, misery and utter despair the man was enduring.

The obvious intention was for him to stay alive, as long as possible. And to send the message that whoever it was tormenting this poor soul were people you simply did not mess with. Ashar felt the tears streaming down his face.

When they had finished Robert's whole body was blood red. A blurred black and reddish haze had started to appear around his feet, working its way up his calves. Then there was the sound of multiple insects being picked up by the camera's mic and these could be seen settling on various parts of his body. By the height of the afternoon heat, there was a perceptible cloud of flying insects around his bloody, constantly quivering body. The haze around his feet, a hoard of red ants, worked its way further up his mutilated, twitching torso.

The last 20 minute time-lapsed the final hours of the torture, which was to let him hang and suffer under the bough of the tree. By early evening his entire body was lost in a moving cloud of flying insects. Anything that wanted to sample his blood or flesh. A perceptible layer of mosquitoes arrived as the sun started to go down.

Then, the rope holding him under the bough was shot away, with the short burst of automatic fire vaporizing his wrists and hands. He crumpled to the ground, knees bending grotesquely outwards.

Robert Jaeger, man of means and power, could still be seen occasionally convulsing beneath the assault of wildlife at the end of the film. The camera was kept on him as his tormentors slowly drove away, until he became an insignificant and irrelevant hump on the ground under a Eucalyptus tree in the Australian outback.

Hallucinating through unspeakable agony his dying thoughts were of the mother he had hardly known and the beloved father who had suffered shame and penury for his future.

+

The time stamps showed that the man's torture had lasted a full day and a half, condensed into just over an hour of video. Few who watched it had been able to turn it off, and Ashar was no exception.

He sat immobile. Shocked and mesmerised as he tried to absorb Robert's suffering. He felt no 'survivor's guilt', just grateful thanks that he had been far away when Robert had been taken.

He sat in a stupor until the plane landed at Antigua. If nothing else, he could at least have a quiet meal in memory of Robert, and he would execute his program immediately after that with a prayer to Allah for his soul and the successful completion of his mission.

His jet landed just before 4.00pm. He got a cab to his apartment which had been cleaned and the fridge freshly stocked with milk and other supplies, as he had ordered.

He had showered and dressed by 6pm, just as Arlene and Drew arrived at Catherine's Café.

Forty-Eight

Kassab walked outside to his 'force', now milling around in the centre of the courtyard. He could see all the vehicles neatly lined up, with ammunition boxes showing quite clearly in the back of the pick-ups. He needed to get all that concealed as quickly as possible and he detailed off the maintenance guy to take ten men and get it all transferred into the armoury.

He then picked out twenty of what looked like the most likely of his crew and told them to *quietly* position themselves, two each, outside of the ten apartments. The remainder to go quietly into the building and, for the time being, just wait in the community areas. No noise, but help themselves to drinks and whatever else was on offer.

On his command, a referee's whistle which he would sound off from the middle of the stairwell between the floors, the locks were to be shot off the doors to each apartment and the occupants dragged, in whatever they were wearing, or not wearing, down to the common rooms. They must not be given any time to wake up or orientate themselves. He wanted them in total shock.

The whole place, and its occupants, was theirs to do what they pleased with.

+

"Blue Force, Watchtower… stand by… there's some action now… the leader's come out of the building, talking to some of his crew… ok… someone's opening one of the garage doors… hold on… 'scope on him, can see inside… *Strewth*! That's some armoury in there… hold on… about a dozen of them unloading the pick-ups… aaah right, those are ammo boxes, and some weapons still boxed up… they're carting it all into the armoury. I'd be surprised if there's room enough in there for all that lot…"

Silence, then "He's leading um… about twenty armed men…AK47's… into the main building. They look like the best of the bunch, so to speak. The rest of these blokes are just bumbling around. Sorry… no, they're starting to follow him in... The guy who met them is coming across the courtyard to the main gate. Ah… He's going to shut the gates… We don't want that… Blue Force, Watchtower… engage."

Then it was Frankie, matter-of-factly. "Right-oh. Plan A. Advance."

The maintenance man started running towards the gate as he saw Blue Force piling up the road towards the compound. He fell to the ground soundlessly as Watchtower's 8.59mm round let daylight through his upper torso. Blue Force drove on.

+

Arlene and Drew walked back into the restaurant making sure that the CCTV would see them only as work colleagues and not the hopelessly lovestruck couple they had become over such a short time. They took a table just inside from the patio overlooking the marina and decided to have a drink before ordering.

To make it look a bit more work related, Drew pulled the picture of the man in the mirror out of his briefcase and put it on the table together with some other paperwork from the file. They sat back in their chairs as if they were work colleagues out for a meal after a heavy day at the office. Which was not too far from the truth.

The sun had long set and the restaurant, now out of tourist season, was only half full. Fine by them as they both disliked crowds. They took in the view of the marina and onwards, out into the flat calm Caribbean lit by a yellow half-moon and its backdrop of countless stars.

Drew was getting uncomfortably hot with his jacket concealing the Glock and asked Arlene if she would mind putting the weapon into her handbag. He unclipped the holster from his belt and passed it surreptitiously under the table to her, before standing up to take his jacket off and hang it over the back of his chair.

He noticed a cab pull up outside the restaurant, just one person getting out. Casually dressed and carrying a backpack. He sat down again and lost himself once again trying hard, for the sake of the camera, not to give away his true feelings as he looked at Arlene. *Has anyone ever drowned in those eyes?*

+

The first Black Hawk rose up above the cliff. Many of those who had seen the man go down after his chest had imploded in a red cloud were standing stock still, traumatized by what they had seen. For all of them it was the first act of battle violence they had witnessed. Then they felt the downdraft, and turned to see the menacing apparition of the first Black Hawk lift itself from below the cliff edge, thirty meters from and level with the vehicles parked facing out to the sea.

There was even more shock as its fifty gauge heavy machine gun raked along the whole line of vehicles. In an instant fuel tanks were exploding with bodywork and engine parts and whole engine blocks cascading in all directions. The noise was ear-shattering.

They then targeted everyone standing, mesmerized at the vision in front of them. More than one went down under the weight of heavy metal parts and fragments from the exploding vehicles landing on them.

Rule One: Total violence. Shock and awe. As the terrified and confused amateur terrorists finally started reaching for their weapons the Black Hawk dropped out of sight.

Blue Force, now approaching the gate at full pelt started blaring its horns and everyone turned around to see what was coming. As this happened, the second Black Hawk rose up from below the cliff and, once again, raked the row of cars and then hosed everyone else standing, frozen in petrified confusion around the courtyard. Fish in a barrel. Obliging targets.

By now, those who had just gone into the main building had heard the pulsing fire of the heavy machine guns and were running into the courtyard to see what was happening.

Those that were trying to turn back once they had seen the bloodbath outside were pushed further outwards by the rush of bodies behind them.

Now, the first Black Hawk reappeared and, along with the second was letting rip an unremitting firestorm at the crowd pushing each other and milling around the entrance to the accommodation block, creating a pile of bodies in a sea of blood. At the same time picking off other groups huddling around the kill zone. They were careful not to aim at the upper floor where they knew the accommodation suites would be occupied.

The Black Hawks had decimated the terrorist force by more than half in the fifteen seconds it took Blue Force to hurtle through the gate. They dropped back below the cliff and turned away back to base. They had done all they had been asked to do and, now, in the smoke and fire left by their onslaught Blue Force jumped and rolled away from their vehicles in four-man teams to follow through with the action.

No terrorist in the courtyard was left standing, and those still in the armoury were kept pinned down by the Watchtower snipers until a couple of squads could position themselves to rush it. But before that could happen the half dozen that were in there were waving anything they could find that was white around the door and came out with their hands on their heads.

Zip-ties on wrists and ankles immobilized them until Josh Miller and his police could deal with them properly. They had already been called and would soon be waiting back at the junction to come and process whatever remained of the so-called terrorist force.

By now, those inside the main building had got themselves organized. The ones detailed off to break into the apartments had done that and burst through to come out on the veranda and were shooting down at blue force. Well targeted fire was returned from the courtyard, helped along by the Watchtower snipers. Most went down quickly.

Screams could be heard from inside the apartments as the guests were woken first by terrifying clatter of the heavy machine guns and the firefight that followed in the courtyard and then their doors being shot off and ongoing gunfire blasting into their rooms. All the guests, in various states of undress and panic, took up shelter in their bathrooms, which were also built as 'safe' rooms.

The action lasted for a further fifteen minutes, until the last surviving terrorists crawled, trailing blood, out into the courtyard where they were zip-tied and lined up with the rest by the main gate. Just 20 living survivors, all wounded, out of the 100 or so who had come through the gates less than thirty minutes before.

Frankie took stock of his own men and was gutted to see that two had been shot and killed, with a further half dozen wounded. He walked over to the prisoners. All of them shuffled away on the ground from him as best they could while hampered with their zip-ties.

The look of threatening contempt on his face struck fear into all of them. He was seething that two of his good men had been killed by amateurs and his sneering expression showed it. If they were proper soldiers he could at least respect them, but these were nothing more than rabble… losers. Filth. On a par with some inner city gang.

He could not bear to look at them and turned away, thinking about the letters he was going to have to write before the day was done.

The building was thoroughly searched and the guests assembled in one of the downstairs community areas. The men were all fit and the women were stunning. Were they here for some fashion or lifestyle magazine photo-shoot? Swinger's party? Frankie was confused, "Who are you and what are you all doing here?"

There was silence before one of them spoke up.

"We've all paid good money… I mean *seriously* good money to be protected from the shit that we've just seen going on here. We were told that this was a safe place to wait out the meltdown."

Meltdown? Frankie and his team all looked at each other, bewildered but clearly not interested. "Ok. Whatever… Um… I believe your host was a man called Robert Jaeger."

Nods of agreement

"Well… I don't think you'll be seeing him again and, from what we know… well, we don't think he'll be making any more appearances. I assume you all have the means to get yourselves organized and home to wherever you came from? Our work here is done, but the police will be here in a few minutes and they'll probably want statements from all of you."

He was answered with blank stares and silence. Until one of the men spoke quietly. Clearly trying to keep his simmering rage under control. A South American accent. Sarcastic.

"I paid twenty-five million dollars to stay at this… oh har har… *safe* compound. Does anybody see the irony in that? I want to see Jaeger and tell him exactly what I think." And then almost screaming "I. Also. Want. My. *Fucking*. Money. Back!"

A woman, obviously his partner, let rip with a bawdy South London accent. Shouting "Fuck you, Manuel, what kind of – 'oh har har' – resort is this? This is the last time I take any shit from you. I don't believe this..! We were even expected to do our own washing and ironing! Can you fuckin' believe that?!"

This set off further accusations and recriminations between the group and Frankie stepped back, beckoning his soldiers to follow him. They backed out the door leaving these strange people to argue amongst themselves.

Josh Millar drove through the gate with a couple of officers in his car and shook hands with Frankie who said "All yours, mate. And…" nodding back to where he had just come from "…good luck with that!"

Miller rubbed his hands together in anticipation. Real police work at last.

Forty-Nine

Most people came to Catherine's Café to eat and relax. Drew found himself getting mildly annoyed when he saw the man sitting two tables away with his back to him pull a laptop out of his backpack. But he guessed that you could get workaholics even on Caribbean islands.

The man was alone, so had plenty of room to set the laptop to one side while he started on his first course. Drew's mobile sounded off with an e-mail.

Hello Drew,

Thanks for your report this afternoon. Very encouraging and helpful. I passed the Jeremy Hitchens and his Revbay Capital Bank info over to Swift and they ran one of their data checks. The serial number on the access device was an Asus laptop.

We checked it out and it was bought for cash in the UK. It turns out that the same serial number had been accessing Swift through a back door, like Mohammed, and had set up a program that would cancel MT799's on just under a thousand accounts, not just GDWM clients. From what Dez Fox says, if all these were PPP-related, which they probably were, that would have left the host banks exposed for something like five trillion dollars of unsecured debt, maybe much more.

Swift has blocked Hitchens' Asus laptop, although he'll be able to access his account – with some $150 million in it(!) – once he's registered another device.

Had Hitchens, or whatever his name is, succeeded at what he was doing the consequences would have been catastrophic. Ask your Fed contact about wealth games and CEESSEB. That will put you in the picture.

If you see Officer Smith please pass on our deepest gratitude for the initiative she showed at the outset of this enquiry. I'm sure she will be hearing from people on your side of the pond to the same effect.

Good luck in your hunt for Hitchens. We want him alive.

Kind regards

Tony Jackson

He looked up at Arlene with a wide satisfied grin on his face and held out his mobile to her to read the e-mail.

But she was looking over at their waitress at the service desk who was staring at, and nodding hard towards the man with the laptop sitting with his back to them. He realized in an instant that she was trying to tell them that this was the man in the mirror. The man calling himself Jeremy Hitchens.

Ashar had finished his meal *in memorium* to his dear friend Robert Jaeger. With a silent prayer for his soul, and for the misery that was about to engulf the entire infidel world, he entered the link to his back door to Swift and keyed 'enter'.

For a full five seconds he sat, dumbfounded, staring at the message on his screen: *Error 403. Access Forbidden.*

Consumed with blind fury he pulled a machine pistol from his backpack and lurched to his feet knocking over his chair and table. His rage was venting with a primal scream "AAAAARGH…! ALLAHU AKBAR! ALLAHU AKBAR!" and a stream of lead sprayed in a chaotic, wild-eyed frenzy all over the restaurant as people dived for cover or ran screaming out onto the street.

Drew had no weapon other than the chair he was sitting on, which he hurled at Ashar hoping to draw his fire. Arlene had rolled to the floor and away, grabbing her handbag. Ashar whipped round and fired off some rounds while trying to bat away the chair. He hit Drew's right thigh, sending him spinning to the floor.

Arlene pulled Drew's Glock out of her handbag, unclipped it from its holster and rose to her feet. Her training came back to her instinctively. In a stand-up squat, gripping the butt with both hands, checking the safety and taking aim within two seconds she fired off three rounds in rapid succession. She went for 'body mass' but was now tripping over a fallen chair and Ashar was still moving.

Two of the powerful .38 rounds shot out his shoulder and the third the back of his knee sending blood and bone splinters into the air, with the not quite spent third round drilling into Drew's right ankle. Hitchens went down and she was on him in an instant pulling a pair of handcuffs out of her handbag at the same time. Not that he was going anywhere.

She would see to it that this vermin would get the best possible medical attention. She wanted him fit and well for his trial and never-ending incarceration. As she finished cuffing Hitchens, Drew rolled over and lay on his back on the floor next to him. His wounds making him moan in agony.

She knelt down and undid Hitchens' belt, pulled it free and used it as a tourniquet on Drew's leg before standing up to survey the restaurant. After a few moments, she felt herself let out a deep, shuddering sigh of unrestrained satisfaction as she realized she had actually delivered what she had promised the Davey's son in the note she had left for him.

Mission accomplished.

She took a picture of Drew and Hitchens lying next to each other amongst the food, drink and blood on the floor. She could hear the sound of police and ambulance sirens approaching.

She checked around the restaurant and was able to tell the police when they arrived that there were no other casualties, aside from cuts and grazes from what the medics called 'flight injuries'.

Two hours later, Arlene sent her picture to Jackson, from Drew's hospital bedside.

Hi Tony,

Thanks for e-mail. We have our man. Alive as requested.

Arlene.

Fifty

I was still keeping my head down, concealed at the side of the road from where I'd watched Blue Force as they headed into the compound, leaving the Land Rover on the roadside. I knew that there was every chance people were posted around the junction and had no intention of getting caught out by a bunch of amateurs.

It felt strange watching a live firefight in progress from a distance, rather than being in the thick of it, but had no choice as I watched using a pair of binoculars I'd found in the Land Rover.

Jackson's call came as I was watching the action going on in the compound. He told me what had been going on at Swift and how the young cop at DPD and the FBI guy, Drew, had tracked down and managed to apprehend the guy they thought was responsible for the Davey's homicide.

He told me how close he had come to cancelling the MT799's. I went through the consequences of that all over again with him and how it was all spelled out in the CEESSEB lecture he gave me at the hotel in La Hulpe. I heard a very quiet "Yeah…" before he just said "Thanks. And we should also thank that mate of yours, Pat Wheeler was it?" Then "Anything on Kelly?"

The battle was now over, leaving a haze of smoke over the compound. I could see a line of police cars and ambulances pulling up just down the road as Ted Larkin gave me a shout on the radio to tell me there was absolutely no sign of Kelly anywhere in the compound. Not even in the cells in the basement.

As soon as all the so-called terrorists had been accounted for the first task of every man there had been to search every nook and cranny of the place.

I lost it for a moment and, stupidly, limped out of my cover over to the Land Rover and leaned on the bonnet trying to clear my head. That bloody leg was giving me hell. I was starting to see why some guys who've had much the same surgery are actually begging for amputation soon after.

Then I saw one of the snipers up in the hide waving his arms furiously at me. He signalled '23' at me and held up his walkie talkie.

I switched the channel on mine to channel 23 and before I could say anything he said: "Get back in your wagon, mate. I'm bloody sure there's a couple of these bastards lurking around at the junction here."

If they were watching me and I got back in the Land Rover they'd know exactly where I was and could pick me off at leisure. I rolled across the road again and landed on my back in a ditch. In the middle of the roll I'd drawn and cocked the Sig. Strange how training can just kick in. Like breathing.

If these guys were amateurs, like it looked they were, sooner or later they'd make the mistake of sneezing, coughing or even farting which would give their position away. But it wasn't any of those, I heard a rush of two men through the bush, the slamming of doors and an engine starting up. No more than 15 or 20 yards to my right.

There was no way I could kneel or take up any textbook shooting position, but I had enough in my other leg to push myself out onto the road again. I hauled myself up onto my backside, sitting upright, legs spread, leaning against a front wheel on the Land Rover, pistol held in my right hand with the grip cupped in my left. I was settled and waiting by the time their pick-up edged out onto the road.

The passenger was sheltering behind the door, hiding himself in the footwell. I fired off a double tap which went straight through the passenger side window and took out the driver. The vehicle then just dawdled into the middle of the road before stalling.

To be fair, I wasn't expecting the other guy to come bursting out firing off a sub machine gun of some sort in all directions. But I didn't want him dead. I wanted Kelly.

It was a bit of a risk and I felt one round tug at the combat jacket I'd picked up back at the base. But it was only 20 yards. I fired off about half a dozen rounds going for the legs, got one of them and he went down with his weapon sliding across the road out of reach.

He was young and fit, but older than that poor brainwashed little sod who'd done all that damage to my leg. This was just a kid who shouldn't be playing with the big boys, but that wasn't my fault. At his age, I'd been on my first tour of Afghanistan.

With my leg giving me more pain than it ever dished out before I hauled myself up and pulled and pulled my walking stick down from the passenger seat. I leant against the vehicle for a second or two to catch my breath, then made my way back across the road. I looked down at the young pretender and took pleasure in knowing that he was now going to have second thoughts about the cause, whatever it was, he was fighting for. "Where's Kelly?"

I expected him to look confused and scared. And he obliged. So I asked again, "Where's Kelly?"

There were tears in his eyes, but he was putting up a good front. I could see that my .38 round had taken out his right thigh. There were bone fragments showing around the wound. I knew how that could sting.

I balanced on my left leg, held my walking stick over the wound, and asked again, "Where's Kelly?"

He was starting to look really worried. "I dunno do I?! Who the fuck's Kelly?" He looked up at me. Defiant. Mocking. "What kind of stupid old drongo goes losing his Sheila anyway?"

Yep. Definitely Australian. But '*Old*'?

The walking stick found its way deep into the wound in his leg. They probably heard his screams half a mile down the road in Fortress Jaeger.

He was shaking his head wildly. "I dunno!!! I dunno!!! I dunno!!!" on and on he went. Sure enough, he didn't know. I withdrew the stick and stood in the middle of the road looking helplessly around me.

"Oi! Mate!" It was the SASR sniper up in the tree again, shouting at me and pointing back into the bush. "Over there. Red Toyota… SUV… It's the car they dragged Jaeger out of. Try your luck there."

I was itching to sprint into the bush and find the car, but I had to make do with a slow, shuffling limp, leaving the prick with the hole in his leg writhing around in the middle of the road. I caught a glimpse of red amongst the trees and, a few second later, could see and hear the flies around the car.

After lifting the rear hatch and falling back from the stench and mass of flies that pummelled my senses I crawled back to the road and shouted up to the hide. "Knife! Ambulance! NOW!"

The large knife, which I could see wasn't SASR or any other regular army issue, thudded into the ground by my side a second later. I heard the ambulance siren as I was crawling back into the bush.

The paramedics helped me cut Kelly, who was convulsing and in deep shock, out of the coils of Gaffa tape. They sedated her on the spot and I went with her to South Perth private hospital where a bunch of nurses took her into a bathroom and cleaned her up.

I was taken for a scan, where they found no real damage to my leg, just a lot of swelling that would take a while to go down. I'd just been using it too much one way and another. I took advantage of the time in Perth to fix up a couple of meetings in Singapore with the help of Pat Wheeler and his lawyer friend.

A couple of days later Kelly was *compus mentis* enough, with her face hidden behind swathes of bandages after some plastic surgery, for me to tell her what had happened to Jaeger. I'd sent one of the nurses out with my card to buy a tablet so that I could let her see the video. She was in the hospital for a few days after I went onto Singapore.

One of the doctors told me she must have viewed that video a dozen times, always with a really worrying grin on her face. She takes the occasional look even now.

It took a couple of weeks of very careful treatment to bring back her lovely face. But that cock-eyed grin of hers has lost some of its mojo, even if she hasn't.

+

I met with the Monetary Authority of Singapore, MAS, with the lawyer Pat Wheeler had recommended sat beside me, and went through the whole story with them. Finishing off by telling them that there were almost 100 billionaires with PPP trades in progress which, if they were interrupted or failed in any way, would cause untold damage to those billionaires themselves and the financial markets generally. The only solution was to turn GDWM over to me so that I could get it back on an even keel.

The probate was straightforward enough, Jaeger had no relatives. Pat Wheeler, Tony Jackson, Interpol and, unbelievably, our own Chancellor wrote references confirming my suitability to take over the company. As did the U.S. Treasury Secretary, on the prompting of Drew Farron I was later told.

So MAS had plenty of people to blame if I managed to screw it all up. Once the paperwork was dealt with I was able to get an e-mail out to everybody at GDWM:

Dear GDWM staff and retained personnel,

> This is to advise that after the sad loss of our CEO, Robert Jaeger, I have taken full ownership and control of GDWM. All salaries, retainers and commissions will continue to be paid as previously contracted and there are no changes to terms or conditions of employment or contracts.
>
> I have met with the administration staff in Singapore and if you have any problems please contact them directly for support.
>
> While I am CEO, the role of COO is being taken over by Ms Kelly Murchison and she will advise you in due course of any changes to structure.

We anticipate moving head office to London and I will keep you well informed of developments.

Thank you for your continued support of GDWM, which we intend to become a leading global service provider, across the whole wealth management and private banking spectrum, for our clients. We anticipate changing the name of the company to Fox, Murchison Private Bank.

Kind regards

Derek Fox, CEO

There was no need to say anything at all to the clients, their PPP trades were all successfully under way and nothing had changed for them.

After I had finished signing everything off at MAS, I went back to the hotel. We were going to have a quiet night in, and it was that night that it finally seemed like the right time to get the ring out of my pocket and ask the big question.

We celebrated in our own sweet way, with both of us looking forward to getting home to my cottage in 'forgotten England'.

Fifty-One

La Hulpe, Belgium. September.

The long, warm spell that had settled over Western Europe for most of the summer was showing the first signs of coming to an end. The yellows, reds and golds heralding the coming autumn were just starting to show on the trees giving shade to La Hulpe's town square.

Bistros, boutiques and al fresco cafés were doing their usual steady trade. The quiet hubbub of conversation carried around the square on the late-Summer breeze.

Just outside of town at Swift HQ, Dick van Druten was relaxed and confident as he chaired an HR meeting to discuss updated employee pensions matters.

Far different to the meeting he had sat in on a few weeks ago, at which he and his top security team had been given a full de-brief on what had been happening over the past few months by the new Head of the UK's MI6, Tony Jackson.

They all knew about the failed conspiracy by GDWM to relieve a group of billionaires of their wealth, but everyone was stunned to hear about the attempt by North Korea to reduce the global economy to their own level by compromising the MT799 system.

At the end of the meeting everyone in the room, no more than a dozen people, fell into introspective silence as they all realized how close they had come to being complicit in the conspiracy. All averted only through the instincts of a young, unnamed, Detroit cop following through on a homicide case in Antigua, which was the catalyst for the whole enquiry.

They left the meeting, each with their own instructions to introduce further measures within 'Dreadnought' which would block any other attempt to breach Swift's network security.

It was quite natural for van Druten to brief Michel Brun, as Head of Cyber Counter-Measures, to track through the MT799 system to identify and remove every stage of the program installed by the man they knew as Jeremy Hitchens, but Brun knew as Ashar. It had taken him a week to identify each linked stage of the program and uncover at least a dozen booby-traps that would have brought all of Swift crashing down if he had followed the logical path to uninstalling them.

He had now reached the stage where every line of code inserted by Ashar was highlighted in red on his screen. He had watched over Mohammed while he had led the building of 'Dreadnought', ensuring that he would not stray from the instructions Jaeger had given him. The threat to him and his family had been sufficient to force his compliance.

Now, with the biggest threat in all history to global financial stability neutralized, he gazed in wonder at the exquisite coding Ashar had inserted into the system.

All he had to do was delete each red line of code in the order which he had noted down separately, and was now ready to execute. It would take about an hour and the threat to Swift, its 11,000 bank members and the entire world's financial stability would be eliminated.

But Jaeger was gone, after endless hours of diabolical torture, now witnessed by more than 500 million on YouTube. And Ashar was in a cell somewhere awaiting trial through which he, Brun himself, could be exposed. He had no idea whether or not Jaeger had revealed his identity to Ashar. And if he had, how long would it be before Ashar let it slip under merciless interrogation?

He was now on his own, the last survivor, at the end of a road that had taken the whole movement many years to travel. Many decades for Jaeger. Was it right that all that planning and preparation should be for nothing? Nothing but ultimate failure?

He and he alone could still make it all happen, but what if his secret was safe, if he was never exposed, and no-one would ever know of his involvement..?

Perhaps, if he just left the programme sitting buried deep in the system he could come back and detonate it if ever he thought the time was right…

Decisions, decisions.

+

Van Druten decided to go down to the hole to see how Brun was getting on with uninstalling the program that could so easily have set off inconceivable global chaos. He was only now starting to fully comprehend the sheer magnitude of what could have happened. It would continue to bug him until he was sure it had all been properly dealt with.

As he left the elevator and entered the dimly lit subterranean chamber he saw Brun in his glass-walled office. He had his back to him and was staring intently at four large screens, all packed with lines of code. Some in green, some in red.

His finger, seemingly absentmindedly, was stroking his 'enter' key. As if deep in thought.

He was obviously concentrating hard on the job in hand. Best not to disturb him. Van Druten returned to his office.

Epilogue

When we got back to London we stayed at the house in Trinity Mews. I kept on the lease so we have somewhere to stay when we're in London.

While I'd been working on my cottage at weekends, Kelly would come as well when she could. There was usually a bunch of guys from the base who came along to help. I loved it that, despite her model looks and elfin build, she could muck in with the best of them.

Over that summer of weekends spent sawing, hammering and painting they all fell in love with her as she tried to help her crippled, lame duck partner on his building project. It was probably her that brought them all out and got the cottage finished quicker than I had planned.

After a hard days graft we'd all go over the road to the village pub, The Chequers, kick back and sink a few beers to a background of friendly banter and camaraderie. Most of us have days of our lives we can look back on in warm reminiscence. These are mine.

We spent a couple of months recuperating at the cottage before heading back into the fray. Sometimes, Kelly would wake up screaming in the night, but she's making good progress now and even firing off that cock-eyed grin of hers at me sometimes, full blast.

Jackson had forwarded a picture of the FBI guy and the Hitchens character lying on the floor of the restaurant in Antigua. A while later I got a picture of him and Arlene at their wedding and I was surprised when they accepted the invitation to ours. Jackson came too, and was very excited to tell me that Bretton Woods wasn't someone's name, but a conference.

MAS had put things through very quickly and arranged it so that wherever Robert Jaeger's signature had previously appeared, there was now mine. GDWM had cash in the bank of just shy of two billion dollars, with more coming in from fees on the PPP trades, which I had managed to stabilize and keep going for our clients.

PPP's are still being done but the banks have now put a stop to the leveraged loans. But people are still seeing very acceptable profits off them, even it takes a while longer.

Over the course of those couple of months GDWM became Fox, Murchison Private Bank LLP, into which all GDWM's cash and assets were transferred. We found some classy offices, big enough for 20 people and the same again if necessary, on Cannon Street, in the City.

I arranged with Josh Miller to have Jaeger's antique mahogany desk shipped over to me.

Also a framed sketch on foolscap paper, obviously by JMW Turner, divided into quadrants. It looked like a series of concepts for his 'Fighting Temeraire' masterpiece, sporting a bullet hole through the ship's mainmast on one of them.

Both are now in my office.

+

THE END

Printed in Poland
by Amazon Fulfillment
Poland Sp. z o.o., Wrocław